THE BAIT

THE MILVUS FILES
BOOK 2

N.R. WALKER

COPYRIGHT

Cover Artist: Reese Dante
Editor: Boho Editing
Publisher: BlueHeart Press
The Bait © 2024 N.R. Walker
Milvus Files Series

BLURB

When three men turn up in their sleepy little town of Tallowwood, Harry and Asher know something's wrong. Not because someone could find them, but the fact that Asher's informant and oldest friend, Yunho, failed to alert them. Messages and phone calls unanswered; Harry and Asher go to Thailand to find Yunho is missing.

Harry and Asher find themselves thrown back into the game of shadows and murder, in a race across the globe to find him and find who's behind the kidnapping.

The list of their enemies is long, their web of entanglement even longer, and Harry and Asher are about to find out once and for all who is predator and who is prey.

CAUTION WARNINGS

This book contains on-page violence, torture, and murder. It also mentions past childhood abuse.

Reader discretion is advised.

THE BAIT

N.R. WALKER

ONE

DETECTIVE AUGUST SHAW plucked the can of WD-40 from the shelf, flipping it a time or two as he whistled his way to the checkout at the hardware shop.

Winter was almost here, but the weather was warm today, the sun was shining, birds were singing, and his damn office chair was squeaking.

Not that winter had much to do with that. But the can of WD-40 sure did.

Bill had a customer at the counter, but he brightened when he saw August. "Ah, the good detective here might be more helpful than me," he said. "This gentleman here was wanting to know which access roads into the national park were open." He pointed to the map they were both studying. "This road in was closed, or so he said."

August looked at the man. He was short and stocky, had black hair, thick eyebrows, and dark eyes.

"Ah, yeah. Big storm recently made it impassable. They're doing some grading work on it."

The guy looked disappointed and annoyed.

"You looking to go camping in there?" August asked him.

"Yes," he said. "Camping. Was told it was good for fishing."

He had a thick accent that sounded a little familiar.

"Whereabouts are you from?" August asked with a smile, hoping to sound conversational and not digging for information. "Hope you didn't have to travel too far."

"Come from Sydney," he said.

August didn't believe that. "Nice." He turned his attention back to the map and tapped an access road along the western side. "You can enter the park in through here. Bit of a trek to the river though, but you won't be the only one there. It'll be busy with the nice weather. Say, what type of fish you hoping to catch?"

The man baulked. "Sorry, English not good."

"Ah, sorry," August said, still being cheerful. He tapped the map again. "This road." He went to the front door signalling for the man to join him. He pointed down the road. "Head left, five kilometres. You'll see the signs."

The man gave him a tight smile, took his map, and went to his 4WD. Two other men sat inside it, looking none too happy.

August took in the details of the vehicle, watching it as it slowly drove away.

"Guess we can expect tourists with warmer days like this," Bill said, ringing up the can of WD-40. "Hope they're not expecting to catch dinner. Bit early for fishing. But whaddya expect from city folks."

August nodded and smiled, as unfazed as he could manage, as he swiped his card to pay. "Yep."

"Oh." Bill made a face. "I didn't mean you. I don't think of you as a city type. You're a local now."

August snorted, took his can of WD-40, and walked to the door. "Thanks, Bill. See ya at the pub sometime."

"Shall do."

August got into his patrol car and dialled Jake's number. He answered on the second ring. "Hey," Jake said. "What's up?"

"Do me a favour?"

"Sure."

"Google standard Croatian military-issue boots for me and send me a photo."

There was a pause, then a drawn-out "Okay." He heard some tapping on the keyboard. "Sending you the pic now. It says current this year, but who knows? Do I want to know why you need this?"

August's phone beeped and he opened the image, his suspicions confirmed. "Run this number plate for me." He gave the plate number and the vehicle details.

"Hm," Jake replied. "Rental. Let me see what I can find out . . ."

August sat there a moment, that sinking feeling in his gut getting a whole lot heavier.

"Rented to a Marko Andric, Croatian national driver's licence." More clicking on the keyboard. "Arrived yesterday—"

August started the engine. "Give Michael and Joshua Hill a call and tell them we're on our way."

There was a pause. "We are? Wh-what for?"

He noted the hesitation, and he didn't blame him. "I'll explain on the way. Pick you up in two . . ."

Jake climbed into the passenger seat of the patrol even

before August had come to a complete stop. He was on duty, so his police uniform was par for the course, but August wasn't sure if this visit called for formalities.

"What happened?" Jake asked as August turned back out onto the street. "I take it nothing good."

"Just ran into a man at the hardware. Something wasn't right." August gripped the steering wheel a little too tight, which Jake noticed, of course. He unpeeled his fingers, trying to convince himself to play it cool. "It's just a feeling."

Jake eyed him. "And when have your gut feelings ever been wrong?"

Exactly.

"You got through to them? Let them know we're coming?"

He nodded. "Spoke to Joshua. He sounded happy about it. Said he'd put the kettle on."

August gave Jake a side-eye. He'd said all he could ever say about Joshua Hill. Jake seemed to like him, maybe because they were the only other gay couple in Tallowwood, but August knew better. They were a couple, yes. Of that, he had no doubt. Michael Hill was a giant of a man. Intimidating and hard, but it was sweet little Joshua who scared August the most. Fun and flirty on the outside, cold-blooded killer on the inside.

August was sure of it.

Not to mention that he'd seen Joshua use a McMillan TAC-50 rifle like it was an extension of his own hands, and when he'd made some enquiries, ASIO had shut him down.

Fucking ASIO.

Which had to mean Michael and Joshua were military or black ops or . . . something.

Either way, August wasn't too keen to give unannounced house calls, hence the phone call to warn them. He filled Jake in on what very little detail he had on the drive out to their place.

Their house was secluded, off the road down a drive a few kilometres long. Surrounded by woodlands, forests, and a few hundred acres that backed directly onto the national park.

When August pulled the patrol to a stop, Joshua opened the front door. He wore jeans, a grey sweater, and a welcoming smile. "Let me do the talking," August murmured to Jake before getting out.

They walked over and Joshua held the door for them in invitation. "Please come in. We haven't seen you since just before Christmas. Can I get you a cup of tea?"

The house was warm and cosy, the wooden floors freshly polished by the looks of it. August almost felt bad for not taking his shoes off. "No thanks," he said.

"Not a social visit, I take it," Michael said, nodding to Jake's uniform. He stood in the living room, his stance rigid, ready. It was probably hard for a man of his size to ever look relaxed, August realised, but his eyes . . . his eyes were assessing every single thing.

"More of a courtesy call," August said, as pleasant as he could. "Had some visitors in town this morning."

Michael stood, unmoving. Joshua walked over and, taking Michael's hand, motioned for everyone to sit. "And what does that have to do with us?" Joshua asked, still smiling.

"Three men. One of them at least is a Croatian national. Arrived in the country last night, rented a four-wheel drive, said they were going fishing in the national park. Had no fishing gear, didn't know what fish were local, and his boots were wrong. They weren't hiking boots, or any kind of outdoor boots, for that matter. They were military boots."

Jacob held up his phone screen to show them the photo. "Croatian military boots. They looked like this."

And for the first time ever, there was a reaction.

Michael's eyes hardened, his nostrils flared, and Joshua took his hand from Michael's and sat far too calmly, his hands now in his lap. "Oh?"

"He said they were camping, pointed to a map that was a little too close to your property boundary," August said. "Now, maybe they're legit. Maybe they're here to actually go fishing. Maybe I'm wrong."

"He's never wrong," Jake added.

Michael's gaze went to Jake, and August had to tamp down his urge to protect him.

"I get that impression," Michael said.

"Look," August said, showing his open hands, non-confrontational. "I'm going to be honest with you both. I tried to look into who you both really are, and I got shut down by ASIO. So technically I know nothing."

"Probably just as well," Michael murmured, his gaze hard and flat.

"But what I do know is, these three men turning up here seemed it might be something you'd appreciate knowing."

Michael stared at him, giving nothing away.

"I don't want any trouble in my town," August said. "Not that I expect there will be any."

"Of course not," Joshua said, his sweet smile not reaching his eyes. Their cat jumped up on the sofa and went straight for Joshua's lap, purring. Joshua pulled it close, kissing the top of its head. "We do appreciate you coming to visit though."

"I thought you might," August said. "For what it's worth, I sent them to the western entrance. It might buy you some time to . . . do whatever you need to do." August didn't want to think too much about what that meant, but he had to look at the bigger picture. "So, just straight talking here, if the Australian government thinks you should be protected, for whatever reason, then it's the least I can do. I won't be adding this to my daily report, just so you know. It's just a friendly house call, after all."

For a moment, August thought Michael might even smile.

He didn't. "Thank you," he said instead. He stood, their meeting now seemingly over, so August and Jake did the same. "Friendly house calls are always welcome."

When August gave Jake a nod to signal that was their cue to leave, he noticed Jake was watching Joshua. But then he gave August a bright smile. "We good to go?"

"Yeah." He gave both a nod and began for the door.

"Thanks for your time," Jake said as they left. "Might see you in town sometime."

They walked to their vehicle in silence and didn't even speak until they were halfway down the long drive. "What do you make of that?" August asked.

Jake shook his head. "That shit's about to go down. And maybe we gave the good guys a head start."

"I'm not sure any of them are good guys."

"Me either. Did you see Joshua's phone?"

August shook his head. "I saw you caught something. What was it?"

"Messages he sent to someone, about five or six, with question marks, and no replies."

"He's been trying to reach someone?"

Jake shrugged. "At a guess, yes. And someone related to this because why would he double-check a screen with two cops in the room?"

August didn't want to admit he hadn't even seen Joshua holding his phone, let alone the screen.

"Michael didn't give much away," Jake added.

"Yeah, he did. His eyes flinched, and his nostrils flared for maybe a tenth of a second."

Jacob snorted. "You caught that?"

August nodded. "Yeah. Pretty sure we told them something they already knew. Or assumed. Or weren't surprised by. Like we confirmed something. I dunno."

Jake made a face and was quiet for a while. "Did we do the right thing?"

August nodded. "I think so. Like I said, those two men, whatever their real names are, are under ASIO's eye."

"Or watchlist," Jake added. When August told him about the ASIO cease and desist at Christmastime, he'd run through a dozen possible scenarios. Some of them were crazy Hollywood action movie fantasies . . . well, August hoped they were.

"So where's ASIO now?" Jake wondered. "If they are under ASIO's protection, where are they now?"

August sighed. Confused, concerned, and completely in the dark. "I don't know."

A SHRILL CRY woke August and Jacob up in the middle of the night. They both sat upright in bed, stock still and listening. "What was that?" August whispered, reaching for his phone. It was 2:12 am.

Another cry cut the night.

"That's a kookaburra," Jacob hissed. "Get up!"

They made it to the kitchen when a rap on the backdoor startled them both. August's gaze cut to Jake's. Who the hell would be knocking at two o'clock in the morning?

On the back door?

"Detective Shaw, Senior Constable Porter," a familiar voice said. "Sorry to wake you."

Jesus fucking Christ.

"Joshua Hill," August whispered. He put his hand up, signalling for Jacob to go back to the hall, and August waited for him to disappear before he turned the kitchen light on.

He opened the back door to find Joshua with a grocery bag, smiling somewhat apologetically, and Michael standing on the patio steps behind him holding a cat carrier.

Not what he was expecting.

"Uh, it's two o'clock in the morning," August said. He looked again at the cat carrier, quickly deducing what this was about. "Come in." He stood aside just as Jake walked out.

Joshua came in, standing nervously while Michael put the cat carrier on the kitchen counter. "I do apologise for the late hour but we . . . we'll be overseas for a while, and I couldn't bear to leave my poor baby Mala. I remembered you saying you had a cat, and I hoped you wouldn't mind." His eyebrows furrowed with worry. "She's fully vaccinated and she's the sweetest thing. I hope your cat won't mind. I brought all the food we had for her. And there's some money in there to cover any costs." He put the bag of cat food on the counter. "I didn't know where else to take her."

August could see Joshua was clearly upset. "Uh . . ."

"It's okay," Jake intervened. "We'll look after her. How long do you think you'll be gone for?"

"We don't know," Michael answered. "Could be a while."

Right.

Michael put his huge hand on Joshua's shoulder, and Joshua nodded. He leaned down to the cat and whispered something through the cage door. Something not in English. Something possibly in Croatian . . .

Oh god.

August wasn't game to ask about the three Croatian camping fishermen.

They walked to the back door, and it was Michael who stopped. "Uh . . ." He winced, uneasy. "Just so you know, next time someone's at your back door in the middle of the night, don't turn your lights on. You know your house in the dark better than anyone else."

August felt admonished by that. "Uh, thanks."

Michael went out first and he held the door for Joshua. Michael pointed his thumb at the railing. "Uh, you've got some visitors on your patio."

August craned his neck, his heart hammering.

"Oh, kookaburras," Joshua said. "The same that visited us"—he looked back at August and Jacob—"the first day we met you."

"They're here for me," Jacob said simply. Both Joshua and Michael stared at him. So he explained. "They look after us. Probably sounds crazy to you, but—"

"No, it doesn't. It's not crazy at all," Joshua said. He smiled at Jake. "I like you, Jacob Porter."

Oh.

August wasn't sure what to make of that.

Joshua seemed to steel himself again, shaking off his emotions. "Please take care of my baby."

Jacob nodded. "She'll be here when you get back."

Joshua smiled as if that was a beautiful thought, whereas Michael didn't seem so hopeful. The bigger man simply nodded, and they disappeared into the dark without making a sound. Not a footfall, not a breath. The gate didn't make a sound. Pure silence.

Jesus.

August closed the door, locking it twice, and breathed for what felt like the first time since he'd woken up. Fucking hell. He put his hand to his heart and followed Jake back to the kitchen. "What do you make of that?"

"I can guess it has something to do with the three men who turned up in town today," Jake answered. "But why they're now going overseas, or where, and what for, is anyone's guess. Not sure I want to know, to be honest."

August had to agree.

"What are we supposed to do with their cat?"

Jake snorted and opened the carrier door. He scooped the little cat out and held her to his chest, and she immediately began to purr. Jake grinned.

August sighed, scrubbed his hand over his face, and flicking the laundry light on, he turned the kitchen light off. "I'm going to bed. Show her where the kitty litter is. If she craps in the house, you're cleaning it up."

"Why me?"

"Because Joshua Hill said he likes you."

Jake laughed, but August still didn't think it was funny. Not because he was jealous.

But because he was pretty damn sure tomorrow would involve opening a triple homicide case of three Croatian lambs that August himself had led right to the lions for slaughter.

And now, as if that wasn't bad enough, they were babysitting their cat. Correction: they were now the owners of the damn cat because it was extremely unlikely they'd ever see Michael or Joshua Hill again.

And for the life of him, as he was falling asleep, August wasn't sure why that bothered him.

TWO

ANDAMAN OCEAN, OFF THE COAST OF THAILAND

THE WATER WAS RELATIVELY CALM, but Harry Harrigan kept the boat under ten knots. The old fifteen-foot fishing boat was built for open water, but he didn't want to risk drawing attention to themselves. They'd bargained for the sale at the marina, paid in cash, and hit the water before seven in the morning.

The weather was warm; the sun and humidity already biting.

Funny how moderate the temperatures were that Harry had gotten used to. He used to be able to handle the baking heat of the Sahara or the sauna conditions of the tropics.

Not anymore. He'd grown soft these last two years.

He kept his eyes ahead on the water, all while watching Asher intently.

Asher sat at the bow, the wind to his face, staring out across the blue horizon.

Harry had never seen Asher so . . . scared.

Asher had always been confident, cocky, even. Sure of his skills, sure of his ability to read a situation, read people, and he'd never taken a backward step.

But that all changed two days ago.

Yunho had gone silent.

No messages, no phone calls, no contact.

And Yunho never went silent.

He was always awake, always online, always one heartbeat away.

Asher had sent him a message for Memorial Day, July 27th. Yunho had served in Korea's military, after all. And while Yunho didn't have fond memories of that time, he appreciated Asher remembering. They'd expected Asher's phone to ring at any moment, because that's what Yunho did.

The call never came.

Then Asher sent him a text, then another and another. All went unanswered. Harry had hoped when they'd woken the next day there'd be an explanation . . . but no. Asher already wanted to get on the next plane to see Yunho.

But then Shaw and Porter turned up with news of three men, at least one who was Croatian, asking about access that bordered on their property.

And they knew then that something was definitely wrong.

It was also a very blunt reminder of how reliant they'd become on Yunho's intel.

He had ears and eyes on everything. Including on Shaw and Porter. Harry and Asher would normally get a quick heads-up phone call to alert them that the town's good policemen were on their way.

So it was a complete surprise when it was Porter who'd

alerted them this time, and not Yunho. And the horror of hearing of a possible enemy threat from Shaw made Harry feel very uneasy.

Yunho should have seen them coming. The fact he didn't meant something was *very* wrong.

So they'd boarded the first flight to Bangkok and were on their way to Yunho's island.

Harry was scared of what they'd find.

Scared of what it would do to Asher.

Yunho was like an older brother to Asher, or a father. The only family he had. He'd saved Asher's life all those years ago, and in turn, Asher had saved his. They'd been working ops together ever since.

Yunho was the eyes and ears of their team; Asher was the feet on the ground. They were unbeatable. Untraceable.

Until now.

The island came into view and Asher got to his feet, ready. Harry brought the boat around, slowed right down, and edged into the private dock like he'd done a dozen times in the last two years.

He hadn't even cut the engine or tied the boat off before Asher was up on the dock, running toward the main house.

Goddammit.

"Asher, wait!" Harry called, but it was useless. He was gone.

Harry hooked the mooring line around the bollard and chased after him. They had no guns, no weapons, and Asher ran in there without any intel whatsoever.

And Harry could see as he cut across the manicured lawn to the house that something was wrong.

The glass sliding door had been left open, sheer

curtains blowing in the wind. Lights were on, a lamp knocked over, and it was far, far too quiet.

Yunho had never not met them on the dock, so that in itself wasn't good. But when Harry ran inside, it was pretty apparent as to why.

Narong, one of the men who worked for Yunho, was on the floor, dead. A dark pool of dried blood radiated from his head like a macabre halo.

Harry didn't need to check to see how cold he was. He could easily determine he'd been dead for over forty-eight hours. Maybe sixty hours.

Too long.

Asher came running down the stairs. "No one. Nothing," he said, not even stopping before he ran toward the back of the room. Harry knew where he was going, and he was quick to follow.

The basement was a secure room. Fingerprint-coded entry, plated safe room, undetectable on radar. It was Yunho's office, his control centre, filled with screens and state-of-the-art tech that allowed Yunho to keep satellite eyes and ears all over the world. Harry used to call it the *war room*.

It'd put Homeland security to shame.

The door was blown open, sheared off its hinges, half of it hanging to the frame, the other half in smithereens all over the floor. Every screen was black, the room silent minus the hum of hard drives and mainframes. In the mainframe cabinet, one box in particular was missing, a hole and cords in its place. The door to the weapons vault was open but otherwise untouched.

Except there on the floor was Aranya, the woman who had worked with Yunho, with a bullet hole between her surprised eyes. As if she'd stood up from her desk when the door imploded and was shot point blank.

Such a shame.

Harry had liked her. He could almost hear the echo of her laughter . . .

Until Asher let out a strangled cry before he pulled a screen off the desk and launched it at the wall with a scream.

Harry went to him, but Asher pulled his arm free. "The other buildings," he said, racing back up the stairs.

Harry chased after him, following him out into the sun and across the lawn. Into the open space and broad daylight, for fuck's sake.

There were maintenance sheds and gardening sheds. A pool house and a boat shed.

All empty. No signs of any struggles, no damage. Nothing out of place.

Being an island, they had no need for a garage or cars, and given that Yunho was a chronic agoraphobic, the only form of transport they had was a boat that Lucas used to go to the mainland when necessary.

Not that he left the island often. They had everything delivered. All maintenance and cleaners came once or twice a week, by boat.

Aranya and Narong would stay in the main house—it was a mansion, after all—and go home on the weekends or for vacations.

This island was a refuge, a secure and off the map haven where Yunho could live without risk of being found.

Given his inability to step foot off the island also meant he was a sitting duck, should someone ever find him.

And someone had clearly found him.

Professionals. Well-armed, well-informed, and well-trained.

This wasn't good.

Harry didn't need to point that out, because Asher understood it all too well.

Upon finding the boat shed empty—Lucas's boat was still there, but no one was hiding in the hull, alive or dead—Asher jumped back onto the deck and spun on his heels, exasperated, frustrated, frightened. He let out a whine, his hands on his head.

Harry had never seen him so distraught.

"Hey," Harry said, taking hold of his hands, then his arms, and when Asher still wasn't focusing, Harry gave him a gentle shake. "Hey!"

Asher's eyes cut to his. "Where is he? What happened here?"

"I don't know—"

He strung together some biting words in Croatian, his frustration giving way to anger. "Who took him? He cannot leave. Taking him off this island will kill him. I swear to every god, Harry. I will find who did this and—"

"We will find them. You and me. But first we need to take a minute to assess the situation."

"What isn't clear to you, Harry?" He threw his hand back toward the house. "Whoever did this knew exactly what this place was and where to find him. They executed Aranya and Narong. They weren't tortured or interrogated, they were executed. Which means whoever did this did not need information or access. Which means they have Yunho and Lucas."

"Exactly," Harry countered. "Which is why we need a plan. You running out into the open like that was stupid. You could have been shot."

"I don't care!" Asher yelled at him. "I had—"

"I do!" Harry yelled back at him. "I care! You cannot die, you hear me?"

Harry wanted to pull his hair out. He wanted to shake some sense into Asher or punch the living shit out of something. But he knew Asher wasn't thinking clearly out of the panic and concern for Yunho.

So Harry tried again, more gently this time. "I need you, Asher. Yunho and Lucas need you. We need to think and work out a plan of what we do next. We cannot stay here. We cannot be seen here. We need to move."

Asher blinked a few times, then squinted his eyes shut. When he looked at Harry, his eyes were focused.

Murderous.

"We will find who did this," Harry promised. "And we will find Yunho and Lucas. We know they're alive." Because they weren't dead on the floor, not that Harry needed to say that. "Likely taken. For information or money, I don't know. But we will find them. We just need to think, and we need to be smart. We can't find them if we're dead."

Asher nodded. "Yes. We need to find them." He swallowed hard, his jaw clenching. "I'm going to kill every last one of them, Harry."

Harry almost smiled. "And I will help you. Plan first. Now, let's think. Who knew about this place? Who knew about the war room?"

"His other staff. Groundskeepers, cleaners."

Harry nodded. This was good. Progress. "Yes. And the doctor who came out when you were injured. I don't know if she knew about the war room though."

Asher nodded. "That wasn't her first time here."

"Okay, so she goes on the list."

"We should see if there's any footage," Asher said, looking back at the house.

"Not sure there's anything left working down there," Harry said. "But we can try." He checked his watch. "Thirty minutes, tops. Then we leave."

Asher gave a hard nod, and they ran back to the house. Harry assumed Asher would head straight for the war room, but he didn't. He ran up the stairs.

"Where are you going?" Harry asked, taking the stairs two at a time behind him. "The security cameras are downstairs."

"The system has a built-in kill switch," Asher said, going into Yunho and Lucas's bedroom. It was a huge room, probably the same size as Harry and Asher's entire house. There was a massive bed, made and untouched, a sofa setting, a huge desk and chair. There were doors open, to walk in robes and a bathroom that Harry could see was empty. Asher had obviously checked when he'd run up here before.

This time he went straight for the desk, opening drawers, searching for something.

"Yunho can voice-activate the kill function from his phone, but it will also shut down if he doesn't log in every few hours. The entire system downstairs will be dead. No one but him can access it now."

And as soon as Yunho knew they were in trouble, he would have activated the kill switch. Voice activated on his phone, though? That was some James Bond shit, right there, Harry thought.

"So what are you looking for?" he asked.

Asher rummaged through the drawers, and not finding what he was after, he went for the bedside table. He pulled open the drawer and found a tablet. "This."

"An iPad?"

Asher scoffed at that. "As if Yunho would ever own an Apple product. Do you know how many people Yunho has tracked through their iPhone?" He shrugged. "But this is like an iPad though, yes. A tablet, no account necessary. Lucas insisted he leave the war room and come to bed at least for a few hours, so he'd lay in bed and still watch everything. He called it a compromise."

The screen came to life but required a passcode. Because of course it did.

Asher didn't even try. He sighed and looked around. "Look for their laptops," he said. "I doubt we'll find anything."

Harry checked his watch. Twenty minutes.

He went into the wardrobe, rifling through drawers and anything that looked like it moved. Their wardrobe was so well organised, so neat, and so damn expensive, it looked like a department store.

Asher soon joined him, tossing expensive watches out of the top drawer, looking for something underneath . . . like a false bottom. There wasn't one.

Yunho was hardly about to have a false-bottom drawer in his wardrobe when he had an entire security war room in his basement.

Asher grumbled, pocketing a few watches.

"What are you doing?" Harry asked. It wasn't like they were short on funds.

"We can use these instead of cash. Less traceable," he replied, heading toward Lucas's shoe collection next. It was going to look like a robbery gone wrong, but Harry figured it didn't much matter at this point.

"Let's go back downstairs," Harry suggested.

Asher gave a nod, and with the tablet in his hand, he followed Harry back to the war room.

Whoever had done this hadn't taken anything. Well, except for Yunho and Lucas. But the computers were all there, even the vault of weapons. Asher's baby, his MAC 50 . . .

Asher searched the desks, stepping over Aranya as if she wasn't even there. Then, clearly deducing they were wasting time, he went into the vault.

Asher upended a rifle carry bag, dumping the contents on the floor: a scope and a bag strap. He grabbed pistols and two rifles, boxes of ammunition, and shoved them into the bag. He threw in the tablet before handing the bag to Harry, then took his MAC 50 off the rack. When he turned to face Harry, he had a different expression on his face.

Blank. Not in a devoid way, but in a ready-to-watch-the-world-burn kind of way.

Harry understood. He gave a nod. "Let's go."

They left the house as they'd found it, crossed the lawn to the dock, stepped onto the boat, and a few minutes later were heading back to the mainland.

"Where to first?" Harry asked over the roar of the engine, though he was fairly sure he knew.

"We track down his staff," Asher replied. "Those who worked on the island, who had access."

Yep. Just what Harry thought.

THREE

TALLOWWOOD

NATIONAL PARKS and Wildlife Officer John Kepper put in a call about a vehicle left in the park and the possibility of missing campers.

"They mighta gone for a hike and got lost," he'd said.

August knew different.

He saw the vehicle details and he knew.

The rented Hilux crew cab utility had been left unattended for three days. No sign of the three men who had stopped in town to ask directions. The same three men who August had told Michael and Joshua Hill about.

August knew they weren't lost.

But he had to follow procedure. They were missing until proven otherwise.

The camp they'd set up wasn't really a camp at all. There'd been no attempt at a campfire, no bedding, no fishing gear, no food or supplies.

"Unless they took it with them and walked off a trail," Jake supplied weakly.

He knew all too well those men weren't here to camp or fish. And he knew they weren't missing.

August looked into the surrounding forest and sighed. "We should get the dog squad and a chopper."

Wasted resources, he thought. But protocol.

There was a minuscule chance of the three men being lost campers. But August had to follow procedure.

He made some calls while Jake and Probation Officer Sharp took to the trails to look for signs or clues. Or bodies. Local volunteer search and rescue teams would be arriving soon and the police search team would be feet and vehicles on the ground too. And a chopper, most likely.

Wasted resources and *wasted time*, August thought.

When the search and rescue team arrived, August was happy to hand over coordinating efforts. He wanted to concentrate his own efforts somewhere else.

"You okay?" Jake asked him quietly when they had a minute alone.

"We're not looking for three men," August murmured. "We're looking for three bodies."

Jake looked out into the trees and sighed. "Most likely, yeah."

Christ.

He should have expected as much. He *had* decided to warn Michael and Joshua, after all. A decision August was certain would come back to bite him in the ass.

"We need to take a drive," August said.

Jake nodded. He spoke to the search and rescue coordinator for a moment, and a few minutes later, August and Jake were on the road.

"I don't need to ask where we're going, do I," Jake said. It wasn't a question.

"Probably not."

"They're not there," he said. "We have no warrant. We can't get inside their house, and anything we find is inadmissible without—"

"I know," August said. And he *did* know all this. "I don't know what I'm looking for."

"Do you think they'd leave any evidence behind for what they did or didn't do to those three missing men?" he asked incredulously. "Because if they are ex-military or ex-government spies, or whatever we think they are, they won't have left behind a trace."

"I know," August said. And he did know. He wasn't sure what he was looking for. "And those three missing men?" he said, looking across at Jake. He loosened his grip on the steering wheel. "We'll never find them. They're gone. Speaking of evidence. No bodies, no clothes, no trace. That whole coordinated search and rescue effort is a waste of time and money."

"So what are we looking for? Not the search and rescue," he clarified. "What are *we* looking for at their house?"

"I don't know."

"You know they'll have cameras and shit. Hell, they probably already know we're on our way."

"I know."

After a few moments silence, Jake sighed. "Feels kinda wrong. They trusted us with Mala. She's the sweetest thing. Even Scarlett likes her. Kind of."

August smiled at him. "Wanna know what I think?"

"What's that?"

"I think Michael Hill will be disappointed in us if we don't go check his place out."

Jake cocked an eyebrow. "Disappointed?"

"Yeah. He respects the badge, or the chain of command. I don't know."

Jake snorted. "I don't think Michael Hill would agree."

Their house was quiet, locked up, and deserted. Looking through the window, August could see everything was still in its place, as if they'd ducked out to the store and not left the country, not knowing if they'd ever be back.

He could only guess they were used to living a life where they could walk away and never look back.

August saw the security camera, and not wanting to look like he was snooping, he held his badge up to it. Not that he needed to. They knew exactly who he was.

And where he lived.

August and Jake had a quick poke around the shed; the shovels, chainsaw, and tools all arranged neatly, nothing out of place. Michael's doing, August would bet. Everything was meticulous.

At the back of the house, where the land sloped downward to the forest, there were two large water storage tanks amidst the piers under the large veranda overhead. They were half-buried, which wasn't unusual, but August stared at them, not sure why they bothered him.

"What's that face for?" Jake asked.

"They're what? Ninety thousand litres each?"

Jake shrugged. "Yeah. Metal for fire safety. Ya gotta have them now. What about them?"

"Then what are those?" he pointed to the two other tanks beside the house. "Another ninety thousand litres each. That's three hundred and sixty thousand litres of water storage."

"House usage, gardens, fire regulation," Jake said, shrugging again.

August wasn't convinced. "Hm. Maybe." He walked down to the other tanks. He remembered at Christmas time when they'd been out here last, the expensive excavator, the grounds work. To dig for the septic tank and drainage line, and they'd just put in a bore for groundwater, Michael had said.

He remembered Michael working in the blistering sun in December, trying to fix a water valve. That had struck August as odd back then, like something didn't make sense until now.

August walked around the tanks until he found the water valve in question. It would switch the flow over between tanks; most tanks had them.

"Bring the ladder," he called out.

Jake did as he was asked, but he clearly thought August was reading too much into it. He put the ladder to the side of the first tank and began to climb up. "What am I looking for?"

"There'll be an inlet hole at the top, maybe with a strainer grate to stop leaves," August said.

"Yes, like there is on all tanks."

August resisted grumbling. "Shine your torch in. Tell me what you see."

A few seconds later came his reply. "Water. I see water."

"And this tank?"

Jake climbed across and inspected the second tank. "Uh, water."

Dammit.

Jake climbed down. "Sometimes a water tank is just a water tank." He took his torch and tapped the tank. "See? Full of water." Then he tapped the second tank.

Only the sound it made was different.

Hollow.

What the hell?

Jake tapped it again and his eyes met August's. "What the hell?"

"My thought exactly." August walked around the tank again, looking for any abnormalities, looking for anything out of the ordinary. There was a seam in the metal joined with rivets. Like he'd seen a hundred times before.

The only other thing on that tank was the water valve. It was a lever handle, so August turned it.

Water came out the release outlet, so he shut it off again. Thinking, thinking . . .

"Remember when we came here in December, Michael was working on this. He had a huge wrench, said some bullshit about not being able to open the valve."

Jake nodded. "Yeah. In summer, when connections swell—"

"Why does this have two valves?"

Jake looked at the valve and then he looked twice. "Well, it's a special firefighting fitting, so maybe they have to have a secondary cut-off feature, I don't know."

The valve looked like a standard ball valve on almost every tank in the country; when August turned the lever, water came out of the tap. Exactly as it should have done.

But there was a gate valve at the base of the tank. The type with a circular flat tap that you had to rotate.

So August rotated it. He turned it all the way off. Nothing unusual happened, but then he turned the lever handle.

No water came out.

"You turned the water off," Jake said flatly. "Congratulations."

August gave the lever another heave, pushing it all the

way round—which it certainly didn't do before—and there was a muted beep, the sound of a pressure release, and the metal seal in the tank popped open to reveal a door.

Jake grabbed August, pulling him back at the same time as he drew his weapon. "Jesus Christ," he hissed. "August, get back."

August stood his ground, heart hammering. It was dark inside. Cool stale air met August's nose when he stepped forward.

What the hell . . . ?

"Give me your torch," August said quietly.

"I don't like this," Jake whispered back, but he held out his torch.

August opened the door wide and shined the torch down, illuminating the steps down into the earth. "There's a light switch," he noted. "Stay here; hold the door open."

"August," Jake breathed.

"I'll be okay," he assured him. He unholstered his weapon just in case, holding it and the torch in front of him, he entered the tank.

He hit the light switch, and after a click and a buzz, a blue light lit up the room below. No movement, no sound. August held his breath as he took the final few steps.

He found himself in a room, about four metres by four metres, concrete walls by the looks of it, with ventilation and lighting . . . and a whole fucking armoury.

There were no sensors, not that he could see, though he assumed there were cameras or eyes on him.

He went back up the stairs to an impatient Jake. "What is it? What's down there?"

August held the door for him. "Go take a look."

UNSURE OF WHO TO CALL, August and Jake decided to call everyone. NSW Police Commissioner's office, the Federal Police, and lastly, ASIO.

Not that August expected to get far, but this was too big for him.

While Jake sat on the phone to the Feds in Canberra, August was on hold to ASIO.

He'd first thought he'd get nowhere or be told, in no uncertain terms, to drop his inquiry. "It relates to Michael Hill and Joshua Hill, Tallowwood, New South Wales," he'd explained. There had been a pause; he was told to please hold. He'd since been transferred twice, on hold again.

Jake seemed to be having better luck. He could see him at his desk, talking to a person on the other end of his line at least.

August was beginning to think he'd been given a dead end, that he'd been put on hold with no one intending to take his call at all, in hopes that he'd just get tired of waiting and just hang up.

He passed the time by googling any keywords he could think of. Any news headlines pertaining to ex-military, or currently serving military, or government officials to see if any images popped up.

Most of the images he found had been from that whole military top-brass case a few years back that got blown open: spies, espionage, murder, treason, embezzlement. It had read like a Tom Clancy novel, and August couldn't remember what ever happened to that guy.

The director of Special Operations Command. Parrish was his name. The court case was ongoing, of course. It'd probably take years. Parrish would probably die of old age before convicted, August remembered thinking at the time.

August was jaded about the legal and judiciary system. He couldn't help it. He'd spent his life's work trying to put bad people away and lawyers armed with loopholes got them off.

He was mid-sigh when his call was picked up. "Commander's office," a male voice said. Short, clipped. Annoyed. No name, no rank.

August sat up straight in his seat. He introduced himself and then dove straight to the deep end. "We have a new case of some missing tourists, which I believe you may be interested in. But I understand you're very busy so I'm going to make a very long story short and ask if there's any information you could impart on a Mr Michael Hill and a Joshua Hill."

There was only silence.

August forged on. "And I know I've been told by ASIO before to cease all investigations in relation to Michael and Joshua Hill, but we've had a development in this case, and it's a suspected triple homicide. It's going to attract media attention, and—"

"Detective Shaw, I'm going to stop you right there," Mr Commander's Office said. "Did you say you'd been asked by ASIO to cease all investigations?"

"Well, yes. But that was for a different matter. That was before this new case."

"When? When were you told to cease investigations? And by whom?"

"Christmas morning, actually. December twenty-fifth, last year. It's why I remember it so specifically. And I didn't get a name then," August said. "Much like I didn't get yours now."

Another pause of silence. There may have been a faint clicking of a keyboard or background office noise; it was hard to tell.

Just then, Jake waved his hand to get August's attention. He was still at his desk, still had his phone pressed to his ear. But he gave a thumbs up.

Then Mr Commander's Office said, "Detective Shaw, I'm going to need you to tell me everything. Don't give me the shortened version. Start at the beginning."

"From when? When they first moved to my town and I knew they weren't who they said they were? Or when I watched Joshua Hill use a sniper rifle at a gun show like he was Jason freaking Bourne? Because that's when I tried to find out who he really is, and that's when ASIO shut me down the last time, and now I've got three missing Croatian nationals in my national park."

The beat of silence stretched out, and his voice was low and cold when he spoke. "Detective, I never shut you down before."

"What do you mean you never shut me down before? I sat in this very office and took a call from ASIO, citing under the Australian Security Intelligence Organisation Act that I was to cease all investigations. It was Christmas morning. I have the call log."

"That order didn't come from this office."

"Then who the hell did it come from?"

More silence except for the muted sound of action. Was he walking? "Detective Shaw, I never gave you that order then, but I'm giving it now. You are to cease all investigations on this case, effective immediately. Someone from my office is on their way to you now."

August blinked. "Uh, I'm sorry, what?"

The line went dead.

Jake came over to August's desk, grinning, his eyes wide. "I think I found something. Remember the defence boss who got busted for all that espionage shit? Parrish?"

August's mind was still reeling. "Uh, yeah. But Jake, listen—"

"Well, there was an agent, a secret ops agent—"

"Jake, stop," August said, louder this time. Jake stopped. "We've just been shut down. Again."

"What?"

"ASIO. But get this. ASIO says it wasn't them who shut us down on this before."

Jake cocked his head. "Then who was it?"

"I have no idea. ASIO's on their way here now."

"Here? Now?"

August nodded. "We need to get everything we have on these missing campers into a job file and make it official. Case numbers logged. I want everything we have put into the system before they get here."

Jake motioned to Kaycee sitting at her desk. "Deans already did. The case is logged and in the system."

"Those men would have had to provide ID to the car rental company. I want copies of passports, names, everything we can get."

Deans spun in her chair and tapped away on her keyboard. "Already on it, boss."

"I'll draft up my report," August said, not knowing what good it would do. But there were other agencies involved. Search and Rescue, Coffs Harbour police, Polair, the K9 squad. Sure, it was rugged wilderness, but they'd found no trace of anything or anyone, not that August expected them to. August wanted his report on the job file and the other agencies reports logged in and officially on the record before ASIO came in and shut it down.

They all got busy at their desks. After calls with the search and rescue coordinator and Coffs' office, August had his head down with his report and had lost track of time. When Jake and Deans appeared at his desk, August noticed it was dark outside.

Shit.

He was holding some papers, printouts by the look of them. "August," he said quietly. "I asked Deans to run with the Parrish case, just googling information. It's all public record anyway, so it's not like we were digging . . ."

August looked at the papers. "And?"

He handed the papers over, and there on top was a photograph. Grainy, old, not entirely clear, but the person in it was unmistakable.

Michael Hill.

Australian army sergeant. Younger, with fewer scars, but the death stare was the same.

Except this had *deceased* stamped across it and a name underneath it.

Timothy "Harry" Harrigan.

"He was military before he went special ops," Deans said. "Dark ops. Assassin working for the Australian government overseas."

Jesus fucking Christ.

"How did you find this?" August asked quietly.

"Google," she said with a shrug. And August knew she'd always been super-fast and efficient when it came to finding anything online. She was a whiz compared to August. "Negative keywords, filters, and knowing what to look for."

He turned the page. It was more on Michael . . .

Timothy "Harry" Harrigan. His military record. Died in 2016 in Syria, apparently.

Which was odd. Because he was standing in August and Jake's kitchen just four nights ago.

"Anything on Joshua?" August asked, though he wasn't sure he wanted to know.

"Nothing," Deans replied.

Just then, two men in dark suits came into the police station. They saw all three officers at August's desk and the one in front showed his badge. "Australian Security Intelligence." He looked right at August and gave a professional smile. "Detective Shaw."

August stood up. "Mr Commander's Office, I assume."

As if that was an invitation to come in, both of them came around the reception desk. Mr Commander's Office put his hand out. "Your case file, please. Including the papers in your hand."

August swallowed thickly, realising far too late that he was still holding the printout.

Fuck.

August slid the printout into the case folder, along with his report and passport photos from the rental company. "My report's been logged," he offered lamely.

"The case is now closed," he said smoothly. "The 4WD has been removed and impounded. All search and rescue efforts have been called off. The three missing tourists were never missing, and Michael and Joshua Hill are just two law-abiding citizens who you don't need to investigate again. For anything. Do I make myself clear?" He shot Jake and Kaycee a hard glare. They both nodded, and seemingly pleased, the two suits turned and walked out, leaving nothing but silence in their wake.

And August seethed.

"The fuck just happened?" Jake whispered.

"We just got silenced," August replied. He hated this. He hated bureaucracy, he hated red tape, and he hated the government agencies that demanded transparency and integrity while having none.

Then his phone rang, the search and rescue coordinator's name on the screen; no doubt he'd just heard the search was called off . . . Then the station phone rang, then another line lit up.

ASIO sure worked fast.

The three of them sighed and got back to work.

FOUR

AUGUST KNEW before they'd even come to a stop at Michael and Joshua's place that ASIO had already been. He wasn't surprised. He also wasn't surprised that the secret door in the water tank had been opened with an angle grinder, by the looks of it.

They clearly had neither the smarts nor the time to figure out the lock.

But the guns were gone.

The house had been broken into, the door still ajar, and that just pissed August off.

So disrespectful.

They didn't care.

And that's when August realised he did. He *did* care.

Not about protocol or government agencies having the right to break and enter—not in this instance, anyway—but he cared about Michael and Joshua.

Not that those were their names.

Not that August knew them at all, apparently.

He tried googling Timothy "Harry" Harrigan and got

nothing. Even his photo that Deans had found had somehow been scrubbed from the internet.

August had a hard time thinking of him as Harry, or Timothy. To him, he was Michael Hill. A newcomer to Tallowwood, moved here with his husband, Joshua. They kept to themselves mostly, and even though August knew there was something dark about them, he'd always assumed they were dangerous and ex-military, he still liked them.

He couldn't help it.

Now, August had no clue exactly what government mess he'd stumbled into. Like, he had no clue just who Michael and Joshua Hill really were, or what they'd done before they moved here. But he couldn't quite believe the two men who'd stood in his kitchen the other night, who had asked them to please look after their little cat, who'd told August to lock the house and keep the lights off, were a danger to him.

As August stood outside Michael and Joshua's house, looking at the destroyed tank, at the broken lock to the house, he realised why.

"What is it?" Jake asked. "You got that scowl that never bodes well."

"Just thinking," he said quietly.

"About? The fact those assholes just left the place wide open? Or the fact they took the case from us? Three missing men and not a fuck to be given, apparently."

August found himself smirking, glad they were on the same page. "Not a single one." Then he sighed. "You know, I was just thinking about Michael and Joshua. Or whatever their names are, or what they've done. And the very little we really know about them at all."

Jake smiled at him. "And you can't figure out for the life of you why you like them."

August laughed. Jake really knew him too well. "I shouldn't. But I do."

"Wanna know what I think?"

"Always."

"No, we don't know who they really are or what they did. Or what made them leave at two in the morning. We know they're dangerous, we know Joshua has sniper skills, and we know that Michael could probably take someone's head off with his bare hands."

August nodded. That was probably true.

"But they have . . . I dunno, an air of integrity to them that's hard to describe."

August met his gaze then. "Yes! That's what I've been trying to pinpoint. That's exactly it. Like an unspoken integrity. Those ASIO suits were sleazy and shady. And for all the things Michael and Joshua ever lied about or hid from us, they still weren't like that."

"Like if it ever came down to it, you'd want Michael and Joshua on your side over those ASIO dicks."

August snorted. "I mean, yeah. You've seen Joshua with a rifle." He ran his hand through his hair. "Jokes aside, I already chose a side though, didn't I? I mean, I warned them about those three men turning up and put a target on their heads."

"That was different," Jake said. "That was a case of kill or be killed. Would you rather find Michael and Joshua dead here? Or if it escalated in town and involved civilians? Those three men signed their own death certificates when they came here to kill Michael and Joshua. It wasn't your fault."

Well, it kinda was. But still . . .

"If you could go back in time, would you do anything differently?" Jake asked.

August didn't need to answer. It was a rhetorical question, to prove his point. Because no, August wouldn't change what he did.

Jake nodded and let out a sigh. "Whatever they did before they moved here . . . well, whatever Michael did, good or bad, was under orders. He worked for the government doing some pretty dark stuff, no doubt, in the name of this country. And that's a loyalty you respect. You wouldn't have warned them otherwise."

August thought about that for a long moment. It was true, mostly. The real question August wasn't ready to answer was would he have done anything differently if ASIO had called him, informed him, and specifically told him *not* to warn Michael or Joshua. What would he have done then?

August wasn't sure he liked the answer.

He shook his head and let out a long sigh. "I think maybe they moved here for a quiet life, to lie low and find some peace. And I respect that."

"And the fact they're a couple." Jake shrugged. "A gay couple. I mean, it's hard enough in our line of work. Can't imagine what it's like in theirs."

August almost smiled. "Can you imagine anyone telling Michael and Joshua Hill they didn't agree with 'their lifestyle'?"

Jake laughed. "Not if they wanted to live."

August nodded and looking out into the trees, he sighed again. "I still wonder who called the first time, back in December. Said they were ASIO but weren't."

"Someone who works with Michael and Joshua?"

"Probably."

"Same person Joshua was trying to text. The same reason the three Croatian nationals turned up. I mean, it's all gotta be related."

"You'd think so."

"Do we want to even guess who Joshua really is?"

August inhaled deeply and sighed. "Nope. Pretty sure we don't want to know the answer to that."

"True." Jake was quiet for a moment. "Do you think we'll ever see them again?"

"I don't know. I doubt it." August felt a little sad about that, even though he knew he shouldn't. "Anyway, let's get this place locked up for them. That way, if they do come back, the forest animals won't have moved in."

"Yeah, okay. Regardless of all the unknowns and all the secrets, I hope they're okay."

August clapped him on the shoulder as they headed for the house. "Same."

RANONG, THAILAND

Harry knew Asher was a ticking time bomb, and there was little he could do to stop it.

Part of him didn't want to stop it.

He wanted to protect Asher, yes. But he was hurting and angry—which Harry totally understood—and if Asher wanted to raze a path of destruction, then Harry would gladly help him.

They'd been out of the game for two years. A lifetime in the killing game. They'd been aging out anyway, which was why they'd had a price on their heads. They'd been loose ends that couldn't be tied off. God knows, men had tried.

Younger men, keen to prove a name for themselves. Thinking they could take out Harry Harrigan and Asher Garin. Fools, they were.

Dead fools now.

Though Harry was certain those younger men's bodies didn't ache in the mornings, joints stiff, and muscles sore.

Well, when they were alive, that was.

Taking those three Croatian men out had been easy enough. Harry and Asher had the element of surprise on their side, thanks to August Shaw.

Those men definitely weren't there to fish or camp. They had knives and rifles. Plastic 3D-printed types they hadn't even got around to fully assemble when Harry and Asher found them.

They also had a map with Harry and Asher's place marked on it. Harry took out the first two with perfect aim, then Asher had tried to get the third guy to talk.

Harry couldn't understand much. It was all in Croatian, but when Asher started to smash the guy's head in with the plastic rifle stock, Harry was sure the interrogation was over.

"He refused to talk," Asher had said. "And to think they were going to kill us with plastic rifles. A fucking children's toy!" he'd cried, duly offended. "I've never been more insulted."

Harry had smiled at that.

He wasn't smiling now.

Like when he had to carry three bodies deeper into the woods. He wasn't smiling then. He was too old for that shit.

Asher had helped, of course, but Harry did the heavy

lifting. They'd taken them into the ravine on their land, where the wild pigs had their dugout. The rutting season was over, the earth was all dug up, trees, roots, leaves. Appetites were frenzied.

See, the thing about wild pigs is that they'll demolish a human body, hair, bones, and all.

It was why Harry and Asher fed them sometimes, adding some bones and blood to their diet over the last two years. So they'd come in handy in a time like this.

Wild pigs had even been known to eat clothes and boots. Not that Harry and Asher risked that, but three naked bodies, slit open and for the taking?

They'd be gone in twenty-four hours.

Not that it mattered.

Because it was highly unlikely Harry and Asher would be returning to Tallowwood, to their little house in the woods. And that made Harry's heart heavy. They'd finally had the perfect place, to live out their perfectly quiet lives.

Until that came to an end.

If he was being honest with himself, Harry was surprised they'd even got two years. And it was a perfect two years.

Until he got complacent . . .

Now he wasn't sure where they'd go after this, if they survived. He couldn't put his finger on it, but this felt final. He didn't know why.

He didn't want to know.

Asher needed his help. Yunho and Lucas were missing, and Asher would stop at nothing to find them. And Harry would be right beside him the whole way.

Till the end.

"You awake?" Asher asked.

Harry shot him a look. "Yeah. Of course." He hadn't

been *asleep*. Jeez. They were walking along a street in broad daylight, for fuck's sake. He'd been lost in his thoughts, that's all. Which wasn't conducive to staying alive, but still. "Wassup?"

"The doctor's office is this way," Asher said, nodding up the alley.

Harry and Asher had watched the two smiling maintenance guys board their boat, loaded up with crates of vegetables and food—Yunho's standard weekly order—heading out to Yunho's island. Well, according to the guy who sold them the boat. And if they were going out there as if nothing was wrong, then they had no clue what they were about to find.

Meaning Harry and Asher could assume they knew nothing.

It also meant they'd alert the authorities, so the police were about to be involved. Time was running out.

The doctor's office was the next visit, and given it was early morning, Harry didn't expect her to be too busy yet. The thing about life in sleepy Thai villages was that everyone was smiling, only too happy to help. So of course the reception lady opened the door for them, telling them to please sit, please sit.

So they sat and waited while the receptionist disappeared and came back with the doctor.

Who *was* smiling . . . until she saw who it was. Harry had to give her props for her stoicism, and she held the door for them. "Come through," she said. She offered them two chairs opposite her desk, but Harry and Asher both remained standing.

"Do you remember us?" Harry asked.

She looked at Asher. "Of course. It's been a while, but it's not something I'm likely to forget." She swallowed hard, studying his face. "Your injuries have healed well . . ."

"Yunho and Lucas are missing," Asher said flatly. "Their house was open, ransacked. Aranya and Narong are dead."

She paled. "Oh my."

"Whoever did it knew about the war room," Harry said.

She squinted a little. "The . . . the war room?"

"The basement," Asher explained.

She raised her hands. "Gentlemen, I don't know anything about a basement or a *war* room. I don't even want to know what that is," she whispered. "Mr Oh is my patient. I do house calls to him and him alone, because he pays considerably well." Then she shrugged. "And because of his condition."

"Agoraphobia," Asher said.

"Right." She nodded. "He can't leave the island. He suffers crippling anxiety at the thought, as I'm sure you know."

"I know," Asher replied. "But he's not there now."

She shook her head. "I don't know anything about that. I'm not sure why you think I would."

"Because you're one of five people who have been there that are still alive." Asher's tone was ice cold.

But from the way she paled, Harry didn't believe she knew anything. "When was your last visit?"

"Ahh, two months ago, probably. Sometimes Lucas will pick up Yunho's prescription to save me the trip. If he comes to the mainland for anything."

"Prescription?" Asher asked.

She hesitated for a second, probably reconsidering her doctor-patient privilege, before she looked at both Harry and Asher and sighed. "He takes medication for anxiety and epilepsy. Only for when he needs it."

"Epilepsy?" That was news to Harry.

"From when he was in Korea," Asher explained quietly. "He was tortured and suffered fits as a result. High-stress situations would bring it on." He gave Harry a dark look. "Like being forced to leave his island."

The doctor gave a sad nod. "He was doing well," she said, then seemed to lose her train of thought. "I'm sorry. I wish I knew more. I hope he's okay. I hope they both are."

"How often did Lucas come to the mainland?" Asher asked. Harry wasn't sure why he hadn't thought to ask that.

"I don't know," she replied. "Every few weeks, I think. I really wouldn't know. I'm not privy to their daily lives. I don't know them that well. I shouldn't even be having this conversation." She shook her head, frustrated and a little frightened. "I'm sorry I can't help you. I know nothing about them, or their basement. I wish I could help you . . ."

They were done here. She knew nothing. It was a stretch anyway. "Thank you," Harry said, heading for the door.

Asher stood there watching her for a few long seconds, looking for a flicker of doubt or dishonesty perhaps. Eventually he turned and, seething, stormed out. The receptionist barely getting out of his way.

Harry had to catch up and pull him to a stop in the alley. "Hey," he murmured. "You need to stop and think."

Asher's nostrils flared, his eyes full of rage. "I need to kill something."

Harry lessened the grip on his arm and rubbed it instead. "We need to put together a plan. We found nothing here, and the cops are gonna be all over this place as soon as those men on that boat get to the island and alert authorities. And we need to *not* be here when that happens, okay?"

Asher sighed, and Harry took that as his acknowledgement.

"We need to think about what we know so far."

"We know nothing."

"Yes, we do. We know Yunho and Lucas weren't killed on sight. That means they were taken because they know something or have something that someone wants."

Asher's eyes narrowed, like that hurt to hear or as if he hadn't considered that.

And he should have.

God, they were so out of practice.

"And the other thing we know for certain is that Yunho and Lucas were taken around the same time three Croatian military guys turned up at our place. That's not a coincidence, and that's all we have right now."

"So we go to Croatia," Asher said.

Harry nodded. "So we're going to Croatia." He thought about that for a second. "I don't know where exactly to start in Croatia, but—"

"I do," Asher said.

There was a coldness in his eyes, a detached and calculating darkness that Harry hadn't seen in a long time. Maybe ever. When they'd been on the run in Northern Africa and Asia, Asher had thought it was the most fun he'd had in ages.

Until he was captured and tortured.

Then it was Harry who was ready to burn the world down.

But this was different. This was Asher on the back foot, threatened and at a complete loss.

Whenever he'd been on an assignment before, he'd had Yunho on call with his intel and insight. Yunho was Asher's eyes in a dark world.

He didn't have that now. But he had Harry.

"We'll find them," Harry whispered. "I promise."

Asher nodded, and there was a flicker of light in his eyes for the briefest moment before it was gone, darkness taking its place. "Let's go."

"We'll need to dump the guns," Harry said. "We can't take them with us; we can't get them into Croatia."

Asher's eyes met Harry's. "We can store them. In case we ever need them. We can get whatever we need in Sarajevo. I know a guy."

Sarajevo?

"Bosnia? I thought we were going to Croatia."

"Sarajevo first."

Harry shrugged, going along with it. "Okay. Sarajevo, it is."

STORING THE GUNS MADE SENSE. They way overpaid the storage company outside Ranong airport, ensuring silence and their storage room would remain off the books for as long as they needed. Harry got the impression this guy had made a few shady deals in his time, but he knew a handsome deal when he saw it. And expensive watches.

He also knew Asher wasn't the type to be double-crossed.

Harry was used to people shying away from him, not Asher. But the murder in Asher's eyes was kinda terrifying, Harry had to admit.

Before they walked into the airport, Harry stopped him again. "Okay, I'm going to need you to breathe and smile. If you look at airport security like you're looking at me right now, we won't be going anywhere."

Asher glowered at him.

"My point exactly." Harry couldn't believe Asher was being so unprofessional. He took him by the shoulders and stopped just short of shaking him. "Fucking stop it. If you want to help Yunho, you need to start acting like it. Where is the Asher Garin capable of reading any situation and then charming his way through? Because I need him right now."

"You don't know what I'm capable of," he murmured.

Harry let out a sigh. "Asher, I get it. You're angry and worried. I know that. I am too. But if you want to help them, you need to play the part. You're smarter than this. So play the fucking part. I know we've been out of the game for two years, but this is simple stuff. We're gonna walk in there, get through security and board a plane to Bangkok, then we're gonna do the same to get to Bosnia. And that's the last place you wanna trip any wires by pissing security off and end up on some government fucking watch list, right? Because if they find out who you really are? It's all over. We can't afford to get caught."

Fire burned in Asher's eyes, but Harry didn't care. This needed to be said.

"Yunho and Lucas can't afford *for us* to get caught."

Anger morphed into hurt in Asher's gaze and he shucked himself out of Harry's hold. But he didn't go too far. Harry put his hand to Asher's cheek, though Asher wouldn't look at him, so Harry kissed Asher's forehead instead.

"I love you. I love the *you* you've let yourself be these

last two years. Happy, carefree. But right now, I need the old Asher Garin back. The Asher who could be anyone he needed to be and then gone in the blink of an eye. A shadow in the dark. No emotions, no mistakes."

Asher still wouldn't look at him but he did half a nod.

Harry kissed his forehead again. "Now let's get our game faces on so we can bring them home."

FIVE

SARAJEVO, BOSNIA

HARRY'S OUTBURST at Asher had earned him the silent treatment. For the plane trip from Ranong to Bangkok and then all the way to Sarajevo. Asher had barely said five words to him the whole time. He just stared at the tablet's password lock screen as if it was some enigmatic puzzle. Or a time bomb, like he didn't want to see what secrets the tablet held.

But he had played his part.

Smiling and charming with the airport staff and security, and even on the plane. Well, correction: Joshua Hill had been smiling and charming.

Asher had been petulant.

He was angry and scared, and Harry understood his reasons. But he didn't play these types of games.

They checked in at a hotel, awaiting Asher's contact to return his call. Harry put a call in for room service, enough food for both of them. He could worry about getting supplies later. It was late, it'd been a long fucking day, and Asher's silence was a cherry on top of a shit-tastic cake.

Harry dumped his bag on the floor and fell onto the bed. He closed his eyes and sighed, scrubbing his hands over his face.

Asher still hadn't spoken to him, and Harry wasn't in the mood for his childish bullshit.

Asher curled himself up on the sofa and stared at the tablet screen, the cursor blinking in the password. He hadn't attempted to enter anything yet, still trying to think what the passcode might be.

It was going to lock them out, and they'd need to track down some tech whiz to access it. Or a teenager.

"We can find someone who can get us access to it," Harry said, nodding to the tablet.

Not that it mattered, because Asher didn't look at him to see it.

Room service delivered their tray of food, and Harry took the lids off. It was burgers and fries, nothing extraordinary, but he needed food, a hot shower, and sleep. "Eat something," Harry said, too tired to fight or argue. "Or don't."

Harry was halfway through his burger before Asher came over. He sat at the table, still sulking, and shoved some fries into his mouth. "You yelled at me," he said.

Harry shot him a disbelieving look. "I did not yell."

"You told me to fucking stop it."

"Because you needed to be told."

"You said—"

"I said what needed saying," Harry snapped. "And I meant every word. We need to be smarter, Asher. We've been out of this world for too long, and they are three days ahead of us. We have no intel, no backup, and no fucking clue what we're looking for. We can't afford the slightest misstep. And I know you're angry and scared. I get that. And you want to unleash hell on whoever did this, and babe, I will be right by your side. But we can't do this blindly, because that's when we make mistakes. We need to be smarter, both of us, because if something were to happen to you . . ." Harry shook his head. "I can't . . . I won't survive it, Asher."

Asher's eyes met his, sadness and fear finding their mark, because god, how it hurt Harry to see that.

"You're right," he whispered. "I'm sorry. Thank you. I just . . . Yunho's the only family I have . . . had. He's the only family I had for the longest time. Until I met you. And now I have you, and I'm so fucking grateful. But . . ." He shook his head, tears in his eyes. "Yunho saved my life, countless times. I owe him this. I owe him everything."

"I know."

"And I lost my head. I wasn't thinking straight. You were right."

Harry finally smiled. "I usually am."

"Don't push your luck."

Harry snorted and nodded to Asher's burger. "Eat up. I want to have a hot shower and go to bed."

Asher pouted again. "Is that an invitation?"

Harry couldn't help it. He smiled and nodded at Asher's food. "Be a good boy and eat, and I'll think about giving you a reward."

That earned him a scowl. "Half the burger and my reward better be a thorough fucking."

"Deal." Harry smiled as he bit into his burger. It was probably what Asher needed. What they both needed, if Harry was being honest.

It'd been a tense and emotional few days, and Harry

knew Asher always felt out of sorts when he wasn't in control.

And this situation they'd found themselves in? They had zero control.

They were three days behind, had no clue if they were even on the right track, and were effectively on the run again.

Someone else was calling the shots, and Asher was stressed and worried. Harry always did know how to bring Asher's mind back into focus. Make him forget all the excess bullshit and strip away the world until all that remained was one single focus.

The pain and pleasure of a thorough fucking.

Hmm.

Maybe Harry needed it more than Asher.

He watched Asher take a bite or two, though it was clear he had no appetite. He was too tired, too stressed, too worried.

He needs to let it all go.

"Hm," Harry began. "Remember when we were in Algeria."

Asher's gaze cut to his, and he nodded. "Which part? We did a lot in Algeria."

That was true.

"Remember when you wanted me to fight and fuck you? You wanted it violent and rough."

Asher raised one eyebrow and licked the corner of his mouth, a smile forming. "I remember. You didn't really want to do it either. The decent human in you kept warring with the animal side." He smirked then. "The animal won."

"No. You won. You got what you wanted. What you needed."

The fire in his eyes ignited. "And so did you."

"I did."

His nostrils flared. "Why are you remembering that now?"

They'd fucked a thousand times since then, and Harry had loved it every single time. The slow tender moments, the lovemaking, the intimacy.

But tonight they needed something else.

"Do you want me to fight you, Harry?" Asher asked. "Is that why you're bringing it up now?"

Harry grinned at him. "I don't want to fight you. I want to fuck you. It won't be gentle, and I won't care if you try to stop me, try to hurt me. The harder you fight me, the harder I'll fuck you."

Asher let out a rush of air, and he ran his tongue over his teeth when he grinned. "Do not make promises you can't keep, Harry," he whispered.

"Tell me now if you don't want it," he breathed.

Asher kept his eyes locked on Harry's, but his hand went to the knife on his plate. Fingers curled around the handle like a weapon, and for a beat, neither of them moved.

Until Asher leapt to his feet and lunged at Harry with the knife. Harry gripped his wrist and holding it high, pushed him backwards until he hit the wall. Asher clawed at Harry's neck, his chest, bringing his knee up, wrestling and pushing.

Fighting.

Harry gripped his other wrist and held him against the wall, hard. He shook Asher's wrist until he finally let go of the knife. But then Asher tried to use his legs as leverage. He kicked and struggled, all while trying to wrestle and wriggle free.

Harry wasn't having it.

He dragged Asher over to the bed and shoved him down, hard. Asher tried to fight him, arms flailing and fists flying, growling and grunting. "Is that the best you can do," Asher bit out. "Fucking weak."

He tried to kick at Harry, connected a few times, and it only made Harry fight harder to subdue him.

He held both Asher's wrists and pinned them to the mattress. Asher tried to wrestle out of the hold, using his legs and hips. So, using Asher's momentum, Harry flipped him over onto his stomach, using his forearm across Asher's shoulders to hold him down.

Harry ground his cock against Asher's ass and it made Asher groan. He was panting, the fight in him gone so Harry held Asher's head, pushing his face into the mattress. "Stay the fuck there," he growled.

Harry got off the bed to collect the lube, but as soon as he had it, Asher was off the bed and lunging at him again. He swung his arm, collecting Harry across the chin and Harry had to counter, driving his shoulder into Asher and tackling him onto the bed again.

He held him down like he meant it this time. They were going to have bruises tomorrow.

"Who's weak now?" Harry hissed, forcing Asher's face into the mattress. He pulled Asher's leg out and drove his erection against Asher's ass. "You're gonna fucking get it now," Harry growled. "As hard as I can give it."

He gave the back of Asher's head a good shove and then, gripping his jeans, ripped them down over his ass. He wasn't gentle, and he wasn't sorry.

With his ass exposed, Asher tried to push up, tried to turn around, but Harry shoved his hand into Asher's back and held him down.

"You're not going anywhere," Harry bit out. He snatched up the lube and tried to squirt it down Asher's crack.

"Want you raw," Asher snapped. "Make it hurt."

Harry undid the fly of his jeans and pulled his cock out. "It's gonna hurt enough," he said, holding Asher down by his shoulders and driving his cock into him.

Asher cried out into the bedding, his hands reaching out blindly before gripping the covers.

Harry pushed all the way in.

Not gentle.

Not sorry.

"This is what you need," Harry ground out. His cock inside him to the hilt, he held him still, and Asher cried out, trying to pull away, trying to turn his hips, to escape, to lessen the pain.

Harry gripped Asher's hip and held him right fucking there. "You'll fucking take it," he said, pulling out a little only to slam back in again. "You'll take every inch of me, and you'll take every fucking drop I give you."

Asher moaned, the fight in him easing away; the tension leaving his body with every thrust, every slam of Harry's hips.

With Asher's jeans still around his thighs, his tight ass was exquisite. The pleasure so intense, so consuming. Harry couldn't stop, even if he'd wanted to. He drove into him, over and over, ecstasy building higher and higher, his cock so impossibly hard. He drove up into him until he tumbled over the edge.

Pleasure exploded behind his eyes, down his spine, detonating pure bliss. He came, burying his load deep inside him.

Asher gasped as he took it. Harry groaned with every pulse, finally collapsing on top of him.

The room spun, his vision skewed, and the only sound was their laboured breathing. Harry kissed the back of Asher's neck, unable to move, unable to think.

"Jesus," Harry mumbled.

"Don't think for one second you're done yet," Asher said. He rolled his hips. "You'll be done when I say you're done."

Harry snorted. "Is that so?" He wasn't feeling like fighting right now . . . He was far too boneless.

Asher squirmed underneath him, squeezing Harry's sensitive cock. "Ah," Harry hissed.

"Finish what you started," Asher bit out, trying to move from underneath him, still trying to fight him.

Harry pulled out, making Asher cry out again. He yanked Asher's jeans down some more and flipped him onto his back, then folded his legs up to his chest. Harry sank his cock back into him and held his hand over Asher's throat.

"I'll finish what I started when I fucking want," Harry rasped.

Keeping his hand on Asher's throat, he gripped his cock with his other hand and began to stroke him.

Asher's eyes rolled shut, his face going red as Harry choked him a little. He didn't need to come again, but his cock was still half-hard and it felt soooo good to be buried inside him.

And apparently Asher wanted Harry's dick in his ass when he came tonight. Harry was only too happy to oblige. He held Asher down by his throat, buried his cock in his ass, and jerked him off until he came with a strangled cry.

Harry tightened his grip on Asher's neck as his orgasm rolled through him. Asher's eyes rolled back, his cock spilling ropes of come across his stomach and over Harry's hand.

He convulsed and trembled for the longest time until he sagged, and only then did Harry lessen the hold on his throat.

Asher sucked back air, a lazy smile on his lips, his eyes slowly closing.

Serene.

Harry pulled out of him and rolled him onto his side, and Asher moaned contentedly. Harry cleaned him up, pulled the covers up and over him, and let him sleep.

A few minutes later, showered and feeling so much better, Harry crawled into bed, Asher quick to snuggle in. Harry kissed the side of his head. "Wanna have a shower?" he asked quietly.

"Hmmno," Asher mumbled. "Sleep."

"'Kay," Harry murmured. He rubbed Asher's back, holding him, kissing his head every now and then, waiting for sleep to come. Until he remembered something. "I can't believe you were going to stab me with a knife."

Asher chuckled quietly, almost asleep. But he never denied it, and he never apologised, and Harry couldn't even be mad. He'd asked for the old Asher back—the Asher who could turn night into day on a dime, who took kill shots without blinking—and that's exactly what he got.

Harry smiled into the dark and sighed, tightening his hold on Asher, and closed his eyes.

THE MORNING LIGHT and the bathroom mirror showed Harry he had clawed nail marks down his neck and chest, a bruise on his thigh, and a mark on his forearm, courtesy of Asher and the fight-sex they'd had last night.

It didn't compare to the very large finger bruises Asher had on his throat.

Asher seemed pleased by all the war-wounds, looking at his neck from a few angles.

Harry, on the other hand, wasn't feeling so jovial about it.

"I could have crushed your hyoid bone," he mumbled.

Asher pointed to the base of his throat. "You know where the hyoid is," and then he showed the finger bruises higher up. "You weren't going to hurt me."

"The bruises on your neck say otherwise."

"They match the stripes down your neck and chest," Asher said, not fazed at all. "I'm actually disappointed that's all I got on you."

Harry smirked. "Your only hope of taking me out is from a safe distance, a good rifle scope, and no wind."

"Or a kitchen knife," Asher added with a blasé shrug.

"I'm starting to think I need to hide the cutlery."

Asher chuckled, then picking up his jacket, he slipped it on. "All right then, let's get this over with. Let me do the talking."

"If it's in Bosnian, I will be, yes."

ASHER SEEMED to know this city with a familiarity that Harry wasn't certain he liked. It was a warm day, the sun shining brightly in a clear blue sky, and the taxi driver, ignoring Harry completely, spoke animatedly to Asher about god only knew what, all in Bosnian, of course. It made Asher smile.

And Harry didn't care much for that either.

He watched the city pass by instead. Beautiful, in the way most European cities were. Where history warred with the twenty-first century, where a now-peaceful life and the scars of war were a contrasting landscape.

Not too unlike himself, Harry thought.

Hidden scars that ran deep, that the last few years of peace and quiet did not do enough to heal.

He wondered if Asher felt that too.

He remembered Asher saying he'd come to Sarajevo years ago in search of his past and how he'd felt nothing.

He wondered what he felt now.

"You okay?" Asher asked quietly.

Harry hadn't realised Asher and the taxi driver had stopped talking. "Yeah, just thinking."

Asher studied him for a moment before he slid his hand over Harry's, giving it a quick squeeze. "We're almost there."

Their destination turned out to be an old warehouse in the industrial part of the city where the scars of war weren't so hidden. Some newer buildings replaced the older ones, which had been shelled beyond repair, alongside older buildings where some walls still bore the damage of a darker time. Pockmarks of bullet holes like acne, and some buildings without roofs or windows, no more than external half-walls like jagged exposed skeletons of mortar and memories of a terrible time.

There were signs of life though. Cars, music from somewhere, the sounds of machinery and construction.

After the taxi drove off, Asher nodded toward the

building across the street. It looked like it may have been an electric power plant at some point. It was large, maybe half the block, with a dozen arch windows fronting the street. It looked maybe three storeys high with a fenced-off loading bay, and Harry assumed it was a depot of some sort.

"And this guy's name?" Harry asked as they walked toward the door.

"Daris," Asher said. He put his hand on the handle and gave Harry a smirk. "Play nice."

Hmm.

What was that supposed to mean?

Why wouldn't Harry play nice . . . unless . . . unless they had a history? As in a *private* history.

Harry stopped dead and cut Asher a laser-like stare. "Did you sleep with this guy?"

He might have asked that a little louder and a little angrier than he probably should have.

The two people in the foyer stopped and stared. They were behind a reception desk, a man and woman, he in his thirties, she in her late twenties. They wore white shirts with a logo on the breast that matched the large icon on the wall behind them.

Jak Logisička.

Harry could figure that out. Logistics.

The man spoke in polite Bosnian, smiling but wary, and trying not to look twice at Harry. Asher replied, fluent and overly pleasant, but then he gave Harry a smile and for his sake, Harry assumed, he switched to English.

"We'd like to see Mr Daris Guli please," he said, still smiling.

"Do you have an appointment?" The woman asked, tapping away on her keyboard.

"No, we don't. We've just got into the city," Asher explained. "I'm a very old friend of Daris's. Just tell him Asher is here to see him."

The woman gave a nod and disappeared through a door behind the desk, and the man stood there watching them. He seemed astute, Harry allowed. He was neat and tidy and probably good at his job, but Harry could tell he was no threat.

Asher gave Harry a nudge. "Smile, you're scaring him," Asher whispered, his lips not moving.

Harry tried to smile, which made Asher have to cover his laughter with a cough. "You still haven't answered my question," Harry said, not giving one fuck who heard.

"I'll tell you later. We're not discussing that now," Asher said.

Which meant yes. Yes, they had a personal history. Yes, Asher had slept with this guy.

It'd been a while since Harry had wanted to kill someone he'd never met.

The door opened and the lady appeared. "This way, please," she said, holding the door for them. The woman turned, Asher following, Harry last, and he didn't like the fact he had no idea what they were walking into.

It was a warehouse, yes. Rows of heavy-duty metal shelving, a man on a forklift, another man with a clipboard, and two small pantech trucks at the loading dock, other staff with hi-vis vests, everyone busy working.

So it was an actual working depot, and not a front.

The woman showed them to an office. Decent sized, an arched window letting in sunlight, bookcases of folders, a long desk at the back wall, and a man, waiting.

He was maybe forty, wearing black pants, a black polo with the same logistics logo. Handsome enough, greying hair, olive skin, full lips with a cautious smile, and a hint of fear with the fondness in his dark eyes.

He stared at Asher for a long beat, then looked at Harry, wincing almost, before his gaze went back to Asher.

"If you were here to kill me, I'd be dead already," he said, his accent similar to Asher's.

Asher laughed and nodded to the window. "It's a big window. You'd make the shot too easy for me."

The man laughed then and gestured to his desk. "It's a beautiful window and I still can't have my desk in front of it because of you." Then his smile faded away to nothing. "It's been a long time, Asher."

Asher nodded and put his arms out, the man quickly collecting him in a fierce hug.

Oh yeah. They had a history, all right.

But from the way they both closed their eyes tight, a moment of pain brought to the surface for both of them, Harry realised that maybe they had more than just a history.

Harry cleared his throat and it made Asher pull back. He had the audacity to smile. "Harry, this is Daris. We were in the orphanage together."

Ah, shit.

Asher looked back at Daris. "And then . . . and then we went to camp together."

Jesus Christ.

Camp. Where Asher had told him boys were taken and trained, military style. Where, as a young boy, he ran drugs and information between camps. No older than eight or ten years of age, shot his first human target at fifteen.

The same camps where many boys never survived.

"Daris," Asher said. "This is my Harry."

My Harry.

Suddenly Harry wasn't feeling so jealous.

Daris looked Harry up and down, approvingly, noting the scratches on Harry's neck. Then he lifted Asher's chin to see the not-quite faded finger bruises on Asher's neck. "A good match, I see," Daris said with a smirk.

"In every way," Asher replied.

Harry felt the need to clear his throat again. "Nice to meet you," he said.

"Likewise," Daris said, but then he looked back at Asher as if he couldn't believe what he was seeing. He put his hand to Asher's cheek. "Look at you. You got old."

Asher laughed. "You can talk. Is that grey hair?"

Daris sighed. "We never thought we'd see it, did we, huh?"

Asher shook his head and whispered, "No."

"And I take it that's not the happy reason you're here now?"

Asher shook his head again. "No."

Daris nodded, and looking back at the desk, he gestured to the seats. "We should sit, I have a feeling this might take a while."

They sat, and Asher cut straight to the chase. He gave a bullet point rundown on Yunho and Lucas being taken. He showed him photos in his phone of the three dead Croatian men being their only lead, and the reason they were here.

"I need guns, ammunition, and any information you can find out," Asher said.

Daris winced and sighed. "I run a legit business now. And I have a daughter, Asher. I can't go back to that life."

"But you know people," Asher tried. "Give me names. I'll ask them."

Daris studied him and then Harry before he turned his attention to the window, but seeing what, Harry couldn't guess. He had a far-off look in his eyes.

"How old is your daughter?" Harry asked.

"She's nine," Daris replied quietly. His smile was genuine and warm when his eyes met Harry's. "And she's my entire world. And my wife. I have a life I don't deserve, and I can't bring them into this. I just can't."

Harry looked at Asher as he stood. "We'll find another way," Harry said. Then he looked at Daris. "Thank you."

Asher clearly wanted to argue, but he stood and conceded a nod. "It was good to see you, Daris. And for what it's worth, I'm happy for you."

They headed for the door, but Daris sighed. "Wait. Asher . . ." He shook his head. "I'll . . . I'll see what I can find out. Give me your number." He mumbled something under his breath and blew out a long frustrated breath. "Goddammit."

Asher shook his head. "No, it's all good, brother. Stay out of it. I don't blame you."

Daris stared at him and a dozen emotions crossed his face. "Look, there's a guy. Ivan Ćosić. Works out of a bar on Splitska in Kovačići. He's small-time, but he can get you what you need. But you didn't hear it from me."

Asher gave him a nod. "Thank you."

"Asher," Daris murmured. "You're asking the wrong questions. Forget Croatia. Those men might have spoken Croatian but that doesn't equate to loyalty. To some people in these parts, borders don't matter." His eyes flinched. "I think maybe you should be asking *why* Yunho?"

"What do you mean?" Harry asked. What Daris had asked wasn't really a question, more like he wanted them to think about the why, not the who.

"We don't know why they took him," Asher said. "That's why we're here. The three Croatian men gave us nothing. My guess is they were contracted out, paid a bunch of money they never got to spend. Yunho had a lot of enemies; the kind of enemies you don't want. Before now, they didn't know who he was. He was always ten steps ahead of them."

Daris shook his head. "That's my point. How did they find out who he was and where he was? And how did he not know they were coming?"

"We don't know," Harry replied.

Daris looked at Asher. "My guess is they don't want *him*."

"He has access to a lot of money and information," Asher said. "Maybe he stumbled into something big—"

Daris laughed at that. "Big? Bigger than ruining politicians and oil tycoons? Bigger than squandering billions from the bad guys? No, Asher. The one thing he has that no one else has," he said, "is you."

Harry didn't like that.

"Me?" Asher asked. "I'm just a pawn. What the hell could I ever be to those people?"

Daris nodded. "That's the question you need an answer to. Because the one sure way to lure you into their web, to bring you to them, is to use Yunho as bait. To bring you back here, to this place."

"Then why send men to kill us?" Asher countered.

Daris shrugged. "I don't know. Maybe I'm wrong. Like I said, it's been a long time since I was involved." He sighed then. "Just be careful."

Asher nodded. "You too." He opened the door and gave Daris a parting smile. "Maybe we shouldn't leave it so long next time."

Harry and Asher left, not saying a word until they were half a block away. "I know what he said seems unlikely," Harry murmured. "But fucking hell, Asher, I don't know if he's wrong. Maybe they are after you."

Asher cut him a quick glance. "I don't think so. Yunho's more valuable than me. And if they wanted to lure me here, why try to kill me?"

Harry wasn't sure about that. He was unsure of a lot of things. They had more questions than answers and he wasn't even sure if they were on the right continent or if he trusted Daris at all. But there was no point in arguing speculations with Asher when it got them nowhere.

Instead, he gave a nod. "We need to find Ivan Ćosić."

SIX

THE STREETS of Sarajevo were so different from the last time Asher had been there, yet familiar enough that he didn't need a map. As they made their way to Kovačići, he saw how people noticed them.

Well, they noticed Harry.

Because of his size and the murderous glare he shot at anyone who dared look at them. Well, at anyone who looked at Asher.

Daris had made an interesting point, but Asher didn't believe he was the target. Yunho was worth an immeasurable amount of money. The information he had access to, the footage, the data—the evidence—was enough to topple empires.

Governments, cartels, oil tycoons, war lords . . .

And what did Asher have?

Nothing compared to that.

He could testify to the hits he'd done, who put the orders in, who'd paid. He could name names but had no evidence. Yunho had it all.

Yes, Asher was good at what he did. He was good with

a rifle, he was good at walking over bodies, he was good at compartmentalising the cold reality of the world he'd grew up in.

But he was nothing: a mere pawn in this game.

If anything, he was a loose end.

Nothing more.

"This way," Asher said, taking a hard right and entering an alley. The concrete walls were painted, dirty, with ripped posters glued and falling, torn. The street was dirty, the gutter pooling puddles of rain and god knew what.

The stench was cloying, the people loitering might have looked twice at them, but if they considered approaching them for drugs or sex, one look at Harry and they quickly reconsidered.

It made Asher chuckle. "You're frightening the locals again."

"I don't like this," Harry murmured. He nodded to the windows up on the third or fourth floors above them. "Too many vantage points and easy escapes."

That was true. But he didn't feel threatened here. It was seedy, yes. But the most dangerous person in the neighbourhood was walking beside him.

"You look like my bodyguard," Asher said.

Harry shrugged. "Kinda am."

"Bodyguard with benefits," Asher mused.

"Not really feeling the funnies right now."

Asher gave up trying to lighten the mood. "It's the place with the pink sign and the doorman."

"See it."

He really was in pro-mode.

And maybe it was justified. Asher wasn't sure how to feel. He'd been so angry and scared, and Harry had warned him to get his head right. But they were being proactive now, getting somewhere, he hoped, anyway. And he felt better for it.

He also felt better for the absolute dicking he got last night. The fight and fuck that Harry did so well.

Asher hadn't been on the ground for far too long, and if he was honest with himself, he'd not missed it one bit.

He loved his life back in Australia. The quiet life, being happy in his little town, with Mala to spoil rotten . . .

Mala.

He wondered how Mala was. How Jacob and August were treating her . . .

He wondered if he'd ever see her again.

They approached the door and the security guard blocked the entrance and crossed his arms. He was early twenties at best, wore all black, had a shaved head, and a confidence Asher doubted was worth a pinch when shit got real. He eyed Harry first, the bigger threat, and Harry said nothing.

Waiting for Asher, obviously.

Jesus. Focus, Asher.

"Bar or girls?" the man said.

"Neither. I need to see Ivan Ćosić. It's a business matter," Asher said in Bosnian.

The security guard looked Asher up and down with a smug smile that made Harry growl. Asher met the guy's gaze and held it in the way that usually made lesser men look away.

It took about four seconds.

"It's a very lucrative business deal," Asher said. "I just need two minutes. You don't want to be the reason your boss loses this deal."

The man studied him for a second, and Asher could see

he'd won. The security guard gave them a pathetic pat down and an annoyed nod. "This way. Wait at the bar."

They followed him into the dingy nightclub. It smelled of stale alcohol. The neon lights illuminated stained lounges that Asher wouldn't sit on for any money in the world. They stood at a tall table by the bar and waited.

Asher smiled at the pretty girl behind the bar. She had a severe haircut, big blue eyes, cheek piercings, and tattoos up her neck.

Asher didn't need to look around too much because Harry stood with his back to the wall, watching everything else. There were some people playing pool and an older man with a younger woman in one corner.

And they waited, Harry getting more impatient with each passing minute.

"I don't like this," Harry said again, murmuring so only Asher could hear.

"I know. But we need the merchandise."

Harry sighed. "It doesn't feel like it used to. My nerves and patience for this are gone."

"Because we got complacent," Asher replied. "We got used to being civilians."

Harry's eyes cut to Asher's, fierce and laser focused. "We'll have it again. I promise. Quiet, in the wilderness somewhere. Just you and me."

"And Mala."

Harry's eyes softened. "Of course." Then his gaze cut over Asher's shoulder, to the end of the bar. "Company."

Asher turned and the security guard was approaching with another man, dressed the same, same stupid shaved head, same stupid ego. They walked with their chests out, trying to appear bigger than they were, which was funny, all things considered. They were basically children and

Harry could kill them both with his bare hands—at the same time.

Infants.

Asher wanted to roll his eyes but instead he smiled.

"This way," idiot number one said, implying they should follow.

Asher went first, then Harry, then idiot number two followed behind.

They went through a series of doors, then up some narrow stairs to a hall. Three doors, one window, and an exit sign that Asher assumed led to a fire escape. At the end of the hall was an idiot number three by an open door, and he stepped aside so they could enter.

A guy sat behind a desk, and for the most part it looked like an office to a nightclub and nothing more. But if Daris said this guy was the one who could get them weapons, Asher believed it.

Ivan Ćosić was mid-thirties, maybe. He looked a lot like the guy from that *Trainspotting* movie—Asher couldn't remember his name—but the shaved heads seemed to be a popular style.

He never stood up from his desk, though idiots one and two never moved, framing them like idiot bookends.

Oh, how Asher wished for a gun.

Then Ivan nodded to the idiot bookends who then proceeded to give Asher and Harry another pat down. *So ridiculous.* Harry extended his arms, growling again, but Asher found this supposed weapon supplier's amateurish display of security funny.

Once they'd found nothing, Ćosić seemed mollified. "You said you had a business proposition," he said in Bosnian.

Asher considered speaking in English for Harry's benefit but decided against it.

"Yes. I need merchandise and I was told you were the man to get it for me."

He stared at them. "What kind of merchandise?"

"I need three SIG Scorpions, suppressors, thirty extended mags. Two HK G36s with Steiner T332 optics, and all the ammunition you can get, some hunting knives," Asher said simply. "Oh," he added with a slight chuckle. "And a McMillan TAC 50."

Ćosić stared at him, then he glanced at idiots one and two before his gaze went back to Asher. He was clearly sizing them up, trying to determine if they were undercover cops or something.

God, people like him were so tiring.

"I don't give a fuck about the hookers or drugs you're running downstairs," Asher said flatly. "I need guns, and I need them ASAP."

Ćosić shook his head again. "I'm not sure where you heard that I can get that kind of merchandise—" he began.

"I don't play these games, Mr Ćosić," Asher said, his voice cold. "And who I heard it from is irrelevant. If you don't want the money, I'll find someone who does and tell my informant you're not reliable. They won't like that."

He opened his mouth to respond, but Asher wasn't done. "I also want information and will pay very handsomely."

"Information on what?"

Asher took out his phone and opened his photos to the pics he took of the three very dead Croatian men. He put the phone on the desk so the two idiots could see it too. "These three individuals. I want to know who they are, who they worked for. Do you recognise them?"

The photos weren't too gruesome, but the men in the photos were clearly dead, very pale, with smears of blood and surprised and blank expressions.

"This one," Asher pointed to the first photo. "He was the leader and refused to talk. Even after he watched the other two die."

Ivan Ćosić looked at Asher, not so smug now. Eyes a little wide. "I don't know who they are. Why would I know who they are?"

Asher scrolled to another photo. It was gruesome. The guy's naked torso, gutted like a fish, his innards now outtards. "Sorry, don't mind the mess," Asher said, zooming in to the tattoo on the dead man's arm. "This tattoo. What does it mean? Is it some special forces mark?"

It was a poorly done tattoo of what looked like a star, possibly a sword, and something that was illegible. Most special forces tattoos were recognisable and professionally done. This one, apart from looking like a prison tattoo, was neither.

Ćosić looked a touch green. "Jesus Christ," he mumbled in English.

"Ah, you speak English. Good, good," Asher said, in English this time. At least Harry could listen now. "You know this tattoo?"

He gave a nod. "ZBK. It stands for *život bez kajanja.*"

"Life without regret," Asher explained.

Ćosić nodded again. "It's part of the oath for the old JNA."

"The JNA?" Asher squinted, not expecting that. "Yugoslav People's Army?" They were disbanded a long time ago . . .

"Yes, or so they started off that way. But these guys," Ćosić nodded his chin towards Asher's phone. "These guys are crazy sons of bitches. It has nothing to do with Yugoslavia, new or old. They're loyalists, separatists, believe in a whole lot of conspiracy theories."

"Right-wing ideologies," Asher prompted.

He shook his head. "Oh, they're way beyond that. They started off like that. Twenty years ago, maybe. Small, quiet, peaceful. Then some ex-general got hold of it, turned it into a money-laundering, drug-running, mercenary faction of white supremacists. Guns for hire."

"Well, three of them are dead now. Who would hire them?"

He shook his head. "I don't know. Someone with a lot of money." He shrugged. "I honestly don't know."

"I'd honestly like you to find out," Asher said, almost cheerfully. He pocketed his phone. "And I'd also like you to find out any information you can on a man by the name of Asher Garin."

Asher noticed a slight change in Harry's stance. He didn't flinch exactly, but there was the smallest of movements. No one else would have noticed it, but Asher did.

He also noticed a change in Ćosić. "What are we talking? Fifty grand?" It was more than generous.

Ćosić blinked a few times. "Uh . . ."

"I'll pay you a hundred grand. Oh and we'll need a vehicle—nondescript, registered, nothing the cops will notice, with a full tank of fuel—and we have ourselves a deal." Asher took a decent wad of euros out of his jacket pocket. "Twenty thousand to start."

Ćosić blinked a few times at the money.

"You have twenty-four hours," Asher said, the deal done. He and Harry went to the door.

"H-h-how will I contact you?" Ćosić said.

Asher stopped and gave him a smile. "You won't. We'll find you."

A little threat never hurt any deal.

He and Harry walked out, back down the stairs, through the bar, and to the street. They walked on the shadowed side of the street to the end of the block, and got into a cab. Asher gave the name of the hotel and thankfully, this guy didn't seem the chatty type.

"That guy was a dick," Harry grumbled.

"Yes, he was. And his two henchmen were ridiculous."

"They were barely out of diapers."

Asher snorted. "We're not that old."

"We're not that young, either."

"You could have ended the three of them before they'd blinked," Asher said.

"Maybe a few years ago," Harry said, looking out the window. "Now I feel like . . ."

When he didn't continue, Asher prompted him. "Like what?"

"Like I'm out of step. Like my rhythm's off."

"I can assure you, your rhythm's fine." Asher meant it as an innuendo and thankfully Harry took it as one.

He almost smiled before he sighed. "It doesn't feel like it used to."

"Because we got used to a different life these last two years. But I assure you, with the likes of Ćosić and his two idiots, we're miles in front."

"You asked him to find out information on yourself," Harry murmured. Then he shook his head, his gaze finding Asher's. "It's risky."

Asher shrugged. "No one knows what I look like. And if they do have a photo of me, it's from fifteen years ago. I don't look like that scrawny, dead-eyed kid anymore."

"Your eyes were never dead," Harry whispered.

"They were," Asher replied. "Before you."

Harry's lips twitched in a half smile. "Smooth talker." Then his brows furrowed. "And what's with the two G36s?"

"They're grossly underrated," Asher replied. Then he smirked at Harry. "Are you seriously doubting my knowledge on the effective firing range of a weapon? Because we have no idea what situations, terrain, or temperatures we're going into. I went for the more versatile—" Having to say this out loud to Harry made Asher mad. "I can't believe I have to explain—"

Harry put his hands up in surrender. "Sorry. I would never question your far superior knowledge on the effectiveness and versatility of a rifle."

Asher relented a smile. "Thank you." Then he let out a long sigh as they passed some restaurants. "You know what I feel like?"

"What's that?"

"Brudet. Then we can spend the rest of the day in our room, doing internet things, and you can fuck me thoroughly." Then Asher spoke to the taxi driver in Bosnian. "Change of plans. Please take us to the best brudet in the city."

The taxi driver's face lit up and he spoke very loudly, using his hands and excitedly telling Asher all about this little place he knew . . .

Harry sighed. "What is it with you and taxi drivers?"

LATER THAT AFTERNOON, Asher needed a shower after Harry had thoroughly had his way with him. He relished the ache in his ass, stretching his very relaxed muscles, and he caught himself smiling . . .

Until he remembered the reason they were here.

Yunho. And Lucas, of course. But Yunho was somewhere—somewhere in the world—most likely suffering anxiety and possibly stress-induced seizures.

Almost certainly beaten. Probably tortured.

Nothing he hadn't endured before, but still . . .

Asher dried off and redressed, finding Harry sitting at the table with a phone. "Whatcha looking at?" Asher asked.

Harry frowned. "I checked the news back home," he said. "Searched for anything on Croatian men in or around the mid-north coast." Then he pointed to his phone. "I found this. A small article on page three of the Coffs Harbour newspaper, four days ago. 'Search efforts of the three men reported missing in the Tallowwood National Park have been called off. Local authorities say the matter is resolved and would like to thank the public for their diligence.'"

Asher stopped. "Resolved? What does that mean? It wasn't resolved. Unless they call finding three carcasses *resolved.*"

Harry scowled. "This has got feds written all over it."

Asher sat down beside him. "Why would they cover it up?"

"To protect us," Harry said. "Me, anyway. While Parrish's case is still pending. They were happy for my Harrigan identity to be announced killed in action with that fake record Yunho provided. They can't have me turning up alive in the middle of the biggest espionage cases in Australia's history. It'd derail the whole thing."

Asher thought about that for a while.

"Do you think they knew it was Yunho who provided that false record?"

Harry considered it. "No. There'd be no way to trace it back to him anyway. Even if someone did wonder where it came from." Then he frowned. "Do you think whoever took him has something to do with Parrish's case?"

Asher sighed. "Not really. But we can't rule out anything."

The more he thought about it, about Yunho, the bleaker it all looked. "We need to find him, Harry."

Harry slid his hand over Asher's. "I know. And we will. Why don't you try unlocking the tablet," he suggested. "You haven't tried any passwords yet. You just keep staring at it."

"I know," he whispered. "I don't . . . I don't know what it would be. It's alphanumerical, seven digits. It could be letters or numbers, both. Knowing him, none. I don't even know."

The truth was, all Asher could think of, after wondering what this password could be, was just how much he didn't know Yunho at all.

Harry looked at the tablet and shrugged. "Try his birthdate."

"Jesus Christ, Harry." Asher couldn't believe Harry just suggested that. "Please tell me you don't use your birth-date as a password for anything."

He winced. "Well, I might have Harry's birthdate, but considering all my ID is now Michael Hill, his birthday isn't mine."

Asher sighed. That was probably true.

"What about something from his old life," Harry then suggested.

Asher almost smiled. "He always did have a warped

sense of humour. And it's seven digits." Then he added in a passcode, C3S1A63, but didn't hit Enter.

"What's that?" Harry asked.

"North Korea law code," Asher replied. "What they'd charged him with. Chapter three, section one, article sixty-three: treason against the state. He'd probably use that as a code because he'd think it was funny."

Because evading death by firing squad was hilarious, according to Yunho.

"Well try it," Harry said, nodding to the tablet.

Asher hit Enter.

Incorrect password.

Shit.

"What else," Harry wondered out loud. "Something that means a lot to him."

"Lucas," Asher replied. "Me." This was so stupid. "He could have used the word parrot because a bird was in the garden at the time. He could have used some random syntax code that changes every twelve hours for all I know."

Harry stared out the window, scowling into the distance. "What if it was a message? Something he'd use that only you would know. Something that only you would guess because he knew you'd come looking for him."

Asher thought about that, hating that it might be right. He thought about all the significant things. The date they'd met, dates they'd escaped, the names of aliases, fake IDs, fake passport numbers, his old North Korean ID number, his military ID number.

"If you get it wrong, we'll just take it to someone to hack into," Harry said. "Not like we aren't resigned to doing that anyway."

Asher waved off at Harry's phone. "You do your thing. Let me think."

So Harry went back to his phone, making some notes, and Asher let his mind wander back over the years, to the time he'd spent with Yunho. The things he'd said, what he'd divulged, the things from his past he'd let slip.

Admittedly, it wasn't much. Mostly a comment here and there when Asher was on some stake out or on the move in the middle of the night, and Yunho would tell him of the juk his *halmeoni* would make for him when he was a boy and how he'd have to make it for Asher one day. Or about the first time he travelled abroad, to Japan, and how enamoured he was with the outside world.

And the Japanese men-only baths and hotels.

Oh yes, he'd liked those a lot.

Or how he was faring once Asher had left him in Thailand to do some jobs for him in Europe. He used to venture out to the market for food back then—not that he'd liked doing it—but his reclusiveness steadily got worse. The more money he made, the more he could pay to not leave, and as technology accelerated, so did his agoraphobia.

Asher had thought finding Yunho's island, and the small house that was on it back then was a godsend for him. Now with hindsight, maybe the isolation fed his agoraphobia and made it worse.

But then, when he'd decided to upgrade his house to the mansion it was now, he'd hired a construction manager to oversee the project, making all the necessary trips back to the mainland on his behalf. Trips that Yunho couldn't make.

And that construction project manager was a sexy Englishman named Lucas Edwards. And Yunho's life improved tenfold. Lucas adored him. Didn't put up with any of his shit, either. Asher could recall a time or two when Yunho was sulking because Lucas had put his foot down. Usually about ludicrous things like buying a helicopter or—

"Your friend Daris," Harry said, interrupting Asher's thoughts. "From the warehouse depot."

Asher remembered how Harry had assumed they'd been lovers. "Yes," he replied. "I will just say you being all jealous was a lot of fun. I'd like to do that again."

Harry glowered at him. "Yeah, I wouldn't recommend that."

Asher smiled. "What about him?"

"You knew him from when you were young . . ."

Asher had expected this conversation, only that it got waylaid because of the visit to Ivan Ćosić. "Yes. We were in the same training school in Serbia together. We had a lot of similarities, so we stuck together."

"Similarities?"

"Orphans. He was from the same orphanage. We were all orphans. He was smart and older than me. I looked up to him. We moved around a lot together." Asher sighed. "I haven't seen him in a long time. I knew he was here. I'd asked Yunho to run a check on him a few years ago now. Thought he'd be dead for sure. But living a good life. Has a wife and daughter." Asher couldn't believe it. "He deserves some good things."

"Yeah. When he mentioned his daughter," Harry said quietly, "I knew we had to leave."

Asher nodded and sighed loudly. "Three years ago I wouldn't have given one fuck. Well, maybe . . . because it was him." He shrugged. "Now, it's different. I'm different."

Harry's eyes met his, and he nodded. "You are. We both are. We had a taste of a normal life. Two years of peace." Then he winced. "And food. I must be twenty kilos heavier now than I was when I lived in Europe. When we have to take down the pieces of shit that took Yunho, I hope I don't have to run over a long distance. Once upon a time I could run for days. Now . . ." He shook his head sadly. "Now I'm old and got too used to eating cheese and crackers with a glass of wine while we watched a movie. Twenty-year-old me would be appalled."

Asher chuckled quietly. "Twenty-year-old you would be amazed you're still alive."

"True."

"I know twenty-year-old me never thought I'd make it this far." He sighed again. "Hell, five-year-old me didn't expect to make it to six."

Harry's eyes softened, and he lifted his hand to Asher's face, thumbing across his cheek. "You know, for as shitty as life's been, at least my childhood was okay. I used to ride a bike down to the river, spent summer holidays with friends, and didn't have a care in the world." His smile faltered. "I mean, it all went downhill when I turned eighteen and found myself disowned and homeless. But I didn't have to go through what you went through. From such a young age too. I hate that you went through that."

"It wasn't so bad," Asher replied flatly. "I survived, at least. Many didn't. Boys that were my friends that didn't make the cut. I don't know what ever happened to them; if they were sold or killed. Probably killed. Less evidence that way." He sighed and tried to brighten the mood, managing a smile. "You know, Yunho would donate money to the orphanages in Thailand and Cambodia and Myanmar, so the children don't suffer as much. He said he did it for me, but also for himself, I think. He never spoke of his childhood often. Mentioned his grandmother a few times. She would cook him porridge. But he tried to give back." Then Asher laughed. "He told me he once set up a ghost secure data—"

Asher stopped.

Could that be it?

"A ghost secure what?" Harry asked.

Asher tapped the tablet screen to bring up the passcode window. "Oh god, Harry. This could be it. He set up a secure data vault . . . it's like one of those old-fashioned safe deposit boxes but it's online. Like a portal to access his mainframe. 'In case the worst should happen, Asher'," Asher imitated Yunho's voice. "But I never thought about it in years, because nothing was ever going to happen to him. I forgot all about it. It would give me access to all his information, all his money. I told him I didn't want it . . ."

Harry nodded along at Asher's excitement but still seemed confused. "What does it have to do with the password to the tablet? Do you think it's the same?"

"It could be. A message, like you said. If it's the password for this, then he's telling me to access the portal as well."

"So what's the password?"

God, it was so long ago . . .

"Uh . . ." Asher tried to wrack his memory. "He told me the password was the sun god. He said it was me because I saved him, or something. It was more 'like a ray of sunlight in a dark world' or some bullshit. He's always sentimental like that. He said it was a password just for me."

"So what's the password?" Harry asked again. "Which sun god."

"The Korean one."

"Yes, but what's its name?"

"How the hell would I know?" Asher said. He nodded to Harry's phone. "Look it up."

"He never actually told you?" Harry asked while typing into his browser.

"Well, yes. But it was a long time ago, and I honestly thought I'd never need it. He talked about a lot of spiritual stuff like that, but I was his darling ray of sunlight."

Harry showed Asher the screen with the name on it.

"Yes, that's it!" Asher said, about to type it into the password screen but stopping on the first letter. "Should I use a capital?"

"Oh Jesus Christ, Asher."

"Okay, okay." He typed it in. "Haemosu." He took a breath and hit Enter.

Password correct.

They were in.

SEVEN

THE TABLET SCREEN OPENED, producing a dark screen with icons and folders and files. "Oh god," Asher whispered. Harry knew he was reluctant, and truth be told, Harry totally understood why.

Afraid of what they might find.

"CCTV," Asher mumbled, clicking on a folder. There were hundreds of folders, filenames with dates Harry deduced were the dates of security footage. Asher clicked on the last entry. It was dated just days ago . . .

The footage began to play, the screen quickly dividing into separate boxes. Each box was a camera view of different locations within Yunho's house and the island.

The first was of the boat house and dock, other cameras focused on the grounds area. Then inside the house was the living area and kitchen, the back of the house, upstairs hallway, and of course inside the war room.

Oh god.

Around six in the morning, Lucas entered the upstairs hall from the main bedroom. He wore sleep pants, a T-shirt, and slippers. He left the bedroom door open, went downstairs to the kitchen, and proceeded to make coffee and set the patio table with fruits and yoghurt, some bread, and condiments. He shuffled back and forth in a well-practiced routine. He looked . . . happy. Normal.

Then Yunho appeared in the hall, showered and dressed. He skipped down the stairs, breezing over to where Lucas was standing in the kitchen. He was fixing a plate of meat and cheese by the look of it. Yunho pressed a kiss to Lucas's shoulder, murmured something the audio didn't quite catch, then carried the juice to the table on the patio.

Asher sighed, frowning at the screen. "They look so happy," he murmured.

They picked at their breakfast, sipping their coffee. Yunho pointed to and talked of a pair of birds who were back for the breeding season, they discussed the lawn maintenance, and they discussed the stock market.

Then at 7:03 a.m., Aranya appeared from a downstairs guest room. She walked out, fixing her hair. Harry had forgotten she stayed there while she worked to save her travelling by boat every day.

"Sawadee ka," she said as she went outside to the table.

"Morning," Yunho and Lucas both replied. They made small talk briefly about the beautiful day, and what their day ahead looked like: the market in the middle east, a data breach in China, leaking international finance fraud in Washington. All normal, everyday stuff for cyber hackers.

When, in reality, they had no idea what was coming.

Asher sighed. "Lucas will now go and shower, Yunho will go downstairs. Aranya will finish up breakfast and clear the table, like they do every morning. Lucas will come by later and wash up." He shook his head. "I'll fast forward to the end. We can go back and listen to the whole day later."

Harry nodded. "Good idea."

Asher scrolled to the end, and when there was a flash in the dark at the south side of the house, Asher paused and rewound it. It was pitch black, 10:12 p.m., and there was definitely movement at the south side of the house. Something glinted in the camera. Something metal.

Then four men dressed in all black crept into view. They dressed like navy seals, moved like it too. Professionals. Three of them had AK-74s and one had a black laptop bag slung over his shoulder.

Yuhno, Lucas, and Aranya were all still in the war room. All three of them spun to look at a security screen, only now seeing the intruders enter, as Harry and Asher could see on a screen. Yunho launched at his keyboard, the door to the war room slammed shut, and a second later, every screen went black.

On the screen of the living room, the intruders entered the house, heading straight for the door to the basement. The guy with the laptop bag pulled something out of it, stuck it to the keypad, pressed something, and the door opened.

Some kind of code breaker?

They went down the stairs, the guy with the backpack went in first.

One door done, one to go . . .

Meanwhile, in the war room, Lucas ran for the vault, coming out with handguns, and he handed one to Yunho.

"Aranya, get in there," Lucas instructed. "Close the door. Do not open it for anyone but us. Arm yourself."

But as she went toward it, the war room door exploded inward and the three of them spun to face it, recoiling.

Two intruders slid into the room. One of them shot Aranya right where she stood—one shot, right to the forehead, perfect aim—and before Lucas could even raise his gun, the other intruder had his rifle at Yunho's head. "Don't fucking move," he warned Lucas.

There was an accent.

"Put your gun down," he said.

Russian?

"Shoot him," Yunho hissed.

The Russian pressed the end of his rifle to Yunho's forehead. "Shoot me, he dies on reflex."

"Shoot him," Yunho yelled.

But Lucas couldn't do it. What the Russian said was right. His finger was on the trigger. If he was shot, his muscles would retract in an instant, shooting Yunho.

The other intruder came around the desk, his gun trained on Lucas.

He spoke fast, his voice rough like he'd had a throat injury. "Put your fucking gun down," he barked.

Lucas put the pistol on the desk and the guy slid it away, then turned his rifle around and cracked Lucas in the side of the head with it. Lucas stumbled and Yunho flinched, but the guy closest to him grabbed Yunho's arm, twisted it up behind his back, and kicked the back of his knee, forcing him to kneel.

Asher growled.

The third and fourth intruder came in then. While the first two zip-tied Yunho and Lucas's hands behind their back, intruder number three went to the mainframe cabinet and took the box that had been missing.

Harry had wondered who'd taken it. The intruders, or even if Yunho had destroyed it.

Now he knew.

"They knew how to get in," Asher murmured. "They knew exactly what to take."

Harry nodded. "They had inside information."

Then intruder number four went over to Yuhno and Lucas. He took out a small black box, no bigger than a pack of gum. He flipped the lid, took out a small circular pad. No bigger than a dollar coin. He whacked Yunho's neck with it, hard. It stuck to the side of his neck and Yunho slumped forward. Lucas fought against his restraints, one of them cracked him again with the butt of his rifle. He fell back. Intruder three stuck one of those circular pads on Lucas's neck, and he never moved.

"The fuck was that?" Harry asked.

"Some kind of sedative," Asher deduced.

Then they hauled both Yunho and Lucas to their feet and all but carried their listless bodies up the stairs. They got upstairs, one intruder on either side of Yunho and Lucas, and hauled them outside, into the dark.

And they were gone.

It took less than four minutes.

The cameras kept recording, though Asher pushed the screen away. They'd see if anything moved, but for now, not even the curtains blew in the breeze where the doors were left wide open.

"They never tripped the alarm system," Asher said. He was so livid his voice was like ice. "They must have disabled it before they arrived. They knew the top door was a PIN pad. They knew the door into the war room would need a PIN pad and explosives."

"And they knew exactly what mainframe box to take," Harry added. "And where it was. They knew everything."

"Like they had eyes in there," Asher said. Then his eyebrows knitted in a scowl. "Or had someone on the inside, feeding them intel."

Harry didn't like that idea as much as Asher clearly didn't like it, but it was a possibility.

He shrugged. "Aranya? They cleaned up that loose end real fast, didn't they? If it was her . . ."

"I'd like to think it wasn't. I liked her, as did Yunho. He trusted her and paid her so well that any money some asshole offered for information wouldn't even compare."

"Unless they took her family, threatened her that way," Asher added.

"A possibility," Harry said, because it was. And at this point, they had to consider anything. "I'll google the news around the Ranong area to see if there's any mention of Yunho's island."

Asher nodded. Then he rewound the footage back to the first sighting of the intruders' gun glinting in the dark and watched it again, looking at anything he might have missed the first time.

"They came in from the south," Asher said quietly. "Each of them had a specialty. Two for the hostages, one for the keypad and to blow the door, one for the main-frame and the tranquilliser."

He listened to their voices and rewound it, and listened to and rewound, several times over. "Belarusian," Asher said. "Maybe Latvian. Or Russian." Then he sighed. "I can't be certain. I'm out of practice. The old me would have known."

Harry gave Asher's arm a squeeze. "It's likely they were just a team paid a lot of money. Their accents aren't indicative of anything. I'm Australian and killed people all over."

Asher shot him a pointed stare. "We came to Europe because those men were Croatian. Are you saying it was wrong? Have we wasted time? Time Yunho doesn't have?"

"No, we came here because it was the only lead we had at the time. And if those guys are Russian or Belarusian or Latvian, and if that's the only lead we have, then we'll go there too."

Asher frowned, almost sulked. "I hate not knowing."

Harry's heart hurt for him. He hated that he felt so helpless. "Then look at what we do know," he tried. He knew Asher would get stuck in his own head, mad at himself for what he deemed a failure on his behalf. "What can you tell me about the footage?"

Asher's eyes went back to the screen, where Yunho was now on his knees, sedated with that pad on his neck. "That those men are going to die."

"Yes."

"That one of them has or had an injury with his larynx."

"Yes."

"That I'm going to make it a whole lot worse."

"Good. And?"

He paused, his voice quiet. "That I'm glad they sedated him, so he wouldn't freak out when they dragged him off his island. So his anxiety didn't kill him."

Harry ran his hand up Asher's back and gave his neck a squeeze. "Do you think they sedated them to make transportation easier? Or because they knew of his agoraphobia? It's much harder to transport someone when they're having a medical episode. It's risky and unknown, and those are two things no transport team wants."

Asher sighed again. "If they knew about the war room, then it's likely they knew about his condition."

Harry nodded. "Good. Okay, what else can you tell me."

"They came up on the south side of the island, so they definitely knew they'd have more cover than if they used the dock. That means it was likely a rubber dinghy so it could come ashore and they had a larger boat further out."

Now they were getting somewhere. "A safe assumption."

"They had intel on the island."

"Agreed."

"And they likely made landfall in Myanmar. Thailand's coastguard is better and there's more chance of going undetected or even paying their way through Myanmar."

"Okay, good." Harry wanted to ask, *where would they have gone next*, but that was a complete unknown and he needed to focus on what they did know. He tapped the screen. "Tell me what else you know about these intruders."

"Trained. Professional. Efficient."

"What else."

He looked closer at the screen. "Kalashnikov rifles. AK-74s, which tells me they're either from Russia or they were armed by the Russians. So that means likely Russian but not conclusive."

Okay, good. "What else?"

Asher pressed play again and waited until one of the intruders, the one with the gravelly voice, turned around. Asher paused the screen and zoomed in. It did pixelate a bit but it was clear enough. "That's a Kizlyar knife. That's Russian."

"Good. Anything else?"

Asher studied the screen before he shrugged. "Nothing. They're covered, have no VDMs, no old Yugoslav army tattoos on display. They look like a standard special forces op."

Harry agreed. "They do look military. Not just some hired loyalist, separatist nutjobs. They've been trained properly."

Asher's brows drew together. "Don't assume anyone with proper training and certain skill sets is military. I never enlisted, but I assure you, I was trained."

Harry conceded that point with a nod. "Fair enough."

"And our friend Ivan did say that ZBK group was taken over by an ex-general," Asher added.

"True." It was Harry's turn to sigh. "We need to find out what we can about them. Location, factions, chapters, however they operate, and who we need to question. I'm sure they assume their three men they sent to kill us are dead, but I'd like to tell them in person."

Asher almost smiled. "And I'd like to be there when you tell them."

"So our next call to action, before we pay Ivan a visit to collect our guns, is to find out everything we can." Harry tapped the screen that still showed the scene in Yunho's war room. "And what else Yunho has in these files. See if we can find out what he discovered recently or who he might have pissed off."

"He pissed off a lot of people."

"Yeah, but why now? Something must have happened in the last six months to bring this about. It might be an enemy from a decade ago who just found out he's still alive. But something must have recently tripped a wire somewhere. Because after all this time of Yunho being untraceable, they suddenly found him."

Asher nodded, frowning. "I hope he's okay," he whispered. "I'm trying not to think about what they've done to him . . ."

Harry put his arm around Asher's shoulder. "We will find them. But we need to focus, and we need to think like Yunho. He gave you the access code to all his information. He wants you to find what we're missing."

Asher seemed bolstered by that, determined to search and find whatever that was. The thing was, it was like searching for a needle in a haystack, if the haystack was a few exabytes of data and they had no clue what the needle even looked like.

Harry busied himself with his own research. Google was a godsend, even though he could remember a time very early in his career when any information he needed to find had to be sent to him. Intel arrived via text or yellow envelopes, or a burner email account. Christ, Harry didn't even know what a VPN was back then . . .

Now he could find out information, get compound aerial views, street views, data records, addresses, and identification photos with just a few clicks of his keyboard.

Yet compared to Yunho and Lucas, Harry was as computer literate as a potato.

Asher was much better at it than Harry could ever be.

Harry was better on the ground, doing the grunt work, doing whatever he was told needed doing. But he could find some stuff easily enough: ZBK names, known locations, info on their new friend Ivan Ćosić. Like his known associates, tax records, and his home address.

Which came in handy at four in the morning when they broke into his house and woke him up. Poor guy almost crapped himself when Asher stood at the side of his bed. "Wakey wakey," he said.

Ivan woke up and shot backwards, bumping into the headboard. "Wh-wh-what the fuck!"

Harry hit the lights and Ivan recoiled from the brightness, but also from the fact that Asher and Harry were in his bedroom at four o'clock in the morning.

Luckily Ivan lived alone. They didn't need to account for anyone else in the house. No wife and kids, and for that Harry was grateful.

Something that, ten years ago, he wouldn't have cared too much about. Sometimes it even worked in his favour; it made the target more compliant. But now Harry was happy no one else had to suffer.

Christ, this is bad, Harry thought. Would he hesitate now because he'd somehow grown a conscience in the last two years?

He really wasn't sure.

"What the fuck are you doing in here? How did you get in?" Ivan said, clutching at his bedding like that would protect him.

"I know I said twenty-four hours," Asher said cheerfully as he sat on the edge of Ivan's bed. "But I do like to keep people on their toes. It's good for business, don't you think?"

Ivan blinked a few times, still confused. "How did you get in here? How do you know where I live?"

"I know all about the people I do business dealings with, Ivan. Now come on, get up. I have a merchandise order to collect."

"Y-you said I had twenty-four hours," he tried. "I don't even know what time it is."

Asher patted Ivan's leg. "Mr Ćosić, if you didn't have everything I'd asked for six hours after I'd asked for it, I'd be very disappointed."

It was the cheerfulness, the buzzing excited manner with which Asher delivered his threats that made them more unnerving.

"Well it's not here," he said, pulling his leg away. "I don't have it in my house."

"I should hope not," Asher said. "You know, your security system is terrible. So easy to disarm. I thought you'd at least have a dog. I love dogs."

Ivan looked at Asher as if he were insane.

Asher clapped his hands, making Ivan jump. "Come on, time to get up. We're going for a little drive."

"D-drive?" He said, eyes wide. "Where to?"

"To wherever my merchandise is."

Harry picked up the jeans and a sweater that were on the floor and tossed them onto the bed. "Get dressed. And don't leave your clothes on the floor. What are you? Eight years old?"

He shook his head, pulling the sweater on, mumbling about getting home late, how he only left his club a few hours ago, blah blah blah.

Harry didn't give one fuck. "Just get fucking dressed."

Asher stood up. "And we're going to need the keys to your car."

Two minutes later, they drove out of the underground car park in Ivan's Audi. Asher drove, Harry sat in the back with Ivan, and while the car was nice, it wasn't built for a man Harry's size to sit in the back. Ivan kept looking up at Harry, their size difference very noticeable, and if he considered for one second trying to escape, Harry could break several of his bones without too much trouble.

Ivan seemed to know this.

The city was dark. Yellow streetlights in the blackness of night, a garbage truck a few blocks over, and the lights on in a bakery they passed were the only signs of life. That's why they were doing this before dawn.

Harry could remember a time when this was his favourite time of the day. Or days and weeks on end when he never saw daylight, not even once.

It was a different life back then.

"So, Ivan," Asher broke the silence. "What did you find out about a Mr Asher Garin?"

He made a face, and it was an expression Harry had seen a hundred times on his victims. He didn't know much, and his answer was not going to go over well. But there was something else in the way he swallowed hard . . .

"That he disappeared a few years ago. He had a price on his head but no one claimed the kill."

He looked up at Harry then, his eyes shifty, hands fidgeting in his lap.

"He knows more," Harry said to Asher. Then he looked down at Ivan. "You can't lie for shit."

"I don't know," Ivan said. "I don't for certain, and I don't like retelling shit that might not be true. You said you wanted information, not rumours."

Harry growled at him. "What rumours?"

Ivan shrank back from him, his hands up. "Okay, okay. There's been rumours. But it was about some other guy tied to Garin, not Garin himself. That the guy he worked for, who he got his intel from, was some guy that supposedly died years ago. They were running some big-time data funding ring together, him and Garin. I don't know. That guy who was supposed to be dead isn't fucking dead, apparently. Like, no shit. Bit hard to run some billion-dollar black market data farm when you're dead. But they found him. Some Chinese kid found him. I don't know."

Asher's eyes flashed to Harry's in the rear-vision mirror.

Chinese kid?

"Who?" Harry snarled. "The Chinese guy? Who is he?"

Ivan slunk away, his back almost to the door. "I don't know. Some genius computer whiz. He's like fifteen years old or something."

"Who does he work for?" Harry bellowed at him.

Ivan went white, his eyes comically large, his hands shaking. "I don't know! Some guy in Moscow. Super rich. Garin's partner must have pissed him off. Deal gone wrong, how the fuck would I know?"

"You seem to know an awful lot of rumours," Asher said calmly.

"It was hot news this week, apparently. Those ZBK freaks you were asking about, in the photos . . ." Ivan said, grimacing. "The Russian guy hired them. Found some lead in Australia, where they reckon Garin was hiding out, and sent three . . ." Ivan's face went a shade of pale before his crazed eyes danced between Asher and Harry. "Oh fuck," he squeaked.

Harry sighed. "He's just realised I'm Australian," he said flatly. "He put the pieces together. You're a bit fucking slow, mate."

Ivan's mouth opened and closed a few times, and he blinked in Asher's direction. "And y-you're . . ."

Asher laughed. "I'm a paying customer." Then he nodded up ahead. "The address is coming up. Where do I go?"

Ivan could only shake his head, so he clearly needed some help getting the words out. Harry grabbed him by the neck and pinned him against the door. "Speak."

"R-round the side," he gasped. "On the right. There's a roller door. PIN code access. Number is 4375."

Harry let him go and Ivan slumped down in his seat, rubbing his neck. "Jesus Christ," he mumbled.

"I doubt he'd be any help to you," Harry replied flatly.

Asher pulled up at the PIN pad, entered the number, and inched the car forward as the door went up. What the place was, it turned out, was a storage warehouse. There were pallets of different alcohols; beers, cans, bottles, and an older style Jeep parked off to the side.

Asher waited until the roller door was closed behind them, then he got out. He opened Ivan's door and helped him to his feet—he looked a little unsteady—and dragged him over to the wall. "Lights," he demanded. By the time Harry got out and walked around to meet them, the overhead lights flickered on.

"Whose place is this?" Asher asked.

"It's mine," he began. "I get wholesale liquor for my clubs. Bulk discounts and shit. Store it here."

"And our merchandise?" Asher asked.

He swallowed hard. "It's over there," he said, giving a pointed nod to the Jeep.

"Let's see it," Harry barked, and Ivan hurried over.

In the corner were some 44-gallon drums of oil, according to the labels. But Ivan pulled the top off and inside were black duffle bags.

Christ. They were dealing with an idiot.

"Inside the oil drum that has no business being inside a liquor store warehouse," Harry griped. "Really?"

Ivan looked about to apologise, but he was shaking so bad he couldn't even stammer out a reply.

Asher looked in each bag, taking out a pistol. It was still in its box, brand new. Asher took it out and lifted it to his nose and sniffed it. "Ah. I love the smell of rust preventative in the morning."

Harry chuckled and Ivan looked between them again, clearly thinking they were insane. He tried to smile but he also looked about ready to puke so it didn't quite hold.

Asher tossed the hunting knife to Harry. "For you, my love."

Harry caught it easily, unsheathed it, and inspected the blade. "Nice."

"Now," Asher said sweetly. "I did ask for a MAC 50. I know they're hard to get, people tend to ask all sorts of questions. Like, 'Why do you need that kind of weapon?' and 'That's a specialist sniper rifle.' Like I don't already know that." He sighed dramatically. "So while I won't be surprised if you couldn't get one, I *will* be disappointed."

Ivan nodded to the next drum. "I got it, I got it, it's in there." He went to reach for it, but Harry grabbed him, stopping him.

"I'll open it," Harry barked.

Inside was a black rifle carry bag and nothing else. Harry pulled it out, rested it on top of the drum, and opened it.

"Is she pretty?" Asher asked Harry, but he was facing Ivan.

Harry pulled the rifle out to show Asher. "Take a look."

Asher gasped excitedly. "It's an R2. It's an older model," he told Ivan.

Ivan shook his head. "It was all I could get. Like you said, they're not easy—"

"Relax, dear Ivan," Asher said. "The R2 is my favourite. The weight distribution is so much better, less recoil. I don't know why they insist on updating these things when the older model was perfect."

Harry put it back in the bag, zipped it all up, and picked up the bag of ammunition. "The Jeep's ours?"

Ivan nodded. "Yes. Like you asked for. Nondescript, Bosnian plates, registered, should the cops do a spot check, and the tank is full."

Harry began loading their gear into the back of the Jeep while Asher took Ivan by the arm. "Now, let's discuss payment."

Harry checked the Jeep over while they did what needed doing. Asher would transfer the money directly into the account of Ivan's choosing. They both stood there looking at their phone screens. There was a ding, Ivan nodded, and Asher smiled.

"It's been a pleasure doing business with you," Asher said.

Ivan nodded and swallowed hard. "Glad I could help."

"Now, about telling anyone," Asher began.

"I won't tell anyone," he said quickly.

Asher laughed. "It's probably best you don't. If they find out you did a business deal with Asher Garin and didn't tell them so they could claim the bounty on my head, you will have cost them a lot of money, and they won't take that very lightly."

"I won't. I wouldn't," he said, panicked.

"As for the ZBK boys, well, I don't think you'll need to worry about them too much. Because we're about to kill all of them."

Ivan swallowed hard.

"And if they know we're about to turn up, I'll know you warned them. And after we've finished gutting them like we did their three comrades in Australia, we'll come back and do the same to you." Asher grinned at him. "M'kay? Are we clear, Ivan?"

Ivan nodded quickly. "Understood. I won't tell anyone."

"Now, are you sure you don't remember anything else those pesky rumours said about my dear friend who was supposed to be dead years ago, but obviously wasn't, and the Chinese boy computer whiz who found him?"

Ivan stammered a bit and shook his head. "No, that was all. Just that they found him. That's all I know."

"And who told you this?" Asher asked, his tone sweet, his smile cute.

"I know some guys who find out information," he said. "Drugs, guns, that kind of stuff, whatever. I asked one of them if he'd heard anything on Asher Garin—" He paused, stricken. "Because you asked me to, no other reason. And he said he'd heard because he . . . maybe he does deals with the ZBK. He gets them guns and drugs, I don't know. I don't deal with them crazy fucks. I haven't ever. You gotta be crazy to get into business with them."

"I need a name," Asher asked, not so sweetly now. "A name of your informant friend who does business with them."

He baulked, so Harry took a step toward him.

Ivan put his hands up. "Daris Guli. His name is Daris."

EIGHT

HARRY WAS quiet as he drove the Jeep, letting Asher get his thoughts together and his anger in check. The Daris that Ivan had referred to was none other than Asher's friend, the guy he'd been at the orphanage with, at the training school with.

The guy who, just one day ago, had told Asher he lived a clean life now.

The guy who Asher had trusted. The guy who had hugged Asher, looked him right in the eye, and lied to him.

If Asher didn't kill him, Harry would have no problem doing it.

They'd left Ivan at his storage warehouse, alive, and with no misunderstanding about his expected silence. Harry doubted he'd be any trouble; he acted like some smooth-talking big-time dealer and nightclub owner, but he was so close to crapping himself the whole time, Harry had to wonder how he'd managed to do any business dealings at all.

Asher looked up from his phone and nodded ahead. "Turn right at the next block."

This was a residential part of the city. A nice part too. Pretty houses, leafy streets. And as the sun was breaking over the horizon, daylight was beckoning. Harry would have called it serene.

A far cry from what it was about to be for Daris.

"Number eighty-five," Asher said. "On the left."

"Are you okay?" Harry asked.

"I'll be a whole lot better after this," Asher replied quietly.

Harry pulled up right out front, noting the kid's bicycle by the garage. "Seems he didn't lie about having a kid," Harry said.

It was his way of reminding Asher that there was a kid inside, though he wasn't entirely sure Asher cared. Not this time. He kinda shrugged. "Good. Leverage." Then he took the Scorpion pistol, loaded the clip, and slid it into the waistband of the back of his jeans, easily concealed by his coat.

"There's an alarm system," Harry said, nodding to the sensor on the eave outside. "And a power box. I'll pull the circuit."

Asher nodded, and they slipped out of the Jeep. Harry went to the side of the garage, lifted the lid to the power box, and switched the power and light breakers off.

He went back to the front door where Asher stood, leaning against the entry way, casual as ever, waiting . . .

And sure enough, a few moments later, a still half-asleep Daris pulled the front door open, grumbling to himself about the power. Asher grabbed the door, swung it out, and Harry stepped in and grabbed Daris by his pyjama shirt and forced him back inside.

"Shoulda locked your power box," Harry said, walking a flailing Daris backwards down a short hall to a kitchen. He kicked a chair at the table and sat Daris's ass on it.

Daris was pale. Harry towered over him, and Asher leaned down, smiling as if he'd been invited for breakfast. "Good morning, Daris," Asher said cheerfully.

Daris shook his head. "Please, not here. My daughter . . . my wife . . . I'll go with you. Just leave them alone. They don't need to see this."

"Oh, Daris," Asher said mournfully, his hand to his heart. "I appreciate the resignation to your fate. But I don't give one fuck about them."

Daris shifted in his seat, paler now, his mouth working, but no words came out. "I'm sorry. I didn't want you to get involved . . . I didn't—"

"Imagine my surprise when our friend Ivan Ćosić spilled all your secrets," Asher said, still using that sweet voice that was kinda terrifying.

Daris shook his head. "I didn't want to get involved, Asher. You have to believe me. I tried to make you ask questions about why, not who. You don't want to be involved with these people, you have to understand."

"Understand what? That you're in bed with the ZBK? A group of terrorists. Makes sense now when you said some folks around here don't care about borders. A group of fucking terrorists who believe in the old days—"

Indignation flashed in Daris's eyes. "They're not terrorists—"

"Oh, so you're a sympathiser," Asher said, pulling his gun out. He kept it on his thigh but Daris's eyes went wide. "Explain, Daris. You have three seconds."

"For what this country did to me," he said. "What they

did to you. How can you not hate them? How can you not want them to pay?"

"I don't blame a whole country," Asher said. "I blame people. I blame individuals, Daris. And right now I'm looking at you. When I asked if you could get me weapons, you lied to me."

"I didn't . . . I can't . . . Asher, please."

"Start talking faster," Asher hissed.

"I didn't want you to know about them," he whispered. "And I don't want them to know about you." He shook his head. "If they knew I knew you, if I did a deal with you . . ."

"They'd what? Kill you?" Asher asked. "Did you think your deals with them would end any other way? Christ, how are you so stupid? You set up a legit business only to cater to factions that run guns and drugs. Do you transport everything for them? Tell me, do you transport people too?"

"It's not like that," he whispered.

"Bullshit," Asher snapped. "When I asked you if you'd heard anything about my friend who was kidnapped, you said no," Asher said. His voice was calm but the grip on his pistol told Harry otherwise. "But Ivan told me everything. Leaked like a sieve, Daris. Now I'm gonna ask you again. Where is Yunho? If I find out you had anything to do with transporting him, you're gonna need a new definition for pain. What those assholes did to us in Turkey will be a fucking walk in the park."

"I don't know," he replied, shaking his head. "I don't know."

Asher put the pistol to Daris's forehead. "Wrong answer."

"I don't know, Asher," he said again. He was teary now

and sweating. He shrank back, a pitiful excuse. "I promise."

Harry kicked Daris's leg. "Sit up straight. If you're gonna get shot in the head, have some respect for yourself and look him in the fucking eye when he does it." Daris sat up and Harry towered over him again. "I should rip your tongue out for lying to him the first time. I don't need a second time. I will do it right here, and you will bleed to death on your kitchen floor. Now answer his fucking question and *do not* lie to him."

"I don't know *where* he is," Daris said, almost crying. "But I know who took him. Vadik Istomin. He's from Moscow. He's some political army head, but he's based in Belgrade. He has some kid working for him who's some genius computer hacker. He's the one who found Yunho. Once they got a location, Istomin sent in a team of guys to extract Yunho. They're Russian mercenaries, ex-black-ops. They're the real deal."

"And how do you know this, Daris?" Asher asked. "How involved are you?"

He shook his head. "I know because . . ." his face fell. "Because Radovic works for him."

Asher went stock still, even a little pale. "Radovic? How the fuck is he not dead yet?"

Daris nodded, shook his head, and shrugged, all at the same time. "He joined the army, found his calling there. He was a sick fuck. Still is. Asher, I'm so sorry."

Harry had no idea who Radovic was, but it changed something in Asher.

"And the three men who came for us?" Asher asked quietly.

"ZBK." Daris shrugged. "They weren't . . . they weren't pros."

"They were pathetic," Asher said. "And stupid. And now they're very dead. And I showed you that photo and you recognised them, or the tattoo, and you lied to me."

"I didn't want you to get involved," he said, shaking his head. "You have to believe me. I didn't want you to see any of this. But then you came here, asking about them, and I knew you'd find out I was involved. You have to believe me. It never started out with them or what they stood for. It was—"

"About the money," Asher said. "It's always about the money. Blah blah blah, I don't give a fuck. Tell me how I find Istomin."

"You don't. No one does."

"I absolutely will," Asher replied.

"He's based in Belgrade, but if that's where they took Yunho, I don't know, I swear."

Asher sighed. "The ZBK leader. I need a name."

Daris sobbed pathetically. God, how Harry wanted to kill him already.

"Josip Rozga," Daris mumbled.

Asher sighed. "And? What else do I need to know?"

"He's going to kill me," Daris whispered.

"The moment you went into business with him was the day you sealed that fate," Harry said. "It's no one's fault but yours."

He nodded pathetically, but then he looked at Asher. "He has three men with him at all times. They're his lieutenants. The one with red hair, he's the one you have to watch. He can fight."

Just then, there was a noise from upstairs. A door opening and soft voices. Daris shook his head quickly, his eyes wide and full of pleading.

A female voice said something about the power in

Bosnian. Harry could hear her trying the light switches. "Daris? There's no power."

Then a woman appeared, wearing a nightgown, her hair in a messy ponytail. She stopped cold, and when a small girl appeared behind her, the woman kept her hands out to stop the girl from seeing. "Daris," she whispered.

"It's okay," he said, trying to smile. "These are some friends of mine."

"Old friends," Asher said, smiling. "We were in the orphanage and training school together, which I'm sure he told you all about." He patted the table, the pistol back on his thigh, hidden from view. "Come in, take a seat at the table."

Daris gave a wild look at Asher before he tried smiling again for his wife and daughter. The woman kept her gaze on Harry and kept her daughter behind her as she edged to a seat at the table. She sat down and pulled her daughter into her lap, holding her tight.

Cute kid with messy brown hair and pink sparkly pyjamas, and Harry hoped this didn't go pear-shaped.

God, he hated when there were kids involved.

Then Asher spoke in Bosnian and Harry missed a lot of it. He picked out a few words here and there; orphanage, six years old, training.

The wife was staring at Daris as Asher spoke, and Harry got the feeling she knew nothing about his past.

Daris was pale, his hands were shaking.

Then Asher spoke in English. For Harry's benefit, or if the kid didn't speak English and Asher didn't want her to hear, Harry wasn't sure.

"I'm surprised," he said. "After everything we went through, after everything we swore we'd get away from, when we were no bigger than your daughter is right now, that you'd bring that life into your own house where your wife and daughter sleep. You deserve everything that's coming for you, Daris, but they don't. If you weren't so selfish you'd send them somewhere far away. You have no security here. We came in through your front door, Daris. Your front goddamn door. Your house alarm is wired into your main power, and you got a kid's bike in the front yard, so anyone who wants to hurt you knows he's got leverage. Did you learn nothing?"

Daris scrubbed at an errant tear, shook his head, and said nothing.

"Tell me something helpful, Daris," Asher said. "I'm running out of reasons to stay."

He shrugged, hopeless. "I don't know. Rozga has a chapter meeting every Wednesday at ten o'clock, at his compound. There'll be twenty or so men there. It's out of town, on the R446. He arrives in the final convoy of three vehicles. Middle car, at exactly ten o'clock, every time."

Asher smiled at him. "Now that is helpful, thank you." He stood up and both Daris and his wife's eyes went to the pistol he slid into his waistband. Her hold on their daughter tightened, shielding her tiny face, chin wobbling.

"We'll be going now," Asher said cheerfully. "Daris, walk us out."

Asher and Harry waited for Daris to stand. He did so, reluctantly. His legs seemed a little shaky and his wife was now crying.

Harry felt sorry for them. Not that they'd entered her house and upset her. He was sorry that she had no clue who her husband was, or who he was doing business with.

When they got to the front door, Asher spun on Daris and pushed him against the wall, his forearm to Daris's neck, the pistol pressed to the side of Daris's head. "I should shoot you right now," he whispered. "It goes against my better judgement to leave you breathing. But I promise you, if I hear your name uttered one more time in any fucking circle, I will kill you, your wife, and your daughter. Do you under-fucking-stand?"

Daris nodded, chin wobbling.

Then Asher spat a string of Slavic obscenities at him, gave his throat one last hard shove, sending him wheezing to the floor.

Harry and Asher walked back out to the Jeep. Asher was livid, Harry could tell. "Feel better?"

"No," Asher seethed. "I really want to kill something."

"Good. Because that's what we're going to do."

THE COMPOUND HEADQUARTERS were twelve kilometres out of the city on the R446 highway to the Mount Trebević region. The tree-covered mountains were popular with hikers in summer, skiers in winter; there were resorts and hotels dotted throughout.

"And tunnels," Asher said. "The War Tunnels. All through the mountains, but I think the mines are all cleared now."

Harry shot him a look. "Mines? Gold mines? Tin, copper? Or landmines?"

Asher snorted. "Landmines."

"You know they're cleared, or you think they are?"

"Supposedly all cleared. Jeez, Harry. I can't personally verify."

Harry sighed. *Landmines. Awesome.*

"From the map," Asher said, zooming in on the screen.

"Their compound has one tunnel to the north of their property."

"Are they usable? These tunnels?"

"For storage, maybe. Hard to say. A lot of them were closed or collapsed."

Harry nodded, considering this. "We should watch them. I know they have a meeting in—" He checked his watch. "—two and a half hours, but—"

"No," he replied flatly. "We find our best position and take everyone out before we get Rozga."

"We need to be able to question him."

Asher shrugged. "So we kill him last."

Well, Harry allowed, at least Asher wasn't suggesting they go bursting in through the front gates, guns blazing.

Finding their best position in a wooded, mountainous region with numerous hiking trails and parking bays was easy. Especially given the compound was secluded, had a lower elevation, and cleared vegetation around the building. From what Harry could find online, their compound was once a wellness-retreat-type place with one large hall. It was a wooden cabin style construction, and there was a newer, large outbuilding near the line of the woods.

And looking through the rifle scope, the difference between the Google Map view and the one they had now wasn't that much. The trees were thicker, taller, but not much else had changed.

They were three hundred metres away, atop a small ridge that sloped down, with the cover of heavy trees.

Until the firing started, that was.

Then they'd have to move down to the compound for closer contact and to grab Rozga. When it was all over, they'd need to retrace their steps, back up the mountain to the Jeep in the hiker's parking lot.

Harry felt useless and restless while Asher set his rifle up, lying on his belly, adjusting everything to perfection. He knew better than to pace or wander, so he sat his ass down and ran through some observations while Asher fine-tuned his rifle.

"The drive into the compound is approximately eight hundred metres from the road. There doesn't seem to be any cameras outside. Not that I can see, anyway. There's an old power box on the telegraph pole twenty metres to the southwest of the main building. A single gas tank outside the main building, under what looks like a kitchen window."

"I see it," Asher said quietly.

Harry studied him for a long moment. "How does it feel?"

Asher had been adjusting every turret cap on the rifle with the precision of a surgeon. He kept his eye to the eyepiece and smiled. "It feels good. Temperature's good, low humidity, no breeze." Then he paused, looked at Harry for a second as if he was contemplating his next words, then put his eye back to the scope. "It's been a long time since I've sighted in on a live target. I thought part of me might find it difficult . . ."

"And?"

"And I wish I could say I did."

Harry nodded, unsure of what to say. There really wasn't anything he *could* say. This was the mental tug of war they played. The separation of guilt, the detachment from humanity to get the job done. "We do what we have to do," Harry said eventually.

Asher nodded and moved back from the rifle. "What you have to do is set up the 36s and go get into position. We should be expecting company at any time now."

"I could stay here with you," he tried. "I don't like the idea of being separated from you."

Asher made a face. "Awww, that's so sweet." Then he shoved Harry's shoulder. "And fucking stupid."

Harry sighed and snatched up the G36. "Fine."

NINE

HARRY TOOK one of the G36s along with two mag clips and moved around the left of Asher some hundred metres through the thick of trees and forest.

Two vantage points was the smart thing to do, but Harry was loath to be separated from Asher.

It was foolish, and stupid to think Asher couldn't handle himself. Especially when he was armed with a MAC 50.

But still . . . Harry was a different soldier now.

He was a different man.

Like when he was in the special forces, when he was a squadron leader, he knew what made tactical sense, but leaving his unit always felt wrong.

Like leaving Asher felt wrong.

Asher was his unit now. His partner.

His entire fucking world.

Having separate vantage points made tactical sense. They would wait until the ZBK men arrived. Then when the final convoy of three vehicles drove in, Asher would take out the front and rear car, leaving the middle car unable to move. The remaining men would then no doubt run out to see what the hell was going on, and Harry would mow them all down.

That was the general plan. Not that these things ever went strictly to plan. These ZBK guys supposedly had training, which was almost laughable, considering they were making themselves sitting ducks in a heavily wooded location with only one entry and exit that was basically only wide enough for one vehicle.

Idiots.

And they were also drug trafficking wannabe terrorists. But mostly they were idiots.

But they were idiots with information.

The first car arrived, three men getting out. Dressed in long blue cargo style pants, black T-shirts, and the same boots as the three now-dead idiots back home. Harry looked through the scope on his rifle and sure enough, one of them had the ZBK tattoo on his biceps. Another one had it on the inside of his forearm like they were some bad-ass boy scouts.

Christ, they were stupid.

They also appeared unarmed.

Idiots, yes. But Harry knew better than to underestimate them.

Harry had no comms with Asher—they couldn't risk radios being heard or relying on phones in no-service areas—but he knew Asher saw them.

Then a second vehicle arrived, parking alongside the first car, and another three men got out. Dressed the same, same shaved haircuts, same variation of their boy-scout tattoos.

They went into the main cabin and two to the newer outbuilding. Harry had deduced it was a storage shed of sorts, and when the two men lifted the roller door, he used his scope to see inside.

There was a vehicle inside. An old white Ford F250 and shelves of crates and boxes. The two men came back out laughing, then proceeded to unload some boxes from the cars and carry them into the shed.

Another car arrived, four men this time, and they were greeted with their boy-scout-bro handshakes and Harry wanted to just murder them all.

Two of them had pistols in thigh holsters at least. Tactical HS2000s with box mags. Somewhat decent.

Finally. Jeez.

One of them carried a duffle bag into the cabin and they all disappeared inside. Harry guessed the bag had money in it, and that the boxes now in the shed contained illegal goods Harry didn't care about.

Another car arrived. Two men got out. These two were also armed. They wore jackets, and Harry spotted what looked like the same HS2000 pistols in a side holster.

Nineteen rounds at least.

They also had what looked like a laptop bag and a decent-sized box, which they took inside the cabin. It could be full of weapons for all Harry knew.

Hell, it could have a cake in it for all he cared.

The inside of the cabin could be a whole damn armoury, and for the sake of his and Asher's longevity, Harry had to assume it was.

Expect the worst, always.

Even if he was certain they were all boy-scout terrorists who were really just low-level crime idiots.

Harry had to remind himself that three of these men had entered Australia with intel on his and Asher's location, which meant they also knew their new names, which meant they had intel from someone in the loop.

So maybe they weren't all idiots.

Then, sure enough, just as Daris had said, three black Range Rovers came up the drive. Like they were in some James Bond movie.

Harry hated them all.

They got closer to the break of trees in the clearing. Two hundred metres. One-fifty. One hundred.

Come on, Asher. Time to do your thing.

Harry trained his sights on the cabin instead and concentrated on his breathing.

He heard the first shot fired. Even with the suppressor, it still had the familiar *thup* sound. A hole appeared in the windshield of the first car in the convoy, the driver painting the inside with red chunks and mist.

Then, before anyone could even react, a second shot fired and a hole tore into the third vehicle and it exploded into flames.

Goddammit, Asher.

Well, they had everyone's attention now.

The boy scouts raced out of the cabin, wide-eyed and in shock. So predictable.

Harry pulled the trigger. *Tink, tink, tink, tink.*

Four of them all spun to the ground like they'd been electrocuted. Four headshots.

He'd gloat to Asher afterwards, but the remaining boy scouts quickly backtracked into the safety of the cabin.

Four down, eight to go.

He'd hoped for less but he could work with that.

Asher fired another shot and Harry glanced quickly to see a man getting out of the first convoy vehicle fall to the ground. That was his third shot, which meant he only had two more rounds left in the MAC 50.

He had the second G36 with a full clip but Harry hoped Asher wouldn't need to use it. He studied the cabin again. A flash of movement in the window, Harry pulled the trigger, and they were now down to seven.

He'd also given away his location.

There was a lot of yelling inside the cabin, then a moment later one of the boy scouts stuck his head around from the top right corner of the cabin, trying to get a visual.

His head turned to mist.

Asher had shot him with the G36.

He was using both guns? At the same time?

God, Harry was never gonna hear the end of this.

Anyway, the boy scouts were now down to six.

Harry saw movement out of the corner of his eye and turned his attention to the convoy. The driver of the middle vehicle opened his door, and when he tried to get a round off, Harry shot him through the windscreen.

He smirked, knowing Asher would like that.

Someone tried to get out of the first vehicle on the far side, another *thup* sounded—Asher was back on the MAC 50—and the man's entire head disappeared.

Nice shot.

More yelling from inside the cabin and the kitchen window exploded outward and a spray of bullets followed.

VHS-D assault rifle.

Trees splintered above Harry's head. The whizz and whir of bullets far too close.

Asher clearly wasn't fucking with that.

He fired his last round from the MAC 50 into the gas

cylinder below the kitchen window and half the cabin went boom. Flames and debris went up in plumes of flame and smoke, and Harry was on the move.

Boy scouts were now zero, but the target was Rozga.

He ran through the forest, still covered by the dense trees, down to the wrecked convoy. His only focus was the middle vehicle.

They had two minutes to extract their target.

Two minutes to be long gone before the cops and fire trucks started descending. Or, god forbid, concerned citizens.

The rear passenger door of the middle vehicle opened on the far side, and Harry saw three figures. Two men and Rozga.

He has three men with him at all times. They're his lieu-tenants.

That's what Daris had said. Harry deduced that lieu-tenant number three was very likely dead already . . .

Then lieutenant number three stumbled out of the vehicle on Harry's side. He was covered in blood, his own and the driver's most likely. He was clutching at his side and in some valiant last act, raised his gun in Harry's direction, but his head turned to mist before he got off one round.

Asher.

One bullet, one shot.

Perfect aim.

Harry kept moving, breaking cover now. He could see the three men, one lieutenant keeping Rozga bent down as they moved into the trees. The second lieutenant was keeping guard on the flank. But a shot whirred past Harry's shoulder.

Someone was unaccounted for.

Fuck!

Harry ducked down behind the first vehicle and this time bullets went over his head. From Asher this time. Three shots. *Pop, pop, pop.* Then silence.

Jesus Christ.

Harry's heart was thundering.

He snuck to the far side of the fender. He could see now there had been another man in the first vehicle. He was now a smear on the backseat.

The three men were escaping into the trees. Harry didn't have time to aim and fire; he couldn't risk killing Rozga. He had to run. He had to pursue on foot. He would have no cover but the trees now, but he had no other choice.

Asher's sight would be restricted, Harry understood. But he was the best, right?

Harry took off after them. The second lieutenant at the flank spotted him and yelled something, lifted his gun, and fired a spray of bullets at Harry.

Harry ducked behind a tree, splinters flying. *Fuck, fuck fuck.*

Then another shot rang out and lieutenant number two spun in slow motion, a crater where his forehead used to be.

The first lieutenant shoved Rozga behind a tree, taking cover. He yelled something in Croatian or Bosnian that Harry didn't understand.

Didn't care.

It was the guy with red hair. The one Daris had said could fight. The smart one, apparently. Rozga's right-hand man. When Harry risked a quick glance to get an eval, a shot hit the tree, missing Harry by millimetres.

Fuck.

Another shot came from Asher, and Rozga cried out.

Asher had shot Rozga?

Not a kill shot, obviously. But one to change the odds and make lieutenant redhead react.

Harry broke cover, his 36 raised, and he ran toward them. He waited for the guy to make one move, to give Harry one inch of body mass. But when he made his move, stepping out, before Harry could fire one round, the guy's head opened like a tin of spaghetti sauce.

Harry skidded to a stop. "Jesus Christ, can I kill one fucking person?" he yelled. He stomped over to where Rozga was trying to scurry away. He was clutching his shoulder, blood oozing from the ragged gash where Asher had shot him.

"Six out of twenty-two," Harry grumbled. "That's all I got. Twenty-seven percent strike rate. You know what that does to my average?"

Rozga shook his head, still trying to back away from Harry in the leaves and mud.

"Get to your fucking feet," Harry said, pulling him by his shirt and shoving him in the direction they'd come. "Walk." He began to walk, but Harry shoved him. "Faster."

"What do you want?" Rozga asked.

"I wanted better than twenty-seven percent, that's what I wanted. He's never gonna let me hear the end of it."

"I don't understand," he mumbled. "My arm . . ."

Harry shoved him again. "Yeah, your arm. Not your fucking leg. Move faster. Run."

Harry knew making him run would only make him bleed faster, but he didn't care at this point.

They broke through the trees near the convoy carnage

and what was left of the cabin. "This way," Harry said, shoving Rozga forward with the end of his rifle, but Rozga stopped when he saw Asher coming out from the trees. He had his G36 rifle and the backpack, but not his MAC 50.

He looked pissed off. Like really fucking mad. "This way," Asher snapped. "North."

They headed back into the forest, away from the clearing, away from the mess they'd just made, and away from the emergency services that would be no doubt arriving soon enough.

Harry couldn't hear sirens yet, but they'd be coming.

"What do you want?" Rozga asked as they walked. "Who are you taking me to? I won't talk so you may as well kill me now."

Asher rounded on him in a millisecond, in his face and seething with rage. "You have no idea what you're about to endure," he whispered. The wildness in his eyes even scared Harry a little.

He was fucking livid.

Harry nudged Rozga with the muzzle of his rifle. "Walk."

So they walked on, down into a valley, through a creek, and up onto the other side. About half a mile later, they came to a small entrance in the mountainside. Covered by trees and overgrown forest, the tunnel entrance was almost fully concealed. It was old concrete, cracked and crumbling, the entrance was five by three feet. Inside was roomier, more cave-like, made of dirt and rock. It was cold and damp and smelled of earth and rot.

Rozga stopped at the entry, and he turned to Harry, pleading, as if he was the good cop in this good-cop, bad-cop routine.

"Get in the fucking hole," Harry said, kicking him into the tunnel.

He stumbled in, still clutching his bleeding shoulder. He fell and staggered back on his ass, leaning against the wall. Asher took out an LED lantern from the backpack and put it on the ground, then turned his attention to Rozga.

"You're going to tell me everything you know about the kidnapping of a Mr Oh Yunho and Lucas Edwards. And Vadik Istomin, the Russian man responsible, and the Chinese kid computer whiz that works for him."

Rozga shook his head. "I don't know . . ."

Asher took one of the hunting knives and unsheathed it. "Yes, you do."

Rozga eyed the blade. "I don't . . . I mean, I . . . he'll kill me. You don't know who you're dealing with."

Asher laughed. "Okay, first things first. You don't need to worry about him killing you. You're already a dead man. And I know exactly who I am dealing with. Do you know who you're dealing with? Do you know who I am?"

He shook his head. He was sweating despite the cold, and whether his paleness was from blood loss or fear, Harry couldn't say. Maybe it was the mood lighting.

Asher leaned over him, the hunting knife pressed into Rozga's cheek. "Do you know how many bullets almost hit him just now?" Asher asked, pointing his free hand back to Harry. Rozga's eyes went to Harry, then back to Asher. "Do you know how many of your men fired bullets at him? Almost killing the man I love most in this world?" Asher said.

Oh Jesus. So that's what he's mad about.

"They weren't *that* close," Harry mumbled.

Asher looked at him like he'd lost his damned mind.

"You have wood chips in your hair from where they hit the tree by your head, Harry. By your head!"

Harry brushed the bits of wood from his hair and sighed. "You could have let me get more kills than twenty-seven percent."

Asher's nostrils flared, and Rozga made the mistake of speaking. "Look, I—"

Asher had the knife pressed to the corner of Rozga's eye so fast he couldn't even blink. "Look at what?" Asher said. "I will cut out your fucking eyeballs if you tell me to look one more time."

"Asher," Harry whispered. "We don't have time."

"Asher . . ." Rozga mumbled, his eyes wide, recognition dawning. "Asher Garin. Who works with Oh Yunho . . ."

Asher smiled. "The one and the same. Now you know who you're dealing with. Tell me about Istomin, and for every second you choose silence, I'm going to choose a tendon in your body and slice it. The pain will be like nothing you can imagine. There are about four thousand tendons in the human body and we don't have that much time, and truth be told, I'm not that skilled with a knife, so hopefully you won't bleed out before I'm finished." Then Asher took the knife and pressed the tip to Rozga's kneecap. "Honestly, that'd be a blessing for you."

Rozga looked at Harry, panic clearly starting to kick in. "He's insane."

Harry chuckled and squatted down next to him. His smile faded slowly. "Call him insane one more time, and I'll start ripping your tendons out with my fucking hands."

Rozga looked between them like a psychopathic tennis match.

"Oh Yunho," Asher said. "Where is he?"

"I-I don't know," Rozga stammered.

"Wrong answer," Asher said. He pulled Rozga's boot off and held it up. "Did you get a group discount on these? Because those three idiots you sent to kill us in Australia were wearing these. They're dead, by the way. Gutted like fish." Asher tossed the boot, twirled the knife, then lifted Rozga's foot and sliced through his Achilles.

He howled, hissing through the pain, and even frothed at the mouth a little. So Harry stripped Rozga's shirt over his head and used it as a gag to muffle the sound.

"Now he can't talk," Asher said, looking at Harry like he was an amateur.

"Let's just fucking kill him already," Harry grumbled. "He's not gonna tell you anything."

Asher gritted his teeth and snarled at him, mumbling something not in English as he ripped off Rozga's other boot. "Take the gag out, for fuck's sake," he said, now pointing the boot at Harry. "How can he talk like that?"

Harry snatched the gag out, making Rozga choke a little. "Happy now?"

"Happy? That you almost died several times today? No, I'm not fucking happy, Harry. Do I look happy?"

Rozga made a pathetic groaning noise, still sputtering. Asher picked up his other foot and looked at Harry. "How many tendons do feet have? Toes have to have tendons, right?"

"I guess so," Harry said. "And I didn't almost die several times today."

Asher glared at him, holding Rozga's foot. "One round missed you by half an inch!" Then he sliced under Rozga's big toe.

He howled again, doing that hiss-breathing thing.

Harry sighed. "You didn't even ask him another question."

Asher looked at the guy, who was now torn between which foot to hold. "Oops."

Harry took the knife off Asher and kneeled down in front of Rozga. "Istomin took Yunho and Lucas. Yes or no."

Rozga nodded. "Yes."

"He sent in a team of mercenaries to extract them. Where did he take them?"

Rozga hesitated, so Harry, holding the knife vertically, pressed the tip of the knife into his bare shoulder, the tip pooling blood.

"Where?"

Rozga hissed but shook his head, so Harry pushed the knife in, blood pooling around the blade. "There's a point between the shoulder humerus and the scapula, where if you slice through the three tendons, the ball joint just pops and renders the arm useless."

Rozga was foaming at the mouth again, trying to breathe through the pain. Harry pushed it through the final resistance. Rozga wailed and his left arm drooped. "There it is," Harry said. "Kinda like deboning a chicken. Just gotta get the right spot."

He gave Rozga a few seconds to compose himself. "Have you had enough yet?" Harry asked. "Because I found your parents' address online. I mean, I usually don't like to fuck with the elderly, but I will. They make it quick anyway. And honestly, the fact I could find out everything about you using fucking Google makes you the stupidest fucking idiot I've ever met. And I don't want to threaten your elderly mother, but if you don't tell me what you know, I will."

Rozga's whole face changed.

"Now, I'll ask you again," Harry said. "Where are they?"

"B-bel-b," he began, but seemed to be having a bit of trouble speaking.

"Belgrade?" Harry prompted.

Rozga nodded.

"And you do work for him? Guns and drugs, that kind of thing."

He nodded again.

That didn't make much sense to Harry. "What does a low-life piece-of-shit drug and gun peddler want with the likes of Yunho?"

He shook his head. "I don't know. Never ask why."

"When he asked you to send three men to Australia, he gave you the names and addresses?"

He nodded.

"The kid he has working for him, the computer whiz. What's his name?"

He shook his head quickly. "I don't know. Yixing, I think."

"And how does Istomin contact you?"

"Text."

Harry patted down Rozga's pockets and pulled out his phone. He held it up to his face, unlocked it, then handed it to Asher. "Disable the Face ID and passwords."

Then he turned back to Rozga. "Tell me everything you know and I'll make your death quick."

He shook his head again, tears, sweat, and spittle marking his dirtied face. "Please don't hurt my mother. She—"

"Then start talking," Harry barked.

"Pukovnik Radovic," he said. "His name is Alen Radovic."

Harry heard Asher gasp quietly. He looked up at him, and Asher shook his head. "Pukovnik means colonel." He swallowed hard, then focused on Rozga. "The founder of the ZBK, the piece-of-shit colonel who took over a political activist group and turned it into a faction of white supremacist fuckwits, is Alen Radovic?"

Rozga nodded. "Yes. He knows Istomin."

"They retired government buddies or something?" Harry asked. He was kinda lost.

Rozga laughed. He actually laughed. "Not retired. Still active."

"Istomin is active in the Russian government?"

"Long live the USSR and Yugoslavia, and the new cold war," he said, smiling. Pale, defeated—knowing he was about to die—but smiling. "Život bez kajanja."

Harry wanted to kick his teeth in. Instead, he drove the knife into the elbow crease of his good arm and severed the joint and tendons in one go. He watched the tendon curl and pull up under the skin of his biceps. "Ouch," Harry mumbled, grimacing. "That's gotta hurt."

Rozga screamed through clenched teeth.

"Tell me what you know about the abduction of Oh Yunho," Harry tried again. "And I'll make the pain stop."

Rozga's head fell back against the concrete wall behind him. He was pale, sweating, and clearly in a lot of pain. He tried to laugh again but he was in no shape for it. "You keep asking about Yunho," he said, panting, groaning out another laugh. "You have no idea."

Asher took the knife then and held it to Rozga's crotch. "If you want to go to the afterlife with your dick intact, you'll speak."

"Not just Yunho," he said. He was slumping now, fading fast. The pain was too much. "They didn't want just the Korean."

Not just Yunho . . .

"Lucas?" Harry said, shaking him. "They wanted Lucas?"

Rozga sneered, the life in him almost gone. "Don't you know? He's MI6."

Harry and Asher stared at him, shocked into silence.

MI6.

No fucking way.

Harry couldn't get his head around it. He couldn't believe it.

Rozga groaned out a mocking laugh. "You don't even know who you're trying to save."

The sound of sirens far off in the distance spurred Harry into action. He stood, pulled an equally stunned Asher back. "We need to leave. Grab the lantern."

Asher nodded and collected their gear. Harry used Rozga's shirt to wipe their fingerprints off the knife handle, then he wrapped the shirt around the handle and plunged the blade into Rozga's heart.

"Let's go," Harry said, taking the lantern from Asher so he could lead the way. And they walked in silence into the darkness of the tunnel.

TEN

ASHER WAS REALLY FUCKING MAD.

Mad at a lot of things. Mad at how this whole day had gone from bad to worse.

First, before the sun had even come up, he'd found out that Daris had lied to him, tried to fuck him over. Daris, the one person Asher had known the longest in his miserable fucking life, and he'd lied to him.

Then they go shoot a bunch of wannabe terrorists, and Harry almost got himself shot several times. Once by the trees, so Asher had to blow the gas tank on the cabin. Yes, it killed the assholes who'd shot at Harry, but it also risked exposing them. The fact that Asher's aim had been off with the third vehicle... He hadn't meant to hit the fuel tank, but he did. A rookie mistake, and that pissed Asher off too.

Then Harry almost got himself shot when he was down by the vehicles. Had he not even thought to check if any of those fascist fucks were still alive? No, he just ran in without thinking and got shot at.

Asher had to take that fucker out too.

And then when Harry ran into the far side of the trees, chasing the men trying to escape on foot, Asher didn't have a clear line of sight. A fact Harry should have realised and didn't.

Or didn't care.

And that pissed Asher off too.

Three times. Three fucking times Asher had almost lost Harry in one day.

It was reckless and stupid.

And then . . .

And then they learned that Lucas is MI6.

Lucas, who had been by Yunho's side for a decade. Married him, cared for him, helped him, understood him. Lucas, who Yunho trusted above all else.

Asher had trusted him too.

And it was all a lie.

Not to mention the fact that they had to crawl through that wretched tunnel for what felt like forever. They'd cleaned up in the river, washing off any splatters of blood and mud, then walked for goddamn miles around the freaking mountain onto the hiking trails, pretending to be happy-go-lucky hikers to any other hiking passers-by, back to where they'd parked the Jeep.

It'd taken hours.

But it had got them out. And by the time they got back to their hotel, Asher was really tired, really hungry, and really fucking mad.

Harry ordered some dinner to be delivered and Asher tried to shower and scrub away his filthy mood.

He came out of the bathroom wearing nothing but a towel.

"There's some pasta here," Harry said. "Have some. I'm gonna have a few bites, then I'll grab a shower. We need to see what we can find out about Lucas. Do we believe what he said? Do you think it could be true?"

Asher had thought he was hungry, but now facing food, he wasn't sure. "Are we going to talk about how you almost got shot today? Three times, Harry. I almost lost you three times."

Harry put his fork down with a sigh. "I didn't almost get shot," he muttered.

"You almost fucking died today and you don't care," Asher said. He was so wound-up, so upset, he could barely contain his tears. "And you don't even care. You don't care what it would do to me. You didn't think about me at all. It would fucking kill me, Harry, and you don't even give a shit."

Harry stood up and collected him in a fierce hug. Asher tried to pull away, to fight him . . . Yes, a good fight would make him feel better. A fight that ends with fucking. Getting railed into the mattress would make him feel so much better, so he fought a little harder, trying to kick and thrash.

Harry only held him tighter. "We're not doing that today," he murmured.

Damn him for being so much bigger, so much stronger.

Asher struggled to get free. "Need you to fight me," he bit out. "Hold me down and—"

"No." Harry was completely still, gripping him in his vice-like hold. "We're not doing that today. I won't fightfuck you. Not today."

Asher tried to fight him off one last time but Harry was too strong, and Asher didn't have the strength or the will to keep trying. He stopped and sagged, a sob escaping him, and Harry's hold on him became a warm embrace.

"I'm sorry," Harry whispered. "It's okay to be scared.

I'm sorry I was foolish today. I'm not as agile as I used to be. I can't think like I used to. I'm sorry it scared you."

Asher let himself cry for a second, Harry rubbing his back. "It would kill me, Harry."

"I know. Like it'd kill me if something were to happen to you."

"I missed a shot today," Asher admitted. "I didn't mean for the car to explode; I meant to take out the engine block but I was scared for you, and I've never missed a shot in my life."

Harry pulled back and wiped Asher's cheek with his thumb. "I wondered about that."

"Did they move the fuel tank in those cars?"

Harry almost smiled but then seemed to think twice about it. "I'm sure they did."

Asher nodded. "It was your fault, because you almost got shot and I panicked!"

Harry nodded. "I'm sorry."

"And then you went into the trees and I couldn't get a clear shot. Christ, Harry, I've never been so scared."

"I think I was reckless because I knew you had my back." Harry inhaled deeply. "You know this Radovic guy?"

Asher froze. "Yes. But I can't talk about him tonight."

Harry cupped Asher's jaw, his palm calloused and warm. "Okay. Whenever you're ready, I'll listen."

Asher leaned into it and closed his eyes, his chin wobbling. "I came so close today to losing you. And I'm worried about what comes next because we're not as good as we used to be, Harry. And it's only going to be harder, and I left the MAC 50 behind. I wiped it down, of course, but I couldn't pack it up and bring it with me."

"You were right about the 36s though. It's a good weapon."

Asher sniffed and nodded. "Then you had to take over asking Rozga the questions because I couldn't even slice some tendons properly."

"You did great," Harry said. "That Achilles slice was flawless."

Asher frowned, getting teary again. "I'm just not good at the close-up stuff. You're so much better at it than me."

"And you're better at sniping than I could ever be."

Asher still didn't feel any better. "Look at me. I used to be precise and cold and mysterious, and now I'm a mess, crying, and you won't even fuck me like I need you to."

"I'm not going to hurt you," Harry whispered, lifting Asher's chin and kissing him softly. "I'll fill your ass to the brim if you want me to, but I won't be rough."

Asher frowned again, but he considered this proposal. "To the brim, huh?"

Harry chuckled, brushing his lips over Asher's. "I'll make love to you, bury my cock in you, long and deep. I'll come inside you. Show you how much you mean to me."

Asher groaned, and Harry crushed his mouth to Asher's, kissing him deeply. He held his face with one hand and pulled him close with the other, their bodies flush.

Asher pulled his towel away and Harry groaned, walking him backwards to the bed. He laid Asher down, pulling his shirt over his head, and Asher pulled at Harry's button and fly.

Harry lifted one foot, ripping at the laces. "Damn boots."

Asher laughed and, reaching into Harry's pants, pulled

his dick free. "Leave your boots on," he said. "Leave your pants on. Fuck me like this."

Harry seemed genuinely torn, but Asher reached for the lube, scooted up the bed, and began prepping himself. "Don't make me wait, Harry."

He kneeled on the bed, boots and pants still on, and crawled up Asher's body, between his legs. Asher smeared his hole, slipping a fingertip in, then two, relishing the bite, the push.

Harry groaned. "That's my job."

"Then get over here and do it." He poured more lube over his palm and slicked Harry's cock. "You said you'd fill me to the brim."

Harry gripped Asher's ankles and pulled him down the bed a little, then pushed his knees up to his chest, leaning over him. "I'm gonna fill you," he whispered, his cock at Asher's hole. "With my cock, with my come."

He pushed into him, Harry's blunt cockhead breaching him in a long, slow push. The size of him still took Asher by surprise, that first push, that first slide in.

The intrusion, the overwhelming feeling of being taken, of being owned and claimed. It was everything Asher needed.

That one moment of focus, of clarity, his entire mind filled with nothing but this primal urge.

Harry groaned, his breaths shuddering until he slid all the way in. Asher's back arched and he gripped Harry's back, needing him to stay right there, to never move, to be that deep inside him forever. He couldn't think of anything else in that moment, nothing else in the world existed, until Harry's tongue invaded his mouth and he began the blissful tug of war inside him; cock and tongue, sliding in and pushing back in.

Then it was stimulation overload, too much and not enough at the same time.

Harry held him as he controlled this seesaw, giving him everything he needed. And this was what he needed. Not to be held down and fucked like he'd wanted earlier. This right here, this tender rocking, gentle yet so consuming . . .

Harry always knew what Asher needed, even when Asher didn't.

And by god, he needed this.

Asher reached down to Harry's ass, pushing his underwear over the swell of his ass cheeks, and slid his finger down his crack.

Harry groaned into Asher's mouth, his rhythm faltering. Asher smiled into their kiss and Harry rewarded him with a sharp thrust back in. Punishment for toying with him really wasn't punishment at all when it was what Asher wanted.

"Fuck, Asher," Harry bit out. "You're gonna make me come too fast."

Asher groaned, his blood warming at the thought. "Fill me to the brim tonight," he rasped. "You said you would."

Harry shuddered and drove up into him. God, he was so big, Asher was so full of him, and as Harry began to thrust harder, his cock harder and with a final thrust, Harry rolled his hips as deep as he could go, and he came.

Asher felt the pulse, the rush of warmth, as Harry came inside him. Harry groaned, his neck corded with veins, with power.

When he collapsed on top of Asher, Asher held him, rolling his hips and relishing the feel of Harry softening inside him. Asher loved it all, feeling every bit owned and cherished as he was.

Harry moaned as he slipped out of him. "Jesus," he breathed, collapsing onto the bed beside him. "I didn't even make you come. Just gonna need a minute."

Asher laughed, rolling on top of Harry's back. He'd only meant to cuddle him, to feel close, to stay joined to him. But his erection pressed down the cleft of Harry's ass, and it felt so good.

His pants were now around his thighs, keeping his legs together, making it a tight fit. "Fuck," he hissed.

"What are you doing?" Harry asked. He didn't move so he wasn't bothered. But ass play really wasn't something Asher had ever done with Harry.

They'd never had the need.

Asher was a greedy bottom, wanting nothing more than a good hard fuck, which Harry had always been only too happy to provide.

But this . . .

This was new, and Asher's hips seemed to move on their own accord. The sensation on his cock too good, too pure to stop.

"Gonna come like this," Asher said, thrusting into the crevice of Harry's ass, over his hole, and behind his balls. "Oh god."

He could only imagine what it would be like to be inside him, to push into him, to own him the way Harry owned him. Harry clenched and Asher jolted with pleasure. "Fuck yes," Asher grunted. He lay over Harry's back, thrusting and chasing his orgasm until the pleasure became too much and he couldn't stop until he tumbled over the edge.

He came, his cock buried in the crease of Harry's ass, spilling his seed over his balls. He shuddered through his release, groaning into the back of Harry's neck.

"Fucking hell," Asher mumbled, his head spinning.

He felt the need to apologise, to ask if Harry was okay because this was not something they'd discussed. Asher had never entertained the idea of topping Harry, and even though he hadn't, he'd wished he came inside him.

"Harry," he began.

"Stay there," Harry said, his voice rough. "Feels good, where you are right now."

Jesus. He liked it?

A tremor wracked through Asher. "I wanted to come inside you," Asher admitted in a whisper. "Never wanted to do that before."

"Never wanted that done before," Harry replied, rolling his hips a little. "Wouldn't mind it right now."

Asher's cock twitched, so he gripped Harry's hip, holding him still. "Christ, Harry."

Harry pulled a pillow under his face and laughed into it. So relaxed, so at ease. Then he tried to widen his legs a little but his pants restrained him.

Christ, he does want this . . .

Asher slid his finger down Harry's crack, smearing his come over his hole and pushing a fingertip inside him.

Harry gasped and gripped the pillow, raising his ass, so Asher used his come to slick his hole some more and pushed in two fingertips.

"Fuck," Harry grunted.

Asher couldn't help it. He couldn't stand it another second. He gripped his half-hard cock and pushed it against Harry's hole. He barely got the tip in. Harry was too tight and Asher was barely hard enough, but he drove it in. Harry let out a cry through gritted teeth, and Asher sank inside him.

God, it felt so good.

Tight, hot, slick with his come.

He wanted to deliver it deeper next time. "Gonna come inside you next time," Asher said.

Harry's hands fisted the pillow, his knuckles white, and he grunted. But he kept his ass up and open. Willing and wanting.

"Would you like that?" Asher asked, and Harry groaned. "Then I'll own you the way you own me."

Harry moaned. "You already own me."

Asher kissed the spot between Harry's shoulder blades and pulled back so he slipped out of Harry, wishing like hell that his dick could recover like it used to.

Getting older sucks.

Getting older is a privilege he heard in Yunho's voice. He used to say that all the time. Every time Asher had complained about the aches and pains, or having a birthday, Yunho would remind him that many people weren't so lucky.

God, how he hoped that Yunho was okay.

Asher got up off the bed and pulled Harry's boots off, then taking his pants by the hems, he pulled them off too. "Let's have a shower," Asher said. He felt better than he did before. More focused now, his head clearer and not so caught up on the unspent anger and frustration. "Then we can work out what's next."

Harry rolled off the bed with a groan. "Man, I'm sore."

"Your ass?" Asher asked.

Harry laughed. "No, my legs. Christ." He shuffled as he walked to the bathroom. "How far did we walk today?"

"Too far."

"I'm too old for this shit," Harry grumbled. He turned the shower on and smiled at Asher. "My ass feels good, actually."

"Hm." Asher liked the sound of that. "Not opposed to what I said?"

Harry laughed as he stepped into the shower, under the water. "Never thought so before, but I'm not opposed at all."

Asher gasped, his hand to his heart, following Harry into the cubicle. "I don't mind accommodating your needs, but let's get one thing clear. I'm the bottom in this relationship, and I need your dick in my ass regularly, so don't get any ideas about swapping places."

Harry laughed, and turning Asher around, pinning his back to the tiles, he lifted one of Asher's legs up over his hip. "Oh, believe me, I know what you need, and I'm only too happy to give it. But it was your idea to roll on top of me and put your cock inside me with promises to come in me next time, so you've only got yourself to blame if I like the sound of it."

Asher groaned out a laugh. "Such a bossy bottom already."

Harry laughed and kissed him before he smacked his ass. "Let's get cleaned up. We've got shit to do."

"DO YOU BELIEVE WHAT ROZGA SAID?" Harry asked.

Asher pushed the half-eaten now-cold pasta away. They'd worked out their travel plans for the next day and had watched the local news about the compound explosions and all the bodies, and how known leader Rozga was missing. Authorities believed he was either kidnapped by the culprits, or he was responsible. That told

Asher they hadn't found his body in the tunnel and they had no clue who was responsible.

But it had brought the topic of conversation back to what he'd said.

"Which part? About Lucas being MI6? Or about Istomin being part of the Russian government and long live the USSR and Yugoslavia and the new cold war?"

Harry sighed. "You know, in all my time working for the Australian government, I dealt with my fair share of guys who yearned for the past. But this all leads back to the USSR and Yugoslavia? These government military men want something that no longer exists. Prepared to kill for it. It's fucked up."

"It's different for you," Asher said quietly. "You didn't live through the war. I know you've seen a lot of war, Harry. Been to a lot of war zones. But it's different, living it on your home soil. A lot of people lost loved ones in the name of change. Their cities and towns were decimated, family members, neighbours killed; cultures erased. Life was never the same. And many of them are then expected to coexist with the people who did it."

Harry's eyebrows knitted. "Yeah. Sorry, I just . . . I just don't get it."

Asher sighed. "I never felt love for any country. You know that. I was never in any place long enough to feel at home, to be loyal. Deliberately so. But I am still a product of war. I am who I am because of the war. No family, no way of knowing where I come from. Was taken and trained to kill people when I was just a boy."

Harry reached over and took Asher's hand. "I'm sorry. I know . . . I can't imagine what you went through."

Asher tried to smile, but it was weak at best. "It's okay. I can't understand the need to exact revenge to a country or a government. That's foreign to me." He shrugged. "We each have our causes, I guess."

Harry's eyes met his. "And what's your cause?"

"To keep you safe, always. To bring Yunho home. And to kill anyone who gets in my way of either."

Harry smiled, rubbing his thumb across the back of Asher's knuckles. "Can I ask you something?"

"Sure."

"You said something to Daris," he whispered. "About what those assholes did to you in Turkey."

Asher sighed, his mind replaying flashes of nightmares he'd long tried to forget. He knew he needed to talk about it, but it wasn't easy. "It was a long time ago," he began. "I was . . . I was about eight, I think. Daris was ten. They would beat us, make us run for hours, make us fight for food. We learned languages, and tricks on how to be invisible. They would shoot at us to motivate us. The kids that lost, the slower or weaker ones, were . . ." He sighed. "Sold, I think. Some were killed if they were too badly injured, but most were sold off to the highest bidder. To sick fucks who wanted boys, usually."

Harry closed his eyes, and Asher wished he could block it out that easily.

"We learned to never get attached or make friends. It was easier in the end that way."

"Oh, Asher, baby," Harry murmured.

He tried to smile for him. "But I was fast and a quick learner. I could read people and situations, and be whatever they needed me to be," he whispered. "They'd strip us naked and beat us. Grown men against boys. Then the older boys were made to . . ." He shuddered and let out a long breath, unable to finish that sentence. He took a deep breath and let his memories take him on a different path.

"Radovic was one of them. He was very cruel. But I learned very fast to be a chameleon. Blend in, disappear. One of the leaders favoured me, saw that I had skills. I was taken to Kosovo after that."

Harry lifted Asher's hand to his lips, kissed his palm and then his knuckles, then held it to his cheek. "Did Daris go with you?"

Asher shook his head. "No. We were two out of half a dozen that lasted the longest. I was the youngest in the end. I went with Radovic to Kosovo. Daris went to Hungary. I saw him a few years later in Albania." Asher managed a smile at that. "It was good to see him. Like seeing a brother. We had a week, like a summer holiday. We swapped stories and dared to think of the future. Until a new shipment of boys came in and I went to Italy after that. Then years later when I found myself back in Croatia, I tracked Daris down. I expected him to be dead. But no. He said he worked at a logistics place and he was finally living a normal life."

Harry sighed. "I'm sorry he lied to you."

"Me too. But you know, I don't know if I blame him anymore." Asher shrugged. "We were taught to do whatever it took to survive, and maybe that's what he was doing."

"Still," Harry murmured, "betrayal stings."

"There are very few people I care enough to feel betrayal over," Asher admitted. "Just you, Yunho, and Lucas . . ."

God, he'd almost forgot about that.

Harry scowled. "Do you really think he's MI6?"

"I don't know," Asher replied quietly. "I don't know what to make of that. But I promise, if he's the one who betrayed Yunho, he will learn how much pain the human body can endure before death."

"And I will help you." Harry closed the laptop. "But it's late and we've got a big day ahead of us tomorrow."

"Ah, yes, driving to Belgrade."

"And our plan to track down Istomin," Harry hedged. "It's high-risk, and we'll re-evaluate the situation if we find out any new information."

God, it was times like this that Asher missed Yunho the most. He would've given Asher any information he needed with a few clicks of his computer.

"And there was nothing about Istomin in Yunho's magic data folders?"

"Nothing that I could see, but I'll keep looking while you drive tomorrow."

Harry nodded slowly. "To the Serbian Military Headquarters or the Russian embassy in Belgrade. Or both, perhaps."

Asher sighed. "What could possibly go wrong?"

ELEVEN

THEY WERE in the Jeep before four am, heading out on the M18, Harry at the wheel, Asher supplying him coffee. He was quiet as he scrolled through the files and folders that Yunho had left him, and Harry was happy to concentrate on driving.

There were bank accounts. A lot of them, with more money in them than Harry thought was possible, and those numbers kept clicking over like miles on a speedometer. Every cent of it was theirs if they wanted it.

Yunho had given it to Asher with instructions on how to access it, via untraceable routing funnels that Harry couldn't begin to understand.

There were files of information. Names and personal details on undercover government operatives, high-ranking government officials, from all over the world. Royalty, billionaires, tycoons in the oil, energy, finance, and media sectors. If they had an ounce of power, Yunho had every detail about them.

Information that people would kill for.

Kill because he had it. Kill to get their hands on it.

There were long lists of contacts: people who could get things like passports, tickets, weapons. In almost every country on the planet, and transaction ledgers of every single thing Yunho had.

There were files of photographs and videos of certain officials, politicians, meeting people they should *not* know, handing over files, transferring data and funds. Yunho had proof of certain governments funding wars, and weapon and drug trades. He had proof that would end careers, end wars and start them.

It scared the shit out of Harry if he was being honest.

In all his time under the Australian government, on the ground in foreign countries doing ungodly things in the name of security, he never wanted to know the details. He never wanted to know why someone was in his crosshairs.

It made things messy.

And now he knew things he wished he'd never seen. Things he wished Asher had never seen, because if they weren't already on a most-wanted list, they certainly would be now.

All Harry wanted to do now was go back to his life a week ago, where their biggest concern was whose turn it was to cook breakfast after lazy mornings in bed.

They crossed into Serbia with only their phones beeping to notify the change of carrier. Harry had to turn right at an intersection on the highway and still Asher hadn't noticed. Harry slid his hand onto Asher's thigh, and he'd been staring out the window, so lost in his thoughts that the touch had startled him.

"You okay?" Harry asked.

"Yes, of course." His answer came a little too fast, too automatic, that Harry took Asher's hand and squeezed it.

Then he seemed to look around, only now seeing where they were.

"I need to piss," Harry said. "Where should we stop?"

Asher pointed at the GPS screen on the dash. "Take the next exit, there'll be a service centre on the E75," he said. "We need to get off this highway anyway."

"Okay. You hungry? I'm starving. You've usually fed me croissants with bacon and eggs by this time. Fresh juice, toast with that homemade jam from the local markets."

Asher gave him a small smile. "Simpler times, huh?"

"Much," Harry agreed. "But we will have them again, I promise."

Asher leaned his head on the headrest and watched Harry for a long moment. "It's all I want. A quiet life with you. I don't even care where, as long as I have you. You're my home, Harry."

Harry lifted Asher's hand and kissed his knuckles. "And you are mine. I don't care where we end up either. If you wanted to come back here—"

"No."

Okay then. That was very blunt.

"Not here."

"We could go back to Thailand with Yunho," Harry suggested, aiming to make him smile. "I mean, he might need to buy a new tropical island, but whatever. Or somewhere new. Somewhere warm and far away."

Asher shrugged and sighed. "I want to go home," he said quietly. "When this is done. To our little home in our little town. With Mala. And Jacob and even August. They're our friends. They came to warn us. They had no idea who we really were, but they came to warn us anyway. The only people I have from my old life have all lied to me. Daris,

Lucas, even Yunho." He shook his head. "I don't know what's real or who to believe. All I have is you, Harry. You and our life back in Australia are the only real things I have ever had. Even if it was with fake names . . ." He shook his head. "It was the happiest I've ever been. I need you to know that."

Jesus Christ.

It sounds an awful lot like he's getting ready to say goodbye.

It made Harry feel sick, made his heart thump out of rhythm. He drove into the service centre, pulled up at the closest bowser, shut the engine off, and took Asher's hand. "Asher, baby, I do know that. You know I feel the same. The last two years have been more than I ever deserved." He squeezed his hand. "Listen to me. We will have that again. I promise. No matter what happens today, or tomorrow, next week or ten years from now. You and me, always."

Asher's eyes met his, glassy and sad. God, it almost killed Harry to see. "Thank you," Asher whispered.

"I love you," Harry said. "All of you, Asher Garin." Then he grimaced. "And I will love you even more after I've had a piss. My back teeth are starting to float."

Asher snorted and rolled his eyes. "So charming. Go," he said, shooing Harry away. "Go find the bathrooms and get some food. I'll fill the tank."

Harry unbuckled his seatbelt, took Asher's face in both hands, and kissed him. "Won't be long."

Harry made a dash for the bathrooms, and on his way out, seeing Asher was still at the bowser, he ordered toasted sandwiches, coffees, and grabbed some bottled water.

When he got to the counter, he saw some familiar mints near the register. *Asher used to love these* . . . Harry considered getting the sugar free ones to annoy him, but given how hard it'd been on him, and what he'd been through, Harry wanted to see him smile. He took four tins of them, paid for everything, and was smiling when he walked back out to the Jeep.

Asher wasn't smiling though. When Harry climbed in, Asher showed him his phone. "They found Rozga's body. It's all over the news. They still suspect it's a gang war. Press conference at nine."

Harry instinctively checked the rearview mirror. "I haven't seen one cop this whole trip."

"Good."

Harry held up the bag in an attempt at getting Asher to smile. "I got you something."

"Do I want to know?" Asher asked from the passenger seat, looking at him dubiously.

Harry stuck his hand in the bag and pulled out a tin. "Look at what they have!"

Asher's eyes went to the mints, then back to Harry, and he smiled, even laughed a little, but his eyes became glassy as he took them. "Thank you," he said, his chin wobbling a little.

Immediately alarmed, Harry shoved the bag aside and took Asher's hand. "Hey, baby, what's wrong?"

Asher shook his head and rolled his eyes. "I don't know. Everything. It's being back here, I think. It's not knowing where Yunho is, if he's still alive. Those stupid files he left me raise more questions than they answer. I don't like being back here. This place. And then you give me these," he said, looking at the mints. "I don't know what I ever did to deserve you."

"You didn't shoot me that day in Madrid, remember?

And after that, you annoyed me until I fell in love with you, remember?"

Asher nodded, smiling now. "Yeah. I remember. Though I'm pretty sure I fell in love with you first."

Harry laughed. "Maybe it was a tie."

"Maybe it was."

Harry started the Jeep. "Okay, back onto the highway to Belgrade, yeah?"

Asher sucked back a breath and let it out slowly. "No. Stay on this road. It will take us south of the city." His brows furrowed. "There's something I want to see first."

Okay then.

Asher gave directions, which Harry followed without question. Asher was clearly familiar with this place. He knew which turns to take as if he knew these streets by rote.

Through a small township where Harry had no hope of reading the signs, past an old fuel station, now abandoned. "Turn here," Asher said.

Harry slowed to a stop. "That . . . that doesn't look like a road. Is it a bicycle trail?"

Asher gave him a cutting look, so Harry turned down the narrow path. About fifty metres in, they passed a man jogging with a dog on a leash. He didn't seem to care that Harry was driving on the path, so Harry kept going. It was overgrown, brambly trees scraped the sides of the Jeep in some parts, and Harry was about to question Asher again until he saw his grip on the tin of mints. His face didn't give much away, but his knuckles were white.

Harry knew then, whatever was up here wasn't good.

"There's a turn to the left up here," Asher murmured.

"Okay," Harry replied. The turn was an overgrown dirt driveway that clearly hadn't been driven on in a long time.

There was an old wire fence, which had been, at some point, locked but was now broken and wide open. Harry drove in slowly, the two-wheel track barely visible in the long grass and shrubs.

Asher swallowed hard, his grip on the tin of mints still tight.

Around the bend and down the track some more was another fence, the gate locked. This one chain-link, six foot tall. There was a hole cut through the wire off the trail but the Jeep wasn't going any further.

There was an abandoned building about two hundred metres away. No windows, damaged roof, spray-painted graffiti on the concrete walls. It was a decent size, but grass and weeds were overtaking it now. There was another building behind it that Harry could see had sheets of iron bent or missing.

Asher got out of the Jeep and walked to the fence. Harry followed him quietly, watching as he gripped the chain-link fence and bowed his head.

Harry gently lay a hand on his shoulder. "Asher."

Asher nodded, but then he sobbed and shook the fence. "Fuck them. Fuck this place."

Harry pulled him into his arms and Asher went willingly, letting Harry hold him as he cried.

Harry had never seen Asher cry.

Not like this.

He held him tight and rubbed his back. He wasn't sure what was wrong, though he could guess. He remembered something Asher had said long ago.

"When I was about six, I was loaded into a truck with other boys and taken to a military training school outside of Belgrade in Serbia."

Jesus fucking Christ.

"Is this the training school you were sent to?"

Asher nodded and a sob wracked him, letting his tears fall and his rarely seen emotions pour out of him, letting Harry hold him, comfort him.

Asher had always spoken of his past with such a matter-of-fact aloofness that Harry had wondered if it affected him at all.

It very clearly did.

And Harry knew Asher had survived horrors and atrocities he couldn't even imagine. A comment here and there, a far-off look in his eyes some days. He had frequent nightmares and he'd flinch and mumble in his sleep.

And clearly being here, seeing this place, made it impossible to keep from the surface.

Harry held him tight, kissing the side of Asher's head and rubbing his back while he cried. He couldn't even imagine what Asher had been through.

Barely six years old, scared and alone, made to fight for food, beaten and abused, seeing weaker boys die or get sold for a worse fate.

Harry shuddered to think of what those grown fucking men did to Asher in this place.

Asher grew heavy in his arms as his sobs became quieter and he gave him time to catch his breath. "I hate them. I hate them all," Asher mumbled.

Harry hated them too.

"I'll help you track them down if you want," Harry said.

Asher sighed and pulled back so he could wipe his face. His eyes were red and puffy, his nose and cheeks wet. He held the back of his hand to his nose. "I'm sorry."

Harry put his hand to Asher's cheek, wiping the tears. "What for? You don't ever have to apologise to me."

"For crying, for being a mess." He shook his head and fresh tears welled in his eyes. "I never realised . . . I've been back here before and it never affected me like this."

"Asher, baby, you're not the same person today as you were back then. Not even two years ago. You know what real love is now. You know you deserve to be happy. You deserve to be loved. You've seen a different way to live."

He shook his head and began to cry again. "I've killed so many people. I killed fifteen men just yesterday, Harry. I don't deserve . . . I don't . . ."

Harry's heart ached for him. "Asher, you didn't deserve whatever those fucking men did to you when you were six years old or the decade that followed. You deserved none of that. Everything you did, every life you took, was because of them. They set you on this path. You were just a boy. You had to do what you did to survive. Kill, or be killed. You didn't choose this life. You were forced into it."

"I chose to keep doing it," he said. "When I rescued Yunho and we began working together."

"Because it was all you'd ever known."

Asher looked back at the derelict building, at the overgrown grounds, and shook his head. "There are bodies buried in this forest, Harry. We had to run the trails, in teams, hunting the other teams for sport. There are bunkers farther down . . . where the instructors would . . ." His face crumpled and he shook away the tears. He sucked back a shaky breath. "We learned to compartmentalise the pain, separate our emotions. I learned to not feel anything, to disassociate myself from what they made me do."

Harry rubbed his back, gently stroked the back of his neck, his head.

"I haven't thought about any of this for years," Asher whispered. "Coming back here was a mistake."

"No. You needed this," Harry said. "You've held it in for too long. And it won't be easy to sort through all this shit, but I'll be with you. Every step of the way."

He shook his head. "No, not because of this place. Coming back here was a mistake, Harry. Bosnia, Serbia. I shouldn't have come here. I want Yunho back, but I can't risk you to get him. Losing him would gut me. But losing you . . ." Fresh tears fell down his cheeks. "I wouldn't survive it."

"You won't lose me."

"I don't know what we're dealing with here," he said. "This feels bigger than just Istomin or Radovic. It's about old countries, old political ideals, and that shit runs deep, Harry. And Yunho . . ." his gaze cut to Harry, and it took a second for Harry to realise what he saw in his eyes.

It was fear.

"A week ago, I'd have said I knew Yunho well. I knew what made him tick, I knew what fed his soul, what made him happy." Asher shrugged. "Now I don't know if I know him at all."

What?

"The files?"

Asher nodded. "There's shit in there that's not good, Harry. I mean, none of it is good. But . . . but he was dealing with some deep, dark shit, that I would have sworn he'd never touch. I thought he had some moral high ground, but . . ." He looked back out into the trees. "But now I'm not so sure."

"Dark government stuff?"

He nodded. "Arming terrorists, supplying trade to

both sides of wars. To the point where I don't know which side of terrorism he's on."

Holy shit.

"And there's something else. Something that . . ." He sighed. "Something that I can't get out of my head."

"What is it?"

"The password to access everything."

"Haemosu? The Korean sun god?"

Asher nodded and let out a long sigh. "There's a file in there called Ćiro Savić."

Harry didn't understand. "What is that? Is it a person? A place? Cheerosavick?"

"It's a name. A man's name. There's a photograph of birth records. Born in Sarajevo. He'd be thirty-six."

"Who is he?"

Asher's eyes met Harry's, and he whispered, "I can't be sure, but I think it's me."

Harry's heart fell through his stomach. "What? How?"

He shrugged. "Ćiro means sun. Yunho always called me the sun. I brightened his world, he'd said."

Harry couldn't quite get his head around it.

"It means he knew," Asher added quietly. "For years, a decade or more. He knew my name. My identity, the names of my parents, where I'm from, where I was born. He knew my nationality," Asher said, thumping his chest. "And he lied to me. He kept it from me."

Oh, fucking hell.

"Asher, baby. I . . . I don't know what to say. I'd like to say maybe he had his reasons, but there's no excuse."

"No, there's not." Asher sighed and looked back out the ruined building. "Did he keep it from me to control me? To keep me on his leash, without loyalty to a country, without a home." He shrugged. "I just don't know."

"I'm so sorry," Harry whispered.

"Of all the people I thought would never hurt me."

"Maybe . . . maybe he has his reasons," Harry offered. "I'm not justifying it; I'm just saying I know he loves you. There has to be a reason he never told you, and when we find him and rescue him, you can ask him. If it's bad, if he's part of this mess and held it from you to string you along and hurt you, then I will kill him myself."

Asher gave the barest of nods. "I don't know what I'd do without you."

Harry rubbed Asher's arms. "You will never have to find out."

"I'm scared, Harry," Asher admitted. "I can't remember the last time I was scared. Probably when I was here." He gestured to the broken building. "We're out of practice. We're too old for this. Once upon a time we were at the top of our game, and now I don't even know what our next move is. I always had Yunho to guide me, to send me intel, to get me anything I ever needed. And we don't have that anymore. We're on our own with no idea if we're on the right path. Everything has been a guess, at best."

"What we have is experience," Harry replied. "And we have each other. We are famous in this industry. People fear us. We are good at what we do."

"We *were* good at what we did. You said it yourself, I'm not the same person I was two years ago. Two years ago, I wouldn't have even blinked at a situation like this. Now . . ." He shook his head. "I second guess every single thing because I could lose you and it scares the fuck out of me. The fear, it freezes me. And in this game, if I hesitate for a nano second, I'm dead. Or worse, you are." His chin wobbled again. "And then what? I would have nothing. And you know, before I would have sworn that if something happened to you, I would watch this world burn. But honestly, I wouldn't have the will in me to do anything but eat a bullet myself."

"Baby, no."

"See? I'm not the same person. Not even close. Because I'm seriously considering just taking you home. Just getting the fuck out of here and going home, where we can live out our days in peace. I can't go back to this life, Harry. I just can't."

Harry shook his head. "They know where we live. They found us once, they'll find us again. We need to end this, and then we can live out our days in peace. Okay?"

"I'm scared," he whispered.

"I know. Me too."

Asher's eyes met Harry's. "Why does it feel like this is about me? Taking Yunho and Lucas, Daris said it was to lure me here. What if he's right?"

Harry pulled him back in for a hug, reluctant to admit he agreed with him. Because this did feel like that. Something was off about this whole thing.

But then Asher's phone buzzed in his pocket, the sound startling them both. He pulled it out to see *Unknown* on the screen.

"No one has this number," Asher said. "Except Yunho."

"Answer it."

He took the call, putting the audio on speaker, but he said nothing.

"Ah, Mr Asher Garin," a man said.

"Who the fuck is this?" Asher breathed.

"Is that any way to speak to me, stranac?"

Stranac.

Asher paled and almost dropped the phone.

"I have a friend here who wishes to speak to you."

The next voice they heard was familiar. And Korean. Harry couldn't understand what he said, but he understood the shouting that cut him off, and the muted thud and Yunho's pained groan that followed.

"Yunho," Asher whispered.

Asshole spoke again next. "You're very slow at this game, stranac. I expected better from you. I thought you'd have found us by now."

Stranac, the name Asher was given at the orphanage. It meant foreigner, and until he was four or five, he'd thought that was his name.

Harry wanted to reach into the phone and pull out this asshole's throat.

"Though I assume the little party at the ZBK compound was you. They found Rozga's body, by the way, in the tunnel. The media found out he was tortured. It's caused quite a stir, public panic about gangs and drugs and guns." He sighed. "Did he spill everything when you tortured him? Hm, I can only assume your boyfriend's with you because the torture really wasn't your style, stranac. You're more of a kill-from-a-distance kind of guy. Never did like getting your hands dirty."

"What do you want?" Asher asked, his voice cold.

"Bukovac. You know where. In two hours. Don't be late, and come alone. Or I'll do to your precious Yunho what you did to Rozga. Tell me, which tendon did you slice first?"

The phone went dead, and when Asher looked at Harry, the fire in his eyes was back.

"Who was that?" Harry asked. "He called you stranac."

"Alen Radovic," Asher said.

"He was here with you? At this place?" Harry nodded to the building through the fence.

Asher nodded. "At the orphanage, then here. He was one of the older boys. He was one of them that held me down and . . ." He flinched. "He was sadistic."

Harry's temper burned inside him like a raging beast. "Then we kill him first."

"First or last, as long as he suffers."

Oh, Harry had every intention of making him suffer. "What did Yunho say? I didn't quite catch what he said."

"He said, 'Ojima hajima,' before he was cut off."

"What does that mean?"

"Don't come, don't do it. He was begging us not to come."

Fucking hell.

"Still want to go home?" Harry asked.

He had that blank look in his eyes now. "No."

"How far is it to Bukovac?" He checked his watch. "How much time do we have?"

Asher walked back to the Jeep. "Enough time to kick the hornets' nest first."

TWELVE

ANY HINTS of Asher's self-doubt were gone. He was focused, navigating for Harry as he checked guns, mag clips, pistols, and then he was googling, reading, searching . . .

He was hyper-focused.

And after his emotional outpour before, opening old wounds that had been left to fester with no attempt at healing, Harry was more than a little worried.

Asher had said before he worried that he'd hesitate out of fear and get them killed. But also not taking the time to assess every detail, to charge in blindly out of anger would just as likely see them both killed.

He was like this before. In Thailand, when he was in a flux about Yunho, and Harry had needed to calm him down. Almost shake some sense into him, telling him to get his head in the game.

He needed to do it again now, but he wasn't sure he should.

Asher had spent his entire fucked-up life with his emotions sewn up so tight, and then after spending the last two years living a civilian life, basking in love and happiness. For the first time in his life, he'd allowed himself to feel something. The wound was being unpicked stitch by stitch, emotions festering and bubbling, every other emotion was rising to the surface.

And now, like a dam about to burst, those emotions were threatening to spew out and annihilate everything in its path.

He had so much rage inside him.

Valid rage. He *should* be angry. Hell, Harry was angry for him. But now was the worst possible time. They couldn't attempt any rescue when Asher was about to go nuclear.

As they arrived at their destination, Harry pulled into the parking lot and shut off the engine. "Hey," he said, taking Asher's hand. "Are we good?"

Asher drew his eyes from the building to Harry. "We? As in us? Yes, why would you ask that?"

"I don't mean us . . . I mean are we good to do this?"

"You mean am I good to do this?"

Harry squeezed his hand, his gaze locking in on Asher's. "Are you good to do this? Asher, baby, it's been a crazy few days. Emotional, heavy days. If you want to stop and regroup—"

"I want this to be over," he said. He looked at the building again, where a crowd was gathering. "I don't need to regroup. I need to get this over with, then go find Radovic and rip out his heart, then see what the fucked-up cold-war wannabe colonel fuckface has to say before I kill him too. And then we save Yunho and Lucas. Where they will tell us everything, and *then* I'll decide if I want to kill them as well."

Harry sighed. "Asher."

His eyebrows knitted. "I know what you're going to say, Harry. Please don't. I just need to get through this, then I'll deal with the aftermath . . . God. Fucking feelings. I never asked to feel anything, I'll have you know. I was quite happy living my numb life, disassociating from everything I've done. Everything I've been through. And now I have more questions than answers and more emotions than I know what to do with. And fear. I've never been afraid before."

"I don't think you're in the right frame of mind to do this," Harry tried.

His eyes hardened. "You said before you needed the old Asher Garin. Well, here I am. The only thing that will make me feel better, give me back a sense of control, is to go kill a lot of assholes who deserve it."

There was no point in arguing, Harry realised, because hell, maybe Asher was right. Maybe they did need him hell-bent on killing everyone. Harry would just need to be extra vigilant.

"Are you ready? Looks like the fun's about to start without us."

Harry sighed. "Fine. But if I think for one second this isn't going to work, we leave. Codeword: coffee. We turn and walk, okay?"

"Fine." He put his hand on the door handle. "No guns or knives. There might be metal detectors."

Oh goodie. They were doing this unarmed. Asher did say he wanted to kick the hornet's nest first and, well, this would do it.

Harry wasn't sure exactly what Asher had in mind, and given Harry's grasp on the Serbian language was more than a little rusty, he really could do no more than stand beside Asher, to protect him or to pull his ass out of there, Harry wasn't sure.

But stand beside him, he would.

THE SERBIAN POLICE headquarters in Belgrade looked like any other government building Harry had seen all over the western world. It was teeming with badges, yes. But for all intents and purposes, it was an administration building.

Though as reporters gathered around the steps outside, Harry spotted at least four armed officers. Two to the right, two to the left, and wait . . . two more that came out with the police official made that six.

Awesome.

Harry had no clue what official rank and title this official guy held. He wasn't up to speed on Serbian police ranking insignias, but the stripes and stars on the shoulders of his jacket told him he was a major, at least.

And of course, everything he said was in Serbian.

Now, Harry could understand some passing words. He'd lived with Asher long enough to pick up a few Slavic words and phrases, though to be fair, Asher only normally slung them at Harry in a slew of mumbled curses.

What Harry did know was that this was a press conference regarding the shootout at ZBK headquarters outside of Sarajevo. Why did that concern Serbian police?

Because five of the dead guys were Serbian and the so-called drug-wars-between-gangs bullshit they were spinning for the media had the public concerned. Bosnian authorities were working in conjunction with the Serbians to find those responsible, blah blah blah.

It was all bullshit.

The police major finished talking, nodding to a female reporter to the right of Asher. She was holding a microphone with a TV channel number on it, and she asked her question. The police answered. Then another reporter asked another question, the cop gave his pre-determined response. Another reporter asked, another bullshit answer delivered with a smile.

Harry deduced the two cops beside the police official were ornamental, armed or not, more worried about looking good for the cameras and getting the right angle, nodding along to the bullshit their boss was spewing.

Two of the other armed cops had disappeared around the corner, and the other two police officers inside the door were having a private conversation, laughing, and paying zero attention to what was happening.

This press conference was purely a spectator sport, nothing else.

Harry was too busy getting mad at the entire debacle when Asher raised his hand and spoke.

Harry had not been expecting him to do that, and he did his best to appear as if it had been the plan all along. Not that he had a clue what Asher said, but from the way the major's smile tightened and the way he stammered his reply, Harry could guess he didn't appreciate it.

Then Asher glanced up at Harry before turning back to the front and then he spoke in English. "Can you confirm if the compound where Rozga was found had any ties to the new cold war support group known as ZBK? That Rozga was in fact the leader of a political faction with direct ties to Colonel Alen Radovic and Vadik Istomin? There are also rumours of them being tied to another ZBK compound at the abandoned airbase in Bukovac. Do you know anything about this?" Asher took a deep breath. "I know for a fact that Radovic was involved with the Kowalska House Orphanage. The same group that trafficked children from Bosnia and Kosovo in the war and turned them into drug mules and murderers. I know because I was one."

Harry slow-blinked, or maybe the world stopped turning for a moment. Asher had just kicked the hornets' nest.

Everything and everyone fell silent as if holding their breath, faces and cameras turned to Asher, and then as a collective swarm, the reporters turned back to the police major. He was a mix of pale and livid, stammering and blinking as the sea of cameras, phones, clicks, and reporters all pushed closer.

He might have tried to speak over them, to ask for the name of the man who dared ask such questions, but Harry and Asher were already gone.

HARRY WAS STRUNG tight as he drove, his gaze darting to the rear-vision mirror. "Care to explain what the fuck that was about?"

Asher leaned over to the back and pulled the backpack onto his lap. "That was our backup."

"Backup for what?"

"For what we're about to do," Asher said, as if he were mad at Harry for not catching on already.

"Which is what, exactly?"

Asher nodded to the GPS screen, to the address they were headed to, where apparently Yunho and Lucas were being held. "We're about to waltz into *their* base, Harry. We will be outnumbered and outgunned. Except now, in about an hour or so, there's going to be backup arriving."

Harry looked at him as if he were insane. "Cops who will not be on our side, Asher. Now there will be more guys pointing guns at us. Jesus Christ. Not to mention our faces will be splashed on every news channel, on TV, online, on every-fucking-thing. We're supposed to fly under the radar, avoid detection—" The penny dropped as soon as he'd said it. Harry stared at him. "That was why you did it."

Asher half smiled at him. "Agencies will be running facial recognition right now, and it's gonna ping national security alarms. All while the media is running stories, digging for information the cops and governments are trying to bury. It'll be a shitshow, and Radovic and Istomin now have more political shit to worry about than just us."

Fucking hell.

"A lot more to worry about," Harry grumbled. "Like kill teams, Asher. Guys like us, only younger and with all the guns and ammo they need."

Asher made a face that said he was very well aware and that he didn't exactly care.

"It ends today," he said. "One way or another, it ends today."

"Jesus fucking Christ, Asher," Harry cried. "Is this a suicide mission? Because it's starting to sound like you think we're not getting out of this. We're definitely not getting out of the country, that's for damn fucking sure. Now that our faces are all over the media and we don't have Yunho's contacts for new passports."

"I have his contact list, remember?"

Harry ran his hand through his hair, his mind racing, his blood pumping. He tried to take a few calming breaths, not that it did him much good. "Just tell me you won't do anything stupid. This is not a suicide mission, Asher. Whatever you have planned for this meeting, we need an exit strategy. No exceptions. We must have a way out and a plan B and a rendezvous point should we get separated."

"How can we have a plan B when we don't even have a plan A?" Asher asked. "We're walking into their web. They're calling the shots. Our only plan is to walk into their territory and find out what the fuck's going on."

"And now you've put a timer on us because every government agency in this part of Europe has been put on high alert. You named two high-ranking political figureheads as corrupt, going back decades, and responsible for ultimately planning to overthrow their governments, and you gave them the location we're heading to."

He made a face. "Cops will be too busy in damage control right now. And anyway, the backup I expect to arrive first isn't the police, Harry. Military, special forces, maybe even a swat team."

Harry stared at Asher, only sparing quick glances at the road as he drove.

Christ, he was serious.

"Jesus fucking Christ, Asher. This *is* a suicide mission. Just this morning you said you wanted to go home, you couldn't bear thinking about losing me or anything bad happening to me, and then you go and do this? What the actual fuck?"

"Nothing can happen to you," Asher said, ever so fucking casually.

What the . . . ? What the fucking hell . . . ? How was . . . what the hell does he think is . . . ?

Oh no.

"No." Harry shook his head. "Don't even think about it. Absolutely not."

"Yes."

"Absolutely fucking not!" Harry roared. His grip on the steering wheel made it creak. "You are not going in there by yourself."

"Harry, I—"

"Absolutely not," Harry growled. "There is no way I would let you go in there alone, and the fact you think I would—"

"You don't have a choice. He told me to come alone."

"*He* can get fucked. Whoever the fuck he is."

"His name is Radovic."

"He's a dead man, that's who he is."

Asher was quiet for a few moments. "Harry, it'll be better if I go alone. You can leave. Our rendezvous point will be our house in Tallowwood. I'll meet you there, and I'll know you're safe and—"

Harry swerved the Jeep off the road and slammed on the brakes. "You think that's okay with me? You can tell me that if something were to happen to me that you'd just eat a bullet because you can't stand to think about life without me, yet you expect me to just go home and live happily without you? Is that what you think, Asher? Do you think I don't love you as much as you love me? Do you think for one second that I could live without you?"

Harry was so fucking mad. And hurt. He was so hurt that Asher would think like this.

Tears burned in Harry's eyes. His heart felt heavy and sore. "Does my love mean so little to you?"

Asher wouldn't look at him. "I just need you to live, that's all."

"And I need you to live. Our best chance of doing that

is sticking together, and you know it. You're not going in there alone."

"What if you find a higher vantage point?" Asher tried, his voice quiet. When he finally looked at Harry, his eyes were glassy. "Take the 36s and—"

"No." That would make tactical sense if they had time and intel. But they had neither. And Asher going in alone was simply not an option. "We go in together or not at all."

Asher's chin wobbled and he let out a shuddery breath. "I don't want it to end here. But you have to know something, Harry. If it does end today, if we don't come out of this, I need you to know the last two years have been the best years of my life. More than I ever deserved to have."

Harry took Asher's hand. "Same. I love you, Asher. But you need to stop thinking about dying today. We're gonna get through this. So enough of the martyr bullshit. Let's go in there and kick some ass."

Asher's eyes studied his, then his whole face, as if he was committing it all to memory one final time.

"Okay," he whispered. "I love you, Harry."

"I love you too, Asher."

He let out a long breath and whispered, "I don't like this. Everything feels wrong."

Harry knew why it felt wrong. They were willingly walking into a trap, outnumbered, outgunned. It went against every fibre in Harry's body. Every instinct he had was telling him this was bad.

If this was an op he'd been contracted for, he'd turn around and be long gone. That gut instinct that had kept him alive for a decade was telling him now to bail and be gone.

But he couldn't.

Asher was going in, which meant Harry would be right beside him.

He squeezed Asher's hand. "It'll be okay."

It has to be, Harry thought.

They drove the final few kilometres in silence. The litany of all the things he wanted to say went unsaid.

Because they would survive this.

Harry had to believe that.

THIRTEEN

ASHER HAD BEEN in a lot of situations that felt wrong. Situations where things didn't add up, where that sixth sense told him to walk away or run. He'd lived on his instincts since he was all of four years old, an expert on reading people, reading the room.

Driving up to the property and in through the gates made Asher feel ill.

Don't come. Don't do it.

That's what Yunho had said before he was cut off.

Asher could still hear the muted thud of an obvious punch and Yunho's resulting groan.

Of course Asher would come.

Yunho could be pissed at him all he damn liked, Asher didn't care. Because Asher was pissed at him. He was more than pissed. He was really fucking angry.

And anger was a better emotion to cling to right now than betrayal.

Betrayal was a dangerous thing.

It kept very close company with goodbyes, and as

tempted as Asher was to take Harry and leave Yunho and Lucas behind, he just couldn't.

Not for their history. Not for all the years they'd worked together, relied on each other, and saved each other's lives. Not because Yunho was like an older brother to Asher. Not because they were two lone wolves who found each other when the rest of the world had abandoned them.

The only reason Asher was going in to save Yunho was for answers.

Answers about who Asher really was and why Yunho had kept that from him.

And why the fuck there was a file in that damn secure server about Harry. Not just Harry either. About his work, spanning a decade, about his time in the military, about operatives just like him.

The Milvus files.

Why Harry wasn't the only one, and why it was still active.

Asher had said nothing to Harry about this. He needed answers before busting open a door Harry had only just managed to close.

That fucking court case with Clive Parrish that was still all over the news, that had cratered out the Australian special forces and brought the entire military and its operations into question.

Every case, every agent, every national security issue for the last decade was now under scrutiny, all while Parrish rotted in a jail cell somewhere awaiting trial.

Asher needed answers and for that, he needed Yunho alive.

If Asher didn't like one of Yunho's answers, if Yunho

had hurt or used Harry in any way, he'd hand deliver Yunho back to North Korea himself.

And if Lucas was actually MI6, Asher couldn't guess.

He was definitely English. He'd been a construction project manager when Yunho was building his house on the island. He and Yunho had hit it off, and when the house was complete, Lucas quit his job and stayed.

He cared for Yunho. He loved him, Asher was sure of it. Granted, Asher didn't have much experience with what love should look like, but Lucas adored Yunho. He worshipped him.

Was he too perfect for him? Was their whole meeting a set-up by the British government?

Asher didn't know what to think about anything anymore.

He felt sick.

"I don't like this," Harry whispered as they drove in.

The property itself was quite rural. A long dirt driveway led up to a huge industrial-style shed. There were black 4WDs parked to the side, security cameras everywhere, and no sooner had they got halfway down the drive, a black SUV appeared behind them. And when they pulled up near the huge open roller doors, four men came out to greet them.

Wearing stoic, grim expressions, in black army gear from head to foot, armed with AK-74 assault rifles.

"Welcoming committee?" Harry asked.

"I'm sorry for bringing you into this," Asher murmured. *God, how his heart was aching . . .*

"Are you kidding?" Harry said with a smile. "I wouldn't be anywhere else right now. With you is all I need."

"Together, right?"

"Always."

Two of the armed men opened their doors while the other two pointed their guns at them and ordered them out of the Jeep. One of them barked at them to put their hands up. "They'd like us to put our hands up," Asher relayed in English for Harry.

They got out of the Jeep, nice and slow. They were patted down, their guns and knives removed.

Predictable.

While one guy was on his knees before Harry, feeling around his boots and calves, Harry smirked at Asher. "Do you think while he's down there . . . ?"

The one with the gun stepped closer. "Shut the fuck up."

Asher sighed. He had no idea how Harry could be joking right now. But then the guy with the gun sneered at him and lowered his gun, and before Asher could blink, Harry took his gun, shot him in the neck, then shot the other guy who was supposed to be aiming at them. In that split second of surprise, Asher disarmed the other guy, and before the fourth and last guy could even move, Harry had his gun pointed at the idiot's head. "Don't even fucking blink," Harry growled.

"A little bit of warning would have been nice," Asher said.

"I didn't know I was going to do that until the first guy got into my reach zone," Harry said. Then he spoke to the now-pale unarmed idiot. "First rule of combat. Don't get in my reach zone."

"Well, now the back-up welcoming party's gonna be here any second," Asher said flatly.

"If they wanted us dead, we'd be dead already. The fact

they didn't kill us in the Jeep means they want us alive." He shrugged. "Where is everybody, anyway?"

Asher nodded to inside the shed. "There's a bunker door in here."

"You've been here before?"

Asher gave a nod as a swarm of guys came bursting out of the darkness, but they also came from both sides of the shed. They were outnumbered now and surrounded.

They had nowhere to go, nowhere to hide. If one of them opened fire, they would die right where they stood. Asher knew it, and from Harry's mumbled, "Fuck," he knew it too.

"Put the guns on the ground," one of the masked men ordered.

Goddammit.

Asher did as he was told, and for a brief moment, Asher wondered if Harry was about to send a spray of bullets into the men. He seethed, growled at the closest guy, then reluctantly put his gun down and his hands up.

A tall figure came out of the darkness then. Smiling, smug.

He looked older than his forty-something years, but Asher knew that face. It still haunted his dreams. Radovic. He clapped his hands and held his arms out as if greeting a long-lost relative. "Stranac," he said. "It *is* you."

Harry growled and his fists clenched, but two guys moved closer, directly aiming their guns at his head.

"It's okay," Asher said to Harry, urging him to stay calm.

"Yes, it's okay," Radovic said with his slimy smile. "We are old friends. We go way back, don't we, stranac." Then he looked at the three dead men. "What have we here? You killed three of my men."

"I slipped," Harry said flatly.

Radovic stared at him, his expression now cold and calculating, in a way that Asher did not like one bit. But then he turned to the fourth guy who Harry didn't kill. Radovic took a pistol from the back of his waistband and shot him, the back of his head turning to red mist.

Fucking hell.

"I don't tolerate incompetence," Radovic said, and the words sent a chill through Asher.

Those words had been uttered countless times throughout Asher's childhood. From their instructors, their trainers, their abusers, and as they got a little older, from Radovic himself. When he was put in charge of the younger boys . . . of Asher and Daris.

Radovic waved his hands at the bodies and ordered some men to get rid of the mess before he smiled at Asher and gave a pointed nod to Harry. "I did tell you to come alone. Still defying orders, I see?"

Asher stared at him. "Where's Yunho?"

Radovic stared at him and his cold eyes and slimy smile never faltered. "So impatient. And," he said cheerfully, "I saw your cameo at the press conference earlier." He sighed as if it was a small inconvenience he now had to deal with. "It's made some people rather unhappy with you. Which is a shame, because I was hoping our little reunion would have been a happy one."

Asher hated this overly cheerful demeanour he portrayed, because it was usually followed swiftly with cruelty. He knew it was coming . . .

Radovic's smile died and his eyes hardened, and he gestured towards the inside of the shed. "Walk."

With at least fifteen assault weapons pointed directly at them, it wasn't like they had much choice.

They went inside, and it was just as Asher remembered. The huge industrial sized shed housed goods and machinery, a black van, and a bunker door.

Asher knew where they were going, and he dreaded it.

My god, how he hated this place.

As a kid, when he was forced down into bunkers. And now he was being forced down again.

Of all the fucking places he was likely to die, why did it have to be here?

Asher hesitated at the door, and Radovic laughed. "Oh, don't be scared, stranac. It's had a considerable upgrade since you were here last."

A few of the armed men went down first, then Harry, but not before glaring at Radovic as he went. The stairs leading down were small and narrow, the hum of yellowed lights overhead familiar and as haunting as Asher remembered.

The stairs were so narrow, Harry barely fit. He had to duck his head and turn his shoulders. Asher put his hand on Harry's back, needing to touch him this one last time.

When they stepped into the room at the bottom, Asher could see that it had been updated, indeed.

When he'd last been down here, at all of eight years old, it was cold dirt floors, rooms with dark corners, and a dank and cloying smell that clung to the back of his throat.

He'd had nightmares for years about this place. About what had happened down here . . .

This main room wasn't any bigger—half a basketball court, maybe—but now the floors were concrete, there was proper lighting and ventilation, and desks with computers and screens. It was a control room.

There was a hall at the end with smaller rooms either

side. Asher could see doors now, where once they'd been no more than cave alcoves.

He'd slept down here a few times, in the dirt. In the dark.

Pitch blackness.

Time passes differently when you can't even see your own hand in front of your face.

God, how Asher hated it down here back then.

Like he hated it now.

He and Harry stood, surrounded by men with their guns pointed at them. AK-74s and . . . was that an AK-12? Well, that just added insult to injury. That he would die down here, in this place, by Radovic and a Russian fucking gun. The weapon of choice of the Russian special forces.

So fucking typical.

Radovic came to stand in front of them. "Stranac," he said. Then he laughed. "My god, you hated that name."

"Hated a lot of things about my time here," Asher replied.

"Aw," he said. "Don't be like that. It wasn't all bad."

Asher wasn't even going to reply to that.

"I'm surprised you're still here," Asher said instead. "After all these years. Tell me, is Delić still alive? Are you still his favourite?" Asher smiled at him. "Still sit in his lap?"

Radovic gnashed his teeth like the fucking animal he was. "You'll do well to remember your place," he said, ice cold.

"Must have been so hard for you," Asher pushed. "Wanting the favour of Barta but never being good enough. Settling for Delić must have been so demeaning. Tell me, is that why you hated me? Because I was the favourite? Or because I was always better than you. Half your age and twice as good."

Radovic snarled and produced a knife, not too unlike Harry's hunting knife. He pressed it under Asher's chin, the tip biting into his skin. Harry growled and went to move, but the armed soldiers all moved in, guns aimed at Harry's head.

"I was told to deliver you alive," Radovic said, sneering at Asher, the blade drew blood under Asher's chin but Asher never so much as blinked. "But he never said anything about seriously fucking injured, so I suggest you shut the fuck up." But then he spared an evil side-eye to Harry. "And he never said anything about *him* being alive though."

Asher's blood ran cold, his bones felt like ice. "You said you wanted me, so here I am. You got what you wanted. Leave him out of it."

He shook his head and clucked his tongue. "Tsk, tsk. Asher, you should know better than to show your weakness. And I didn't bring him into it. You did, by bringing him here."

This was why Harry should have listened. He should have stayed away.

"And he went and killed three of my men upstairs," Radovic added. "And the three men we sent to Australia. So tell me, Asher, what do you think is a fair trade?"

"Me," Asher said quickly. "Take me, leave him alone."

"Asher, no," Harry said quickly.

"That's so sweet," Radovic said in a singsong voice. "But I already have you," he then said loudly. "Here, in my bunker, after all these years. Just like old times, huh?"

Harry growled at that, and it made Radovic laugh. Like this was his favourite sport.

Asher felt sick. He needed to regain some control and change the focus of conversation. "Where's Yunho? Who gave you the order to keep me alive? Was it Istomin? Is that who you work for?"

Radovic's eyes drew to his, wide and wild. He pointed the knife at Asher. "You don't ask the questions around here. I asked you what was a fair trade and your offer fell short."

"I'll tell you whatever you want to know," Asher tried.

Radovic smiled, but then he sighed, long and loud. "I don't think you're quite truly motivated yet. I know your breaking point has a high threshold because I helped shape you. Isn't that right, little stranac?"

Bile rose in Asher's throat.

The things Radovic had done to him. He was just a kid himself, a teenager when Asher was just a boy.

The things he'd done to him down here and in Kosovo, and Turkey.

"I said I'll tell you anything—"

"I don't take orders from you," Radovic yelled, pointing his knife at Asher's face. "You, I can't touch. As much as it fucking pains me. But I get the feeling it'd hurt you a whole lot more, Asher, if I hurt your boyfriend instead."

Then Radovic swung his knife and lodged it in Harry's side. "Oops, I slipped," he said.

Harry screamed through clenched teeth, and Asher reached for him just before he was grabbed, his hands held behind his back, and a black hood was put over his head.

The last thing Asher saw was Harry slumping to his knees.

FOURTEEN

ASHER WAS HAULED AWAY with his arms twisted behind his back. He tried to kick and scream for Harry, but it was no use. He could see nothing, only darkness, but he could hear the sound of men and Harry's muffled yelling.

Then Asher had restraints around his wrists, his hands fastened behind his back, the hood still over his head, and he was thrown into a room, the door slamming closed behind him.

He scrambled to his feet and tried to go in the direction he was thrown from. But he had no hands, no eyes. He hit the wall and almost fell backward, but he still screamed for Harry.

Please stop hurting him.

"It's me you want," Asher screamed. "Not him. Take me! Please," he said with a sob. "Please."

He slid down the wall and cried. Helpless.

Responsible.

This was what he didn't want to happen. This was why he'd wanted Harry to leave him. But Harry, so fucking stubborn, had said they'd be together until the end.

But now they weren't together. And they were doing god only knew what to him . . .

Asher banged his head on the wall, crying. He screamed in frustration, in fear.

"Asher?"

Asher froze.

He wasn't in here alone.

"Is that you?"

Oh my god.

"Yunho?"

Yunho sobbed out a cry. "I told you not to come. Why did you come?"

"Where are you? I can't see you," Asher said. "I have a hood over my head. They have Harry."

"I have a hood too, and my hands are tied," Yunho said, crying. "They have Lucas too. I hear him scream every so often. It kills me, Asher. I'm so sorry."

Jesus fucking Christ.

"I'm in the corner, opposite the door," Yunho said, sniffling. "I've seen this room. It's four metres by four metres. There's a chair they use to the right."

Asher got to his knees and crawled over. It was so dark, he could see nothing at all, but he crawled until he hit the wall, then he edged toward Yunho's breathing.

Yunho yelped when Asher's knee touched him and he jerked back, crying some more. Asher turned so his back was to the wall and he slid down next to Yunho, and Yunho leaned into him, wracked with sobs and tears, his body shaking and trembling. "Asher, I'm so sorry. I didn't know. I tried to tell you not to come. Ojima, ojima, Asher. You shouldn't have come."

Asher let him lean into him; the best embrace they could manage. "I came for answers. And you better start with the truth, because so help me fucking god, they have Harry right now. They stabbed him, and they were beating him. I don't know if he's alive or if he's dying on the ground out there," Asher said, unable to stop the tears. "Because I can't hear him anymore, Yunho. Fucking hell." Asher squinted his eyes shut, even though he was completely blinded by the hood. The silence was worse than the screaming. "I told him to leave. To not come with me, but he refused to leave me."

"Of course he did. He loves you," Yunho said, sniffling and crying. He leaned in even closer to Asher, and he was trembling so much, Asher's anger at him dissipated.

"How are you?" his voice a murmur.

Yunho sucked back a ragged breath. "Doesn't matter. I'm so sorry, Asher."

"You need to tell me everything."

"It's Vadik Istomin," Yunho said. "He's behind this."

"I know. What does he want?"

"I found something I wasn't supposed to find. I'm so sorry," Yunho said, almost wailing now, shaking, trembling. "I've done things, Asher. And it brought you here. And Harry, and Lucas. My god, I'm so sorry."

Lucas.

"Lucas," Asher murmured. God, how did he tell him about Lucas. That maybe the man he loved wasn't who he said he was.

Hell, maybe Lucas was the reason they were here.

"I haven't seen him since we were taken," Yunho sobbed. "I've heard him, his screams . . . what they keep doing to him."

Fucking hell.

"I don't know how long it's been." Yunho's whole body tremored. "How many days . . . It's been dark. The hood." He sucked back a ragged breath. "The darkness helps," he whispered. "If I can't see, it helps if I can't see."

His agoraphobia, his anxiety.

God, he was shaking so hard Asher had to wonder how tightly strung his entire body was, how exhausted.

He hadn't even thought to ask him when he'd slept last or eaten. Had they even fed him?

Asher opened his mouth, to say what he wasn't sure, when the door banged open and footfalls stomped into the door. Asher jumped, but Yunho cringed back and whined.

"It'll be okay," Asher said.

But then hands grabbed him and hauled him up. His hood was ripped off and he could see faces in the dark room. He spun around to see Yunho; they'd taken his hood off too, his face all banged up, eye swollen, cut and bleeding. His eyes wide and terrified as he looked at Asher.

"Tranq him before he has another seizure," one of the men said, struggling to hold Yunho.

Then they slapped one of those white patches on their necks, and they were hauled back out under the bright lights. Everything was hazy, swirling, his feet heavy, and he was dragged back out to the main room and up the stairs. He tried to take in details. He tried to look around, tried to look for Harry. He needed to find him.

There was no Harry.

But there was blood on the floor.

Then he couldn't focus, he couldn't think. His head was too heavy and his eyes wouldn't stay open. He tried to talk. He tried to fight the hold they had on him. But then they threw him into the back of an army truck.

And Asher's world went dark.

ASHER WOKE up to the rumble of an engine and the vibration of a moving vehicle. His face was pressed to the cold metal floor and it took him a second to remember . . .

He'd been shoved into the back of an army truck. The troop-carrier kind with the canvas canopy. It was dark and loud. He had no clue how long they'd been driving for or how far they'd gone. Which meant he had no clue where he was. He pushed up with a groan, trying to sit up, which wasn't easy given his hands and feet were still bound.

His body ached, his head was fuzzy.

Then he noticed Yunho, lying on his side, his back to Asher. He still had the black hood on, but Asher was sure it was him. His hands were tied behind his back, his feet bound, just like Asher's. But Asher knew those arms, those hands.

"Yunho," Asher said.

Nothing.

He scooted over the best he could, nudging Yunho. "Wake up," he hissed at him.

Nothing.

He shoved him harder, moving him over so he could lie on his back, and Asher saw the white medical patch on Yunho's neck. The same one that Asher had. The same ones they'd used to kidnap Yunho and Lucas from the island.

Yunho groaned, then he froze for a split second before scooting up and backwards, pushing with his feet and shaking his head, scared as hell.

"It's me," Asher said. "Yunho, it's me, Asher. We're in the back of a truck. I don't know where we are or where we're headed. They took my hood off. It's just you and me in here. I don't know where Harry is." Asher tried not to cry. He felt like he could vomit, and panic was beginning to set in. "If they killed him, Yunho, I will . . ."

He didn't know what he'd do. What he could do, given his predicament.

He shook his head, trying to not think of it.

He couldn't bear the thought of it.

Yunho groaned again, his head falling forward. His breathing was laboured and his whole body was shaking, and Asher remembered Yunho's agoraphobia and anxiety, his epilepsy and PTSD, and how extraordinarily awful this must have been for him.

"You okay?" Asher asked.

No reply.

"We'll find them," Asher said eventually. "We'll find them. I promise."

Yunho's whole body went stiff and he slumped back to the floor. He shook with tremors, and fucking hell, Asher wasn't sure if he was breathing. Asher sidled up close to him, like he had in the dark room they'd been in, letting Yunho lean into him.

The body contact had to help.

And all the anger Asher had felt toward Yunho melted away. Their years of history, their pasts, and everything they'd been through came to the forefront.

Asher loved Yunho like an older brother or a father. The first person who had ever shown Asher kindness. Kindness without expectation of something in return, and that was something Asher had never had before.

Yunho had always credited Asher with saving his life. And it was true. He had.

But Yunho had saved Asher a thousand times. Not just with security and intel. But he'd shown him kindness and friendship.

Family.

And right now, what Asher had found in those damn data files didn't matter.

Yes, he wanted answers.

But Yunho was suffering right now. Physically, emotionally, psychologically. The answers could wait. If they lived through this, Asher would ask all the questions he had.

Right now, his only focus was their survival.

And trying not to think about Harry.

God, how Asher hoped Harry was okay. He had to be. Asher couldn't accept anything less.

Eventually Yunho's breathing calmed down and evened out. "Hey," Asher said softly. "I'm here. I'm here. You're not alone."

Yunho sobbed in response.

The truck slowed then, the road underneath the tyres changing from possibly a highway, with its smooth surface and periodic line breaks in the surface, to a rougher surface like asphalt.

A smaller off-road, perhaps.

Then Asher heard the crackle of a radio, and voices. He couldn't quite make out the words or the language. His head was still foggy, the noise of the truck too loud.

A few minutes later, they came to a slow stop. There were voices outside, a little too far away to hear. Then they started forward again, driving over a grate of some kind.

Asher tried to see out through the small gaps in the canvas canopy, catching barely a glimpse of trees and a metal gate, perhaps.

But they were driving too slow to be on another main road or highway, and Asher could hear voices and . . . a helicopter?

What the hell?

Where the fuck were they?

Then the light in the holes of the canvas canopy disappeared. A tunnel, perhaps? But the truck came to a stop and more voices shouted. Croatian, maybe Bosnian; it was hard to tell the difference because they were far away and were barking orders to remove the cargo.

The cargo . . .

When the back of the canopy lifted up, two men appeared in full black combat gear, pointing guns at them.

More AK-74s, Asher noticed. Russian funded, then.

Another man climbed in and hauled Asher out by his arm, and he barely landed on his feet. The zip ties cut into his ankles and his head felt woozy.

Disoriented.

He tried to take in his surroundings.

A massive open warehouse, not a tunnel. Army trucks. Soldiers in combat gear. Outside looked like . . . an airfield?

A military training compound?

Another truck was pulling into the warehouse but Asher was dragged away. He barely saw them drop Yunho out of the truck. He landed heavily on his knees and shoulder, then was hefted up and dragged behind Asher.

"Stop there," a booming voice yelled. The men carrying Asher stopped and Asher lifted his head as a man stalked toward him.

He was maybe sixty years old, short grey hair under a black cap. He wore black army pants and coat, and a sneer of distaste.

And Russian issued military boots.

Was this Istomin? Asher assumed it was.

"Asher Garin," he said, his English accent stilted by his

Russian tongue. "Take a look everyone," he declared loudly for all his soldiers to hear, "at the infamous and untouchable Asher Garin." He tapped the side of Asher's face. "Not so untouchable now, are you?"

Then he looked behind Asher, his sneer turning more sinister. "And the irrepressible Oh Yunho. Who the whole world thought was dead. Believe me, you're about to wish you were. Take them downstairs."

The two men hauled Asher through a door and down some stairs.

Another bunker.

This wasn't good. Not good at all.

The darkness. Being underground. God, how Asher hated it.

But at the bottom of the stairs, Asher was waiting for darkness and that familiar dank smell of earth, but he found neither. This was a whole new set-up. Another door led into a long corridor. White walls, bright lights, clean smell. Asher wasn't sure if it was a secret government admin office or a hospital.

He hoped it was the former because the idea of a hospital made his stomach roll; medical gear, torture and chemical pain.

Jesus fucking Christ.

They passed doors and Asher tried to see inside the rooms off the hall. He saw desks and computers in one room.

And the fact they'd kept Asher's hood off meant only one thing.

They didn't care what he saw because he wasn't living through this to tell anyone.

Asher cleared his mind, trying to prepare himself for a long and painful path to death. He wasn't scared of dying.

Hell, he'd faced death a thousand times. He should have died more times than he could count. He'd had the gift of years many others did not.

But what he was scared of, what he did regret, was not being with Harry when they met their end.

They were supposed to grow old together in their little house with their little cat.

Asher was sad that was being taken away from him.

He'd dared to believe he could have that, and that candle of hope was being snuffed out in some bunker on the opposite side of the planet.

So far from home.

His home.

His Harry.

He so desperately wanted to know he was alive but was terrified to learn he wasn't . . .

The two men dragged him down the corridor, through a warren of halls and doors and too-bright lights. They stopped at one door and took him into a large room.

Asher half expected tiles on the floor with a drain for easy cleaning, but no. This was an office.

A tactical office?

Whiteboards, computer screens, a wall of monitors, not too dissimilar to Yunho's war room. And there were two wooden chairs in the middle of the room.

They shoved Asher onto one of the chairs and fixed a chain to his zip-tied feet, securing him to a bolt in the floor. His hands were still behind his back, and his head was still foggy.

He did feel a little more alert but not back to full clarity.

Then two men brought Yunho in and threw him into the chair next to Asher. They chained him too and pulled his hood off before they went to join the armed men standing by the wall.

Yunho kept his head down, the bright lights clearly painful after wearing that black hood for god knew how long. Asher could see him tremble.

"I'm here," Asher said quietly. When Yunho didn't respond, Asher repeated it in Korean.

Yunho jerked his head up then, and what Asher saw made him almost weep.

His right eye was swollen shut, purple, and the skin torn like a mangled plum. His lip was split; he had dried blood and dirt over his face. His dark shaggy hair was damp and sticking to his forehead.

He was far too pale.

Anger flared in Asher's core, and that resignation of dying today was quickly replaced with a burning desire to find the men that did that to Yunho and make them pay.

God, how he wanted to make them pay.

But then Istomin came in with a man behind him. No, not a man. A child. Tall enough to qualify, perhaps, but he had a baby face. Asher was certain he hadn't even begun to shave.

Jesus Christ.

A fucking kid.

Then Asher remembered . . .

Yixing, a fifteen-year-old genius. The same computer whiz who had, apparently, been the one to track down Yunho. Same kid who had found Asher and Harry in Australia.

Asher was going to make him pay too.

Kid or not.

Istomin clapped his hands, making Yunho jump. "Look

at this family reunion," he said, gesturing between Asher and Yunho. "How sweet."

Asher ignored him and instead, trained his eyes in on the kid. "How much is he paying you?"

The kid smiled at him. He fucking smiled. "A lot."

"Until it's your time in this chair," Asher said with a laugh.

Istomin took Asher's chin and yanked his face around. His eyes were a cold blue. Icy and dead. "Do not speak to him."

Asher considered spitting in his face and briefly wondered if the painful retaliation that he would no doubt bear would be worth the satisfaction.

Instead he smiled at him.

Istomin stood up to his full height and took a step back. "We're going to play a little game," he declared. "Where Mr Oh here tells us everything we need to know," he said, then smiling and gesturing to Yunho like this was a game show on TV. "And for every answer he gets wrong, or even hesitates," he gestured to Asher, "Mr Garin here loses a body part."

Awesome.

"No," Yunho mumbled, crying and trembling. "I'll tell you everything. Don't hurt him."

Istomin chuckled and tapped Yunho's face. "Yes, you will tell me everything."

"Don't tell him anything," Asher said. They were dead anyway. Istomin was going to kill them regardless, so Asher would sooner give them nothing.

He wanted to know where Harry was, if he was still alive. But then part of him didn't want to know. For if he was dead, even to hear those words, it would kill Asher.

Asher also didn't want to bring Istomin's focus on

Harry on the off chance he was still alive. Surely, he knew Asher's one weak spot was Harry.

And Yunho, yes. He loved Yunho. He did.

But Harry . . . Harry was the entirety of Asher's world. That was never clearer to Asher as it was in that moment; sitting next to Yunho in this bunker, facing certain death. Sitting alongside the man he thought of as family, an older brother, a father. Asher's mind kept an ironclad hold on Harry.

He clung to the hope that Harry was still alive. It was the only reason he had to keep going in that moment. No matter what came next, what he was about to endure.

If Harry was still alive, then he'd endure it.

If he were to learn right then that Harry was dead, Asher's reason for living would die with him. He'd once thought if he lost Harry that he'd burn the world to the ground, to avenge his death with nothing but fire and fury.

But the truth was, he wouldn't. He'd simply crumple to the ground and wait for death to find him. He wouldn't fight it.

Hell, he'd welcome it.

"Let's start, shall we?" Istomin said. He waved a man over. A stoic, hard-faced man, that Asher recognised? He wasn't sure . . . until he spoke in that raspy, larynx-injured voice.

The same man who'd kidnapped Yunho and Lucas. He'd killed Aranya and Narong.

Larynx. Asher wanted to kill him, very much.

Larynx took out a knife from his thigh holster, similar to what they'd used on Rozga in the tunnel, and waited for Istomin's next order.

"Which body part shall we start with?" Istomin said.

"Which appendage would he miss the most?" Then he acted surprised. "Perhaps his tongue, after he spoke to the media today. Hmm," he seemed genuinely unsure of which part of Asher's body to mutilate first. "Ooh, I know! His index finger. A sniper without his trigger finger is like a snitch without their tongue, am I right?"

Fuck.

"I told you," Yunho said, crying and shaking his head. "I will tell you whatever you want to know. Don't touch him, please."

"It's okay," Asher said to Yunho, needing to placate him, to comfort him.

Istomin smiled at Yunho. "Did you hear that? He said it was okay. Though I'm sure he wouldn't think that if he knew what you'd done."

What he'd done?

"How you betrayed him?" Istomin added.

Asher didn't want to hear it. Not from him. If Yunho had betrayed him, then he'd hear it from Yunho.

Istomin turned his attention to Asher and smiled. "Do you know how easy it was? Yunho's a genius, yes. But he's also a little freak who can't leave his house, so you know what that makes him? A creature of habit. Meticulous. Routine, routine, routine. And a sitting duck, unable to leave." He shook his head and clucked his tongue. "Careless, careless, careless."

Istomin made a distasteful face at Yunho and then he pretended to shake, like an epileptic. "God, he's such a freak. Absolute basket case. We had to keep him sedated so he didn't seizure himself to death or hyperventilate, choke on his own tongue."

"He needs medication," Asher said. This asshole was going to die, Asher would make sure of it.

"And you," Istomin said. "You're just as predictable, Asher," he added, clearly enjoying having centre stage. "I knew you'd come to rescue him. I knew you would, like I know the sun will come up in the morning. So predictable. So many people wanted you dead but none of them knew how to get you. When it was really very simple. All I had to do was capture your precious Yunho, and it would lure you right in." He brightened. "Then imagine my surprise when it turns out you have a lover. Someone you love more than your precious Yunho. Someone you'd want to settle down with in your little house, play the gay wife, and pretend you weren't Asher Garin. Well, guess what. You don't get to pretend that you didn't kill all those people. And you don't get to pretend that you didn't kill Sergey Volkov and ruin our plans six years ago and take every fucking cent of our money."

Wait. What?

"Who?" Asher asked.

Istomin grabbed Asher's hair and yanked him backwards. The chair couldn't move because it was bolted to the floor, so Asher's neck strained painfully. His face appeared above Asher's, straining and angry, his dead eyes ice cold. "You know damn well who."

The truth was, Asher had killed a lot of people, ruining a lot of plans. He didn't remember them all. He tried to remember which job six years ago. Russian, at that . . .

Oh.

There was a Belarus job about six years ago . . .

"You're just the lackey who pulled the trigger," Istomin said. "Yunho ordered the kill. You know every shot you fired, every life you took was for his personal gain, yes? You mean no more to him than a pawn in his fucked-up game of chess. He needs someone removed so he can take the spoils. He calls you and you take them out, he takes the money, the data, and the control."

Asher wasn't sure what part of that great revelation was supposed to be a surprise. He almost laughed. "I know all this. Who did you think we were? Batman and Robin, saving the world from evil villains? Newsflash: we're *all* villains."

Istomin didn't think that was funny. He grabbed Asher by the throat, his fingertips squeezing, his face red with rage.

"Did you know that he works for the government?" Istomin asked through clenched teeth.

Asher snorted because *of course* he knew that. "Which ones? There are dozens of countries who pay good money to have pieces in this game of chess with no strings. Yours included."

"Yours," Istomin said, giving Asher's throat a squeeze before letting go.

Asher swallowed and resisted the urge to cough. "I don't have a government," Asher replied. "I have no allegiance to any country."

Istomin laughed, which Asher hadn't really expected. It was a sinister sound. "You don't even know. You are so caught up in it and you don't even know. He hid it from you well, yes?" He gave a pointed nod to Yunho. "You lied to him about his whole involvement, and he has no clue."

Yunho shook his head, causing more tears to fall down his cheeks. He opened his mouth but no words came out. His breathing was ragged, unsteady, his whole body trembling.

Istomin smiled at Asher. "Like it or not, Asher, you now belong to the Australian government. Your precious Yunho sold you out. And your boyfriend, Harrigan. He sold the both of you. You think the Milvus files case being blown wide open was the Australian military's doing?" He laughed and gestured to Yunho. "The mastermind was right beside you the whole time."

No.

Asher shook his head.

No.

Istomin laughed. "Was he helping you and Harrigan escape? Or was he orchestrating your every move? Did he provide information to bring down Clive Parrish, or did he use you to tie up loose ends?"

Asher shook his head again, but he glanced over at Yunho. He had his head down, crying. "It's not like that," he half mumbled, half cried. "I'm sorry, Asher."

It's not like that.

Meaning it *was something* like that.

Asher felt ill.

He'd brought Harry into this, and now he had no idea where he was or if he was even still alive. His Harry could be dead.

And for what?

Betrayal burned through Asher's blood like lava, searing and beseeching.

He snarled at Yunho, his anger uncontained. "The fuck have you done?"

FIFTEEN

HARRY CAME to in complete blackness, his years of training registering everything immediately.

His hands and feet were bound. Silence, but for the ringing in his ears, and utter darkness.

A rank odour of burned metal and sulphur filled his nose.

Welding. Something had been welded.

He was in a room, perhaps. No noise from outside, no windows. He was on the floor. Cold, concrete. His head hurt, his teeth, his jaw, his right eye swollen. Not swollen shut, but the skin was tight and he knew his eyebrow was split, sticky with blood.

His skull hurt, headache throbbing, his whole mind heavy and dazed. Concussed, most likely.

When he tried to sit up, pain shot through him. Ribs, cracked at least. His kidneys had been pummelled, and his left shoulder was . . . yeah, something was definitely torn.

The stab wound at his side screamed as he moved. He sucked back a breath and his chest pulled agonisingly. Sharp and piercing.

Shit.

Punctured lung?

Broken ribs, then.

Not good.

Then he remembered the room when they'd first thrown him here, before they'd kicked and stomped his head and everything went dark. The room was small, a few metres squared, and empty of furniture. Fully concrete. There *had* been overhead lighting but it was off now.

Not even a buzz of electricity, of any kind, that usually rattled through bunkers like this.

Now, there was nothing, except the ringing in his ears.

His head hurt. Everything hurt.

Then he remembered fists and boots raining down on him while he was defenceless with his hands bound behind his back. Some teeth were loose. Back molars, which told him how hard he'd been hit. Explained why his jaw was sore.

Then Harry heard a gasping rattle and he jerked at the sound.

He wasn't alone in here.

"Who are you?" Harry asked, his voice deep, his eyes straining to adjust to the pitch dark.

A soft groan and another breathy rattle.

Whoever it was, was not in good shape.

Fear struck him cold, his pain now irrelevant.

"Asher?"

Another soft groan and Harry scooted toward the sound. In the corner, he could make out a figure lying on their side. Hands also tied behind their back, feet bound, just like Harry.

Harry scooted until he reached them. He knew it

wasn't Asher. Too tall and his hair was too light—he could see even in the dark—but it was a man. Harry had a sinking realisation of who it was. He nudged him with his leg. "Hey," he tried again. "Lucas?"

Another raspy inhale.

Harry knew that sound. A punctured lung. Or two.

Harry knew the position the man was in, on his side, was the best position for breathing. He couldn't assess any other injuries, not in the dark like this. Was he unconscious? Was he dying? Near dead?

That breathy rattle didn't sound like he had much life left in him.

Harry nudged him again. "Lucas. It's me, Harry."

Another shaky breath. "Yunho," he mumbled.

"They have Asher too."

Lucas sobbed and wheezed on the inhale. "No, please. God, no," his English accent soft.

"I don't know where they are," Harry admitted. "They separated us. I think they welded the door shut."

Saying those words out loud . . . Harry knew what it meant.

They'd been left for dead.

No chance of escape. Left to die and rot like garbage. It wasn't the dark and cold that bothered Harry.

It was the silence.

He could no longer hear the voices, the yelling, the boots on the ground as soldier's walked the hall. He couldn't hear anything.

Except Lucas's raspy, too-shallow, too-quiet breaths.

Harry had no clue if Asher was in another room, beaten and bound, behind a welded-shut door. If he'd been taken somewhere else. Or if he was already dead.

He didn't know how long he'd been out of it. How much time had passed? What had he missed?

He couldn't believe it was going to end like this.

So fucking stupid.

It was all . . . pointless. What had they accomplished? What had they done but every single thing the bad guys had wanted them to?

They'd fucking walked into this, willingly.

Harry had known something was off with Asher. He was too resigned, too quick to agree. Harry had put it down to Yunho being kidnapped, to being back in Serbia, to where his fucked-up childhood began. He'd found out Daris, his oldest friend, had lied to him and sold him out, was part of some political faction that did all the shit Asher had spent his lifetime trying to forget.

And Asher had found out that Yunho was keeping secrets from him.

So Harry knew Asher wasn't thinking clearly. He knew Asher was scared. He'd never seen him so scared. But there was no way Harry was letting him walk in here alone. Absolutely no fucking way.

And if he could go back, Harry would do the same all over again.

At least that way Asher would know Harry would choose to be by his side, regardless of the outcome.

God, it was all such a mess. None of it made sense.

"What the fuck happened?"

Lucas's breath hitched, rasped. "Caught." More raspy breaths. "Taken."

"Yeah, I know you were taken," Harry said. He had to lean into his side, with the stab wound. And his sore ribs.

The pain was biting, making him sweat.

"What does Istomin want with Yunho? Or did he want Asher?"

More raspy breaths, faster now and getting shallower and more rattly. He didn't speak.

"Lucas," Harry snapped.

Lucas jolted. "Sorry." He lifted his face some, and Harry saw him better, then. Even in the dark, Harry could see the mess that was Lucas's pale and purple face.

Beaten, almost unrecognisable.

Both eyes swollen shut, cuts on his cheek and nose, split and swollen lips, blood drooling from his mouth.

Jesus Christ.

What had they done to him?

"Fuck, Lucas," Harry breathed.

He slumped back down, his head a muted wet thud on the ground. "I never told," he said, barely a grating breath. "Never said a thing."

Then he went silent, his shallow infrequent breaths the only proof that he was still alive.

He never told. Never said a thing.

Harry wasn't sure what that meant. Harry remembered that Lucas was supposedly an MI6 agent. Maybe it was true?

Maybe.

Harry wasn't getting anything else out of Lucas right now. He could try again later, if Lucas woke up again, that was.

It wasn't looking good.

Harry shuffled around and leaned his back against the wall, his legs outstretched near Lucas's head. The darkness, the exhaustion, the pain settled over him and he closed his eyes.

The unbearable grief of knowing he may never see

Asher again lodged itself into Harry's heart, and as heartbreak overwhelmed him, silent tears escaped his eyes, and he allowed himself to cry.

***

THE PAIN WOKE HARRY. He had no clue how long he'd slept. No clue of the passage of time.

Without a window or a watch—in a dark underground room—there was simply no way of knowing.

Lucas was still breathing. His quiet raspy breaths were no better, but they were also no worse.

It took a long while for Harry's eyes to adjust again, for him to see there was nothing else in this room. No water, no food.

A human body could go seventy-two hours without water, right?

He had no idea how long it'd been already, and there was truly no point in starting to count from now.

It didn't matter.

Not anymore.

Not without Asher.

His mind grew dark, his eyelids heavy. Lucas's weak rasps were a lonely metronome. Harry couldn't believe it was going to end like this. He always thought he'd go out in a gun fight or a fist fight, on his feet, at least.

Then, in the last two years, he'd hoped he'd meet his end with Asher at his side, both of them old and grey.

It was a different kind of grief knowing that that wasn't likely now. And instead of being grateful for the last two perfect years with Asher, he mourned the next fifty years they'd robbed from him.

Maybe he deserved this.

Maybe they all did.

Another silent tear fell from his closed eyes. With his bound hands unable to wipe it away, he let them fall.

THE NEXT TIME HARRY WOKE, it was with more clarity. His body still ached and it still hurt to breathe, but his mind was clearer now.

And he was pissed.

Pissed at himself for wasting precious minutes, wallowing in self-pity and unfounded grief.

The old Harry would have never allowed himself that.

Lucas's breaths remained the same, the death rattle persistent but no closer.

Harry had to do something. He had to try.

He still couldn't see much, the room impossibly dark, but his vision had adjusted. It probably helped that the blinding headache was now just a dull thump. He scooted over to the opposite wall, to the door. Mad at himself for not even trying to open it, certain the acrid smell of metal and sulphur had meant it had been welded shut.

And he was sure it had been . . . but he still had to try.

He pressed his back to the wall, and using his bound feet, he pushed himself up, his torn shoulder protesting loudly. He groaned out through gritted teeth at the pain and exertion, the stab wound in his side leaking fresh blood.

Fuck.

When he was finally upright, leaning his back against the wall, he took a few deep breaths, allowing his throbbing head to stop spinning.

He edged over until he felt the door jamb under his

bound hands, fumbling over, searching for the door handle . . . to find only the hole where the handle should have been.

Goddammit.

Harry tried to ram his good shoulder into the door instead, pain reverberating through his whole body with each slam.

It didn't move a millimetre.

All it did was leave him panting, breathless.

Hurting.

"Wh-what was that?" Lucas asked weakly. He sounded confused.

"Just me," Harry replied. "Checking the door. Pretty sure it's welded shut."

"H-Harry? Harry, is that you?"

Could he not remember?

"Yeah."

"Is . . . Asher . . . here?" He asked, rasping back breaths between each word. "Yunho? Where's Yunho?"

Harry deflated. Any hope he'd briefly had before simply withered away.

"I don't know where they are," Harry admitted. "There's only silence outside. So it's pretty safe to assume we've been left for dead."

Why they didn't kill them both, Harry could only guess.

Maybe they'd be back for them. Maybe their torture wasn't over yet.

"There's no water," Harry said flatly.

Hell, if the door had been welded shut and fully sealed, they had limited oxygen too.

Fuck.

He hadn't even thought of that before now.

He shuffled to the other side of the door, feeling the jamb, trying to feel if a lick of air was coming in.

He couldn't feel anything.

Hopelessness etched around him instead.

He wanted to lash out and scream, and maybe pummel the shit out of something, but there was no point.

He pulled against his arm restraints. He wasn't even sure what they'd bound him with. Zip ties most likely. They felt thin and bit into his skin like a zip tie.

He tried straining his wrists apart, his torn shoulder screaming with pain with the effort. But because of the size of his wrists and his arms, Harry imagined it'd have taken zip-tie cuffs and a third zip-tie chain-linked between them.

It was ridiculous how effective those cheap plastic things were.

Harry hated that he was subdued by something so simple.

Normally he wouldn't have been subdued so easily. If his shoulder wasn't so pained. If he hadn't been stabbed in the side. If his ribs weren't broken, and if it didn't hurt to breathe, or think.

Fuck.

He hated being so pitiful.

The old Harry wouldn't be so fucking useless . . .

"You know what?" Harry grumbled to himself.

"Huh?" Lucas croaked.

"I am the old Harry," Harry said. "I'm not useless. And I refuse to fucking die with my hands behind my back."

Then, with a strength Harry didn't even know he had, he strained to pull his hands apart. Pain ripped through his shoulder, his ribs, the stab wound at his side. His jaw and teeth hurt from clenching with the strain. Starbursts shot behind his eyes.

He roared through the pain, through this one final attempt.

Until one of the zip ties gave way, snapping free.

His hands fell forward, muscles spent. He had to cradle his left arm because his shoulder . . . Jesus. His fucking shoulder burned with pain. The shoulder joint, the muscles across his chest and down his arm and back.

But he got his hands free.

The zip ties around his wrists were pulled so tight, cutting into the skin, he couldn't even get a fingernail underneath them.

"Harry?" Lucas rasped.

"Yeah," he panted. "Just got my hands free."

Then he quickly sat down, feeling around for the broken zip tie. Once he found it, he set about using the tip to unlock the ties around his ankles. He only needed to do one . . .

And presto!

His feet were free.

Harry scrambled over to Lucas and, using the same technique, freed his hands.

Lucas groaned, each breath an effort, as he struggled to bring his arm underneath him. He could barely lift himself up enough, his lungs rattling, and he lay back down, panting as if he'd run a marathon.

"Thank you," he wheezed.

Harry set about untying Lucas's feet. He was barefoot, Harry realised, though his feet were tacky, sticky, and Harry looked at his fingers. It was too dark to really see, but Harry knew it was blood.

Christ.

"What did they do to you?" Harry hadn't meant to say those words out loud.

Lucas only answered with ragged breaths.

Harry shook his head, frustrated and helpless. But he could stand now, and figuring Lucas had probably lapsed back into unconsciousness, Harry went back to the door.

He couldn't feel any cool air around the door jamb. The door handle was gone. There was no light switch, no window. He looked up, squinting at the ceiling for an air vent or ducting.

They were basically locked underground in a dark sealed box.

Just fucking great.

The wet pang at his side reminded him sharply that he'd been stabbed.

With any luck, he'd bleed to death before he died of dehydration or suffocation.

Heavy weariness settled over him once again. Every ache burned, every pain receptor buzzed. He went back to the wall by Lucas, and slid down, his back resting against it.

His thoughts turned to Asher. How he'd sit on the back veranda of their house with Mala, how he'd smile with the forest behind him. The sound of his laughter, how he'd let fly with a string of Croatian curse words at Harry when he was mad. How he'd pout and complain about putting on a few kilos and Harry had kissed him, telling him he'd never been sexier.

How he'd cried at the ruined buildings of his terrible past just this morning—was it this morning? Yesterday? Last week? Harry wasn't sure. But Harry was glad he'd been there with him, to hold him, to tell him he was loved.

And if this was their end, then Harry was glad Asher got to let go of that demon before he died.

Harry was just pissed he hadn't had the chance to kill

that asshole who'd done god knows what to Asher as a boy.

Harry wanted to break every bone in that man's body, peel his skin like a fucking grape, and squeeze his head so hard, with pure rage, that it popped.

Lucas groaned on the floor beside him, coming in and out of consciousness.

"Hey," Harry said loudly. He wasn't going to ask this before. Lucas had clearly been through enough. But now Harry needed to know. If they were about to die, then Harry wanted to know. He wanted to know for Asher. "Hey," he said again, giving Lucas a nudge. "It's me, Harry."

"Mm," he mumbled.

"Answer me, yes or no. You working for MI6?"

Lucas's breaths grated in and out of him, slow and painful. Harry thought for a moment that Lucas was out of it again and maybe he hadn't even heard the question.

But then he answered.

"Yes."

SIXTEEN

LARYNX PRESSED the tip of his blade into the top of Yunho's knee, sinking it in half an inch. Yunho bit back a scream, trying to breathe through the pain.

"Tell him what you did," Istomin said. "Tell him how much the Australian government paid you to string him along in bringing Parrish down?"

Yunho shook his head. "No money."

"No money? You did it for free?" Istomin asked, his tone sickeningly sweet as Larynx twisted the knife.

Asher heard the pop of Yunho's patella, and Yunho tried not to scream. He was panting, spit frothing at his lips.

Larynx yanked his head back by his hair. "Or did you pilfer the funds from another transaction? One set by the British?" Istomin asked. Larynx pulled Yunho's head back harder and Istomin peered angrily into his face. "The fucking British, you piece of shit with your piece of shit boyfriend. You wanna know what we did to him?"

Yunho sobbed.

Istomin smiled evilly. "Or should I show you?"

He nodded to Radovic, who Asher hadn't even noticed. "Untie his hands and hold them up."

He did as he was told, yanking Yunho's hands around and up over his head. Yunho had no fight in him, no resistance.

Then Istomin aimed a sinister smile aimed at Asher. "Did this to your boyfriend too," he said. "But he was so out of it by then. Took one helluva beating, that man."

Fear and dread sunk cold in Asher's belly, spreading like ice through his limbs. "What did you do to him?" Asher asked, bile roiling in his gut.

Istomin grinned at him. "This." He gave a nod to Larynx, who felt down Yunho's exposed sides, through his shirt, along his ribs. "Right here," he said, in his terrible voice. "Between the third and fourth rib, the blade at the perfect angle . . ." He put the tip of the blade where his fingers had been, then thumped the base of the hilt of the knife with the heel of his hand. The blade sunk into Yunho, and he wailed.

"Pierces the lung," Istomin added, almost cheerfully. Then Larynx pulled the knife out and Yunho recoiled and wheezed.

They'd done that to Harry.

And to Lucas.

Jesus Christ, Asher wanted to weep.

His poor Harry.

"What did you do to him?" Asher asked, louder this time. Anger and rage, both rendered impotent and futile by his bound hands and feet. "What did you do to Harry?"

Istomin watched Asher coolly. "You don't need to worry about him anymore." He glanced at his watch. "He's not dead yet. But it won't be long."

No, no. Asher shook his head. "Fuck you. Fuck all of

you with your fucked-up boy-scout operation of wannabe fucking dictators. So desperate to be relevant—"

A hard punch made Asher's head snap back, shutting him up. Larynx loomed over him, fisting Asher's hair, his angry face far too close. "Shut your fucking mouth or I'll cut out your tongue."

"I'm in," a young voice said behind them, and both Larynx and Istomin turned to look at the monitors on the screen, forgetting momentarily about Asher and Yunho.

The screens began to fill with data, pages of it. Codes, numbers, IP addresses, bank account numbers. It looked a lot like Yunho's screens in his war room. Like his data and information.

"It wasn't that difficult to get in," Yixing said, sparing Yunho a smug glance. "The password was Haemosu. A Korean word."

"Haemosu." Asher's gaze shot to Yunho. "Ćiro Savić."

Yunho's head shot up and his eyes took a second to focus on Asher, but when they did, Asher knew.

It was his name.

"You knew. You've always known," Asher bit out, still speaking Korean. He shook his head, eyes burning with unshed tears.

The betrayal seared Asher to his core.

He couldn't even look at him.

"I'll tell you everything," Yunho said in Korean, then repeated it in English. "Everything."

"Are we interrupting?" Istomin yelled, making both Asher and Yunho glance his way. He glowered at them both, then clapped Yixing on the shoulder, smiling at his new favourite pet. "Good boy," he said. "Good job."

Radovic clearly didn't like Istomin praising the kid.

Yixing preened under Istomin's attention, ignoring

Radovic to sniff dismissively at Yunho. "Thought *he* was supposed to be the best. I had it decrypted in under an hour."

Yunho's reply was low and raspy, and he spoke in Chinese. Asher's Chinese was rusty at best, so he couldn't be entirely sure but it was something like *foolish roosters call the fox*.

Yixing stared at Yunho for a long moment.

Istomin looked between them. "What did he say?"

"Nothing," Yixing murmured, shaking it off and turning his attention back to the monitors. He began to explain routing codes to Istomin who listened intently.

But Asher was sure it meant something. What he'd said to Yixing, what it meant.

Foolish roosters call the fox.

Asher looked at Yunho. His head was now lolled forward, his breathing was laboured, wheezy. His swollen face a testament mask to the beatings he'd taken; bruises, cuts, sweat, blood.

"Yunho," Asher whispered. "What did you do?"

Yunho looked up at him.

And smiled.

SEVENTEEN

HARRY WASN'T sure if it was the lack of air in the room or his punctured lung that made it so hard to breathe.

He was sweating, hot and cold, and could barely keep his eyes open.

He longed for sleep, but the idea of falling asleep now and not waking up scared the shit out of him. He'd seen a lot of death. His entire adult life had been a war game of kill or be killed. He'd taken more lives than he could remember.

It shouldn't have scared him to know it was his turn. After all, there could be worse ways to go . . .

But he didn't want to die.

Not like this.

Not without Asher.

Without seeing his face one last time.

He tried to regulate his breathing, slow and steady, minimal use of oxygen. Not that it mattered. Lucas was panting, rattling.

He couldn't fight his eyelids any longer.

HARRY WOKE WITH A START, realising it was Lucas's cough that startled him awake. A wheezing rattle that surely meant Lucas's end was near.

Harry reached out for Lucas's hand. It was cold and unmoving at his touch. Jesus. Were his fingers broken? Fucking hell.

"I'm here," Harry whispered.

No one should die alone.

Harry couldn't join the dots between MI6 Lucas—who had lied to them and was probably half the reason they were in this mess—with the Lucas who had welcomed them into his home. Fed him, laughed with him, cared for Asher when he'd been kidnapped in Oman, helped them escape. Harry had seen the way Lucas looked at Yunho with nothing but love in his eyes. So pure it had made Harry blush.

How were these two Lucases one and the same?

Harry didn't know.

But he had considered Lucas a trusted friend. So it was *that* Lucas's hand he held as he sat there in the dark, his back to the cold concrete wall. He closed his eyes and listened to Lucas's breaths get weaker, further apart, slower.

Waiting for the silence to engulf them.

HARRY STIRRED to find himself slumped to the side. Pain radiated through his neck as he tried to straighten up, through his whole fucking body. He was dazed, unsure if it was the lack of water or oxygen that would win the fight to take him out.

He couldn't hear Lucas breathing anymore.

He couldn't hear anything.

He thought he heard yelling and banging, but he was sure his mind was playing tricks. Everything was muted, far away. Even his thoughts.

His pain was still close though. Nestled in his chest, in his bones.

He could smell that acrid metal sulphur smell again. The same rank odour he'd noticed when he'd first come to.

God, his mind was really going.

He'd read once, a long time ago, that some people experienced aromas from distant memories as they succumbed to death. Things like sunshine or cut grass, or jasmine from a garden they'd grown up in.

Nice things.

He longed to smell Asher. Sandalwood from those terrible incense sticks, or spices from his delicious cooking. Or the smell of his sweat on his skin, lazing in their bed after a summer afternoon of fucking.

But no.

All Harry had was acrid burned oxide, and bright orange sparks dancing across the floor.

HARRY COULD BARELY OPEN his eyes. He couldn't move. Slumped on his side against the wall.

But there was light.

And boots coming into the room.

He tasted fresh air, even though his lungs couldn't

inhale at first. His eyes unable to focus. He felt so unbearably heavy.

"We got them," a booming voice said.

Australian.

Then a face was in front of him. Black combat gear, the static of a radio was close by. "Can you hear me? Sir, can you hear me?"

Harry could hear, kind of. He just couldn't speak.

The man spoke into the radio at his shoulder. "We need a medic, stat. Repeat, we need a medic team in here."

Then there was a water canteen at his lips, pouring a few drops into his mouth. "Drink this," another voice said, accent English.

It registered then what was happening, that this was real, and Harry tried to sit up. Pain stabbed through him everywhere.

A black gloved hand pressed on his chest. "Stay there. Try and stay still."

"Asher," Harry bit out.

The door was open, he realised. Of course it was.

Why was his mind so foggy?

"Asher," he said again.

The man's eyes flinched, just as more men rushed into the room. They had medic packs. Harry realised far too late that there were two men kneeling over Lucas. One medic came to Harry, the other to Lucas.

"He needs help," Harry said.

The medic closest to Harry assessed him, worried eyes looking him over. "Yeah, mate. He's not the only one. Jesus Christ." Then he shoved an oxygen mask over Harry's mouth and nose and quickly rigged up a field IV. Saline, most likely.

Harry wouldn't have minded if it were morphine.

"We need to look at the abdominal stab wound," the medic murmured.

"Just cauterise it," Harry mumbled. "It'll be fine. I need to find Asher."

The medic looked kinda horrified but not altogether too surprised.

"We'll find him," the Australian voice said, patting Harry's leg. Harry hissed, looking down at his legs. He had patches of red and knife holes in the fabric, at his thighs, calves, and shins.

Fuck.

No wonder he hurt all over.

He remembered that sick fuck Radovic jabbing him like a fucking pin cushion. Maybe a knife block was more apt.

Now that there was light in the room, he could see he had blood over most of his body.

"We got a punctured lung here," the medic said.

"We've got two here," the other medic said, working on Lucas. Harry's gaze drew over to where Lucas was. He couldn't see much with the people crowded around him. Just his feet. And with the light coming into the room, Harry could see they were red with blood and dark purple.

They lifted Lucas onto a stretcher, carrying him out of the room, leaving a Lucas-shaped pool of dark blood, congealed and dried at the edges on the floor.

Jesus fucking Christ.

What had they done to him?

Then there were more men in front of Harry. The first man's face was back. "We need to get you up and out of here, sir."

"Need to find Asher," Harry agreed, trying to push himself up.

"He's not here," the guy said.

Harry's eyes met his. "Then I need to leave," Harry bit out, pushing himself up with more determination this time.

Then he had a man on either side of him, helping him. Harry wanted to shake them off, declare loudly he didn't need no help. But when he almost fell face first, his knee crumpling under his weight, the two men at his side held him up.

They ambled him out of the room, the medic alongside him, still holding the IV.

The air was cleaner out here, breathing easier. He'd never been more grateful for air. But he hurt. My god, how he hurt, every-fucking-where.

They got him up the stairs into the warehouse. Harry barely remembering them coming here. But the Jeep they'd driven was still parked by the large doors.

This place had been crawling with soldiers in army fatigues before . . .

And now . . . now there were different soldiers, dressed in black combat gear. Different helicopters. Wildcats.

Different accents.

Australian. English.

As they all but carried Harry a few metres from the stairs, one of the helicopter's rotors whirred to life in a familiar thumping sound but before it took off, a man came in to stop right in front of him.

He was tall, almost as tall as Harry but not as broad. He wore all black, from his helmet and face guard down to his boots. He had a EF88 strapped to his chest, his finger on the trigger guard. Harry could only see his eyes, nothing else. They were blue-grey, hard at first, then flickered with brief softness before hardening again.

"Harry Harrigan," he said. "It's an honour to meet you."

Accent Australian.

"He needs to be on the next chopper to a hospital," the medic said. Harry shot him a glare, but he glared right back, undeterred. Brave, for a medic. "You need medical—"

Harry growled, wrestling out of the hold of the two men who'd helped him up the stairs. "What I need is to find Asher," Harry bit out. "And I need to know what the fuck's going on. What division are you?" He asked grey eyes. "And what the fuck are you doing here?"

Grey eyes stared at him, unblinking for a long second. "My name's Captain," he said. No names, and Harry understood that. He'd been lucky to get a rank. "And we are the Milvus Division."

EIGHTEEN

ASHER'S HEAD smacked back as Radovic punched him. Pain spiked down his cheekbone, in his neck.

So laughing hadn't been the appropriate response when Radovic had asked if the funds transfer would be enough, and Yixing had snorted and said, "Two hundred and fifty is perfect for you," in English. Then added, "Èr bǎi wǔ," quietly.

Radovic clearly didn't know what that meant, but Yunho did, and he'd had laughed at him, sending Radovic into a murderous rage. It was bad enough that he was Istomin's lackey, but now the genius kid had taken over as his favourite.

Radovic was pissed, first at Yixing, and then at Yunho laughing at him. The way he strode over with his jaw clenched and his fist cocked, Asher was sure Yunho was about to cop it. But he didn't punch Yunho. He walked past him and punched Asher right in the fucking face.

Radovic glowered at Yunho. "Every time you say something without being spoken to, your friend here gets hurt. Are we clear?"

Sure, Radovic couldn't touch Yixing, no matter how much he might have pissed him off, but he could punch the fuck out of Asher.

Asher's face hurt, his nose, his cheek, his lip, his brain ached, but he could take a whole lot more than that. Hell, Radovic had done worse than this to Asher when Asher was just eight years old. Asher snorted at him and nodded toward Yixing. "You're still second favourite, I see." Asher glanced over to Larynx who stood beside Istomin and Yixing. "Or are you third? Like when we were kids. You weren't good enough then, either."

Radovic spun to glare at Asher, murder and fire in his eyes. He pulled his knife out, and without a word, still glaring at Asher, he stabbed the knife into Yunho's thigh.

Yunho screamed through gritted teeth, the sound etched forever in Asher's mind. "Untie me and make it a fair fight," Asher spat at him.

Radovic pulled his knife out, red beading at the tip. "Speak without being spoken to again, and he gets hurt. Got it?"

"What do you want us for?" Asher said. He nodded to the monitors where data and numbers were still scrolling on the screens. "You got what you wanted."

It was Istomin who came over then. He smiled at Asher. "Oh, Mr Garin, we haven't begun with you yet. I'm afraid your pain hasn't even started yet."

Asher sneered at him.

Istomin's expression was thoughtful. "Do you remember, about six years ago, you took out Sergey Volkov when he was in Belarus. He was a diplomat for the Kremlin. You shot him in the head." Istomin mimicked a gun with his hand. "You must have been, what? Eight hundred and fifty metres away?"

It was closer to a thousand, but Asher didn't say that.

Istomin sighed dramatically. "Well, he was in a business deal with two Croat and Bosnian senators and a very dear Russian friend of mine, and they lost a great deal of money. A lot of money, Asher." He shook his head. "So I made a deal with him—his money back, and you on a silver platter. And believe me, you won't like what he plans to do with you."

"And what do you get?" Asher asked.

Istomin grinned like a ghoul. "I get two very well-situated men in the senate."

Asher couldn't believe it. He was fucking sick. "For your political agenda, to push the new cold war."

He laughed. "It's not a political agenda, you fool. It's a financial one."

Asher was stunned. "What?"

"I don't give a fuck about the politics of it," he replied. "Do you know how lucrative civil unrest and war is? With this"—he waved his hand at the monitors—"stock markets, weapon deals, and the Balkans in turmoil, with a shove from my Russia, do you know how many billions that will make me?"

Asher wanted to scream at him, to strangle him, punch the shit out of him. He wanted to vomit. "Do you know how many people will die? Do you know how many children end up in orphanages or sold to sick fucking animals?" Asher was almost vibrating off his chair, white hot anger burning in his veins. "The casualties of fucking war that no one talks about? Fuck you," Asher spat. "The ZBK factions, those pathetic wannabe soldiers," Asher said, disbelieving, but the pieces were clicking together. "You're using them to start a war for money?"

Istomin smiled imperiously. "Shall we discuss what

you and your pathetic friend here have done for money? How many people have you killed? How many people have died indirectly because of you? How many orphans did you create? And you think you can lecture me about ethics?"

Yunho snorted out a raspy laugh. His side was bleeding badly, red staining the side of his shirt from where they'd stabbed his lung. "Every person we killed deserved it. War mongers, arms dealers, drug cartels, human traffickers, pieces of shit like you—"

Radovic's fist came down so hard on the side of Yunho's head, the sound of the crack was sickening. He slumped as far as his restraints would allow, his head lolling forward.

Unconscious, red drool stringing from his mouth.

Radovic grabbed Asher by the face, his fingers clawing, squeezing painfully. "Please let me hurt him," he gritted out.

Istomin tsked. "I promised him to my friend largely uninjured. Shame."

Radovic growled. "I want to watch what they do to him."

Istomin sighed. "I'm sure they'll allow it."

Yixing mumbled something and began clicking on a keyboard furiously.

"What is it?" Istomin asked.

"Something's not right," Yixing said, not even looking up.

Istomin went to him, Radovic giving Asher a hard shove before he followed.

"What do you mean something's not right?" Istomin barked.

Yixing was still typing furiously, shaking his head.

"It's . . . wrong. Something is wrong. It's not appearing. The routing . . . the money's transferring but . . . but not to us."

A moment of deafening silence.

Istomin stammered, then he roared. "What do you mean not to us? Where is it going?"

"I don't know!" Yixing cried, his keyboard clicking frantically. Then he stopped and looked back over to Yunho, stark realisation on his young face.

Yunho had done something to fuck them over, Asher was sure of it. God, they were gonna kill him for sure now. But if that was the last thing Yunho did before he died . . .

Hell, Yunho probably did it to make sure it was the last thing he ever did before he died.

Asher had to admit, despite the physical pain and the anguish knowing it meant certain death, it was kinda funny.

And he laughed.

A MAN APPEARED at the captain's side, his hand to his earpiece. "Sir, we have the location."

The location to what?

Harry's heart kicked up, anticipation and dread dulling the pain riddling his body. "Location? For Asher?"

The captain's grey eyes went to Harry's before he spoke to his man. "Two minutes. Both teams."

"I'm going with you," Harry said to the captain.

"You're not going anywhere," the medic said, "but to a hospital."

Harry batted away the oxygen mask the medic was still trying to put on him. He snarled at him, the pain in his loose tooth and jaw barely registering as he spoke through clenched teeth. "I don't need a fucking hospital. I need to find Asher."

"You have a punctured lung, a stab wound, and from the way you're carrying that arm, I'd say your shoulder—"

Harry didn't know whether this fucker was brave or stupid. "So give me a fucking shot in it," he roared. "I don't give a fuck what you do, but I am on that helicopter in two minutes."

He shot the captain a wild look, daring any mother-fucker to argue. He didn't care if he sounded crazy. In that moment, Harry felt like a cornered bear, ready to maul anyone who tried to stop him.

Captain held his gaze before conceding with a sigh. "Fine. But you follow my orders. You do anything stupid, I will shoot you myself."

Before Harry could say anything, the medic jabbed Harry in the shoulder. "What the fuck?" Harry said, looking down at the needle.

"Hold still," the medic said. "Christ. I swear the bigger they are, the bigger the baby. Quit your whining. You wanted a shot. It's just to dull the pain a bit." Then he rolled his eyes. "You're welcome, by the way. For saving your life."

Harry stared at him.

He was at least a foot shorter than Harry, half his width, and twice the attitude. He grumbled something about ungrateful assholes as he packed up his medic pack and walked away.

"The fucking audacity of that guy," Harry said, rubbing his shoulder.

Captain snorted. "He's . . . feisty." Then he nodded to the chopper. "Come on."

Harry followed him onto the chopper, sighing with unforgiving impatience when he realised he was sitting next to the medic. Out of the seven men he had to sit with, it had to be him.

The medic smirked at him.

Harry was too damned old for this.

And why were the team across from him all sixteen years old?

Okay, maybe not sixteen. But Christ almighty, did they have to all be so young?

They were you twenty years ago, Harry.

Harry grumbled at himself as he put on the helmet and buckled in, ignoring the way the men opposite him were staring at him, at his chest, at his legs.

Harry looked down at himself to see what they were looking at. He was covered in blood. Mostly from incisions and shallow stab wounds, dark red circles staining the cut fabric marking each one. His side, under his arm, was particularly red, the dark blood stain leaking down to his pants. He'd thought it was his ribs—lord knows they hurt—but he could see the slice through his shirt now.

"Still wanna cauterise it?" the medic asked.

Harry glared at him. "Yes. Give me a knife and a lighter." The fucker laughed, so Harry turned to the captain. "Can I hurt him?"

Captain grinned. "Absolutely fucking not."

The team across from him all smiled. Harry hated these helmets with mics and audio.

He slumped back in his seat, exhaustion trying to settle in, take over. It hurt to breathe; his breaths were a lot shorter, and his lung hurt, and his ribs. His kidneys hurt too. His jaw, his teeth, his eye, his cheek . . . Hell, his whole body hurt.

But he needed to focus. He was going to get Asher, and he needed to be single-minded. He could push the pain back, for now.

He'd sleep for a week, once Asher was safe.

He needed intel.

He turned back to the captain. "Where are we headed?"

"There's an old military base over the Croatian border."

"How do you know he's there?"

"Location key was activated."

Harry resisted sighing, barely. This was like pulling teeth. He had neither the patience nor the time for this bullshit. There was a very good reason why he'd worked alone for a decade.

"You called yourself the Milvus Division," Harry said. He couldn't believe that.

Milvus. The Milvus Division?

That had been what the Australian government had referred to him as. The Milvus files. And now there was a whole division?

"What the fuck?" Harry asked. "Milvus?"

Captain gave a nod. "You were the first, kind of. The beta test."

"The fuck is that supposed to mean?"

Captain almost smiled as he raised one hand in a pacifying manner. "The Parrish case exposed a bunch of overseas operatives. Not just Australian. Classified documents revealed MI6, CIA, India's IB, and France's DSGE's solo agents."

Harry looked again at the men across from him. So damn young.

Jesus Christ.

"Kites," Harry said flatly. "Like me."

Captain nodded. "A lot of agents like you." He shrugged. "So, to protect them, the governments aligned a program. To bring them under one umbrella."

Harry shook his head. "Not to protect the agents. The governments did it to protect themselves."

"Of course. Can't dispute that. Not anymore," Captain said, and one of the guys across from him shrugged.

Harry still couldn't get his mind around it. "So these *kites*, from all different countries, can now work together?"

Captain gave a hard nod.

Harry shook his head. "Like an elite SAS team. And who gives the orders? Who has control of you? Because I can tell you right now, that kind of power is not good. No good will ever come of it."

"There's a special counsel," Captain said. "No one country can make a call."

Harry still couldn't believe what he was hearing and the fact that Captain was divulging this information so freely. He didn't like any of it.

"Why did you come?" Harry asked. "How did you know where we were?"

"A beacon in the Jeep," he said, nodding to the vehicle. "The tablet."

Asher must have activated it when he slipped it under the seat.

So they could find them.

"And Lucas? Where was he taken?"

Captain paused until Harry's eyes met his, and then he sighed. "A decision on the hospital where Agent Edwards will be taken to will be made en route. Likely London."

Agent Edwards.

So he really *was* MI6.

Harry was almost relieved to have it confirmed. At least now he knew. He wondered if Yunho knew. If Yunho was in on it.

It'd kill Asher.

If he wasn't dead already.

The captain stilled for a second, then said, "ETA eight minutes."

Before Harry could ask, Captain added, "Underground bunker, same as before. Number of men on the ground, unknown. Three truck convoys were let through the border. Military and police have been asked to stand down. Russian politician Istomin is believed to be on site and is to be taken in alive."

"I'll need a weapon," Harry said.

Captain's reply was blunt. "Negative."

Right then. Hands and boots it was.

"You can wait with Medic until we give the all-clear," Captain added.

Harry snorted.

Not a fucking chance.

NINETEEN

THE ENERGY in the room had changed. Istomin and Yixing were panicked, and Radovic was beginning to pace.

And that was never good.

Panic and agitation led to mistakes, rash decisions, and plans being abandoned and changed.

It led to hostages being killed.

Asher knew that.

So did Yunho. Though he wasn't acting like it.

He'd come to a little while ago, moaning with pain, incoherent almost. Until he seemed to remember where he was.

He spared a glance to Asher. "My darling," he murmured. "It'll be okay. No matter what happens, it'll be okay."

"No one gave you permission to speak," Radovic screamed, stopping mid-pace to stalk over to them. His eyes were wild as he took out his knife and held it to Yunho's cheek. "I should give you a matching scar on the other cheek."

He pressed the knife tip into Yunho's cheek as a distant

sound rumbled overhead. Like feet running above them. Like tankers and truck engines. And yelling.

Istomin cocked his head, then he barked an order for his men to go up and see what it was. "Now, now, now!"

Men ran up the stairs and Yunho laughed, blood drooling from his mouth. His face a swollen mess. Asher wondered briefly if he'd lost his mind.

"You stupid fuck, you said we were the bait," Yunho said with a laugh. He looked up at Istomin smiling, panting. A string of blood dropped down from his chin. "We were never the bait. You are."

Then voices shouted, machine guns fired, and a body fell down the stairs with a thud. One of Istomin's men, now staring upward, his chest a gruesome jigsaw puzzle.

And the unmistakable sound of a Hellcat helicopter.

Then a swarm of men in black combat gear came down the stairs, fluid and smooth. The room erupted into chaos. Shots fired, yelling, so much yelling.

But then as if all fell silent and in slow motion, Asher saw Harry.

He came down the stairs like a bull. Like a madman, until he saw Asher, and he stopped.

He was alive. His face beaten, swollen, he was covered in blood. But he was alive. Asher could have cried.

Harry let out a sigh and began to run toward him, just as a wall of black blocked his view.

Radovic had gripped Asher's hair, his knife coming for his throat, his face deranged with rage. Asher tried to pull away, holding his breath as the knife met his neck.

But then he was gone, hoisted up in front of Asher. Harry held Radovic by his throat in one hand, gripping Radovic's hand holding the knife with his other. He forced the blade upward into Radovic's belly and jammed it up and up, bones crunching.

His face was one of shock, his mouth open, eyes wide. Blood streaming from his front, gushing to the floor.

Harry was quickly surrounded by the men in black combat telling him to stand down, but he didn't seem to notice them. He still held Radovic's throat and he snarled at him. "Look at Asher," Harry seethed. "His face will be the last thing you see."

Harry shoved Radovic in front of Asher, then Harry squeezed his hand around Radovic's throat. And squeezed.

His fingertips dug in, skin piercing, bones crushing, and Harry pulverised his windpipe. Radovic gurgled and gasped, blood gushing.

So much blood . . .

"Jesus fucking Christ, Harrigan," one of the men said.

Harry dropped Radovic, discarding him like garbage, his hands then went to Asher.

Soft, cradling, gentle.

"Asher, baby," he whispered. "My god. I'm here. I gotchu."

Asher sagged with relief and exhaustion. He could have cried, but then Harry was yelling. "Get the cuffs off him. Both of them. Now."

A moment later, Asher's hands were freed, his tired and sore arms hurt. Everything hurt.

But then Harry scooped him up, his embrace impossibly tight, as if he thought Asher might disappear. Asher sagged in his hold, unable to stop his tears, and he sobbed with relief and gratitude.

Nothing else mattered, except that Harry was alive. He was here, and Asher would never let him go again. He clung to him, and Harry picked him up and carried him toward the stairs.

Like no one was barking orders, like no bad guys were on their knees with guns pointed at their heads, like no one else existed. Like he needed to take Asher away from this terrible ordeal.

They reached the top, met by more combat men who lowered their guns when they saw who it was. It was bright daylight, the air fresh. Tears streamed down Asher's face. "Harry, I love you. I love you."

Harry stopped and smiled at him, still holding him tight.

Then Harry collapsed to the ground.

TWENTY

ASHER WOKE UP IN A BED, lights bright, machines beeping. The smell told him it was a hospital.

He remembered then . . .

Harry saving him. Carrying him up to safety, then crumpling to the ground.

He remembered the medic fussing over Harry, frantic, barking more orders and jabbing him with needles. They'd been carried to a helicopter. So many strange faces, so many noises.

Until there was only darkness.

And now he was here.

Not that he knew where *here* was.

Harry.

He needed to find Harry.

He sat up and a hand pushed him back down. "Stay there," a man said. A doctor, accent English.

"Harry," Asher tried, his voice hoarse.

The doctor smiled at him. "He's right there." Asher

followed his line of sight and found a bed beside his, Harry's big frame filling the bed.

He was so still, covered in white patches, hooked up to so many machines.

"Is he . . . is he okay?" Asher asked.

The doctor smiled again. "He will be, considering he survived this far. He's rather resilient."

Asher's eyes burned with tears, and as he sagged back onto the bed, his own injuries making themselves known, but he never took his eyes off Harry.

And as the doctor asked Asher questions, checked him over, explained the extent of his injuries—fractured eye socket, broken nose, multiple lacerations, the list went on —Asher never took his eyes off Harry.

Even as the pain ebbed at his consciousness and as the chemical relief swept him under, Asher never took his eyes off him.

THE NEXT TIME he woke up, Asher startled, checking to see if Harry was still in the bed beside his. The nurse reassured him that Harry's condition was stable. He didn't seem to have moved a muscle in the bed next to his, just completely still. A nurse came over and checked Asher's machine.

"Everything okay?" she asked. "Your heart rate went up there."

As long as Asher could see Harry, he'd be okay. He nodded, relaxing back, and the nurse seemed to realise. She gave him a smile. "He's doing better," she said quietly. Then her smile softened. "You know, we were told not to separate you. Said the big guy wouldn't take it well if we did."

Asher half smiled, half cried. "Thank you."

She asked him a few questions about his pain level, how his face and eye felt, if he could see with his good eye. She was English too.

"Where are we?" he asked.

"Royal Hospital in London."

Then he remembered . . .

"What about Yunho?" he asked.

The nurse wasn't sure at first, confusion on her brow. "Oh, the other man that had been held with you?"

Asher had no clue what Yunho's situation was. Or what name he'd been admitted under, and Asher probably shouldn't have used Yunho's real name. Hell, Asher didn't even know which name *he'd* been admitted under. He nodded. "Yes. He's Korean."

Her face softened again. "I can't really say, but I can tell you he made it through surgery."

Surgery.

Jesus.

"And Lucas," Asher asked. "He's English. Was he with Harry?" He glanced again at Harry's bed. He couldn't remember seeing Lucas when Harry had rescued him . . .

The nurse patted his shoulder gently. "I don't know who that is. But I'll see what I can find out."

"Thank you," Asher said weakly.

"You need to rest," she urged. "I'll see about bringing you some soft food."

Asher didn't care for food.

He waited until she was gone, then peeled back the blankets and crept out of bed. He was woozy, dizzy, he hurt all over, and he was so freaking tired, but he took the few steps to Harry's bed, sliding his hand over Harry's and squeezing his fingers.

Harry looked like he'd been through a shredder.

Asher's whole chest felt heavy, the burden of Harry's suffering too much to bear. He sobbed and leaned over him, resting his head on Harry's chest.

"My love," he murmured. "Please be okay."

Two other nurses were there then, urging him back to bed. He didn't want to move. He didn't want to leave him ever again.

"No," he pleaded. He didn't care if he was being pitiful. "Please let me stay. I need to be near him."

"Mr Garin," one nurse said, her gentle hand on his shoulder. "Please."

He reluctantly stood up, his fingers still laced with Harry's. "Harry," he whispered, "I'm here. I'm right here."

Harry's fingers moved, and he squeezed Asher's hand.

"He moved his hand," Asher told them. "He's holding my hand."

The nurses both stilled, watching and waiting, and Asher held his breath.

Then Harry opened his eyes.

PAIN WAS something Harry was used to. His tolerance for it well exceeded normal levels, and he'd had some gruesome injuries in his time. He'd been able to endure pain with no more than a hiss that would have rendered other men useless.

But this felt different.

He hurt all over; bones, muscles, skin.

And he was tired.

So fucking tired.

He wanted to sleep forever. He wanted sleep to ease the pain, both sharp and dull, the stings, the aches. God, even his bones were heavy, aching and leaden. As if a weight was holding him down.

But then Asher's touch, his voice, broke through the surface.

Harry blinked awake, and then there was Asher's face. Still bruised, still swollen, but still beautiful. He sobbed and threw himself at Harry, burying his face in his neck as he cried.

"Hey," Harry croaked.

Asher mumbled something into his neck, the tears and hot breath on his skin felt so good.

But then a guy in a white coat was there, and Asher was gone. The doctor leaned over him, shining a pen light into his eyes that pierced Harry's brain.

If he could have lifted his hand, he'd have grabbed that pen and stabbed him with it.

But he was so heavy.

Morphine, Harry realised.

The doctor spoke, telling him where he was, what his injuries were, but Harry couldn't focus. He closed his eyes and let the blessed drug take him.

WHEN HARRY WOKE UP AGAIN, Asher was sitting beside him. He'd showered, his face, neck, and hair clean from all the blood, he looked better. Still bruised and cut, but better. He grinned when Harry's eyes opened.

"Hey you," he said, gripping Harry's hand in both of his.

"Hey," Harry managed. He slow-blinked, taking in Asher's bruised face. "You okay?"

Asher nodded, then shook his head. "I'm better now you're awake."

Harry took a breath in, his lungs and ribs both protesting. "Tired."

"You need to rest," Asher said. "Your body needs to rest. You . . . you've been through a lot." His chin wobbled. "God, baby. I never thought I'd see you again. I thought you were dead."

Harry squeezed his hand. "I thought you were too."

"You . . . you have a lot of injuries," Asher whispered. "What they did to you . . ."

"I'm okay," Harry said, relishing in the warmth of Asher's hands. He tried to smile, even though his jaw hurt. "We made it."

They had made it out alive, that much was true. But it was only because they had outside help. That team of men almost half Harry's age. They were the reason Harry and Asher had made it.

Asher nodded, tears falling down his cheeks. "We did." Then he swallowed hard. "Yunho's okay. Well, he will be. Lucas . . . Lucas is in bad shape."

Harry remembered seeing Lucas in the light of that small room. His bruises, the pool of blood on the floor.

"He's MI6," Harry whispered.

Asher nodded. "And Yunho was in on it, somehow. Not with the bad guys, but he did things, Harry. Not good things." Asher sniffed, another tear escaping his good eye. "He said he'll tell me everything. But I don't . . . I don't know what to think or what to believe. He's not who I thought he was. Neither of them are."

Harry squeezed Asher's hand the best he could. "Baby.

Let's wait to hear what he has to say. Then if you want me to kill him, I will."

Asher's lip curled into a smile and he chuckled. "You're so sweet."

Harry sighed and closed his eyes. "So tired."

He felt a soft kiss on his forehead. "Sleep, my love."

TWO DAYS LATER, Asher was at Harry's bedside when he woke up again. This time from surgery to repair his shoulder. A complete tear of the acromioclavicular ligament, as well as a partial tear of the coracoclavicular ligaments. How Harry had even managed to move his arm at all without screaming was a testament to his pain tolerance.

How he'd carried Asher up those stairs was a testament to pure will and determination.

How he'd held up Radovic and gutted him and then crushed his windpipe was something else.

Unmatched rage and protective fury, Asher could guess.

Radovic had been one centimetre from killing Asher. He'd also been Asher's childhood tormentor and abuser. One of them, anyway.

He got the end he deserved, and Asher wasn't one bit sorry.

Asher was sitting on the edge of Harry's bed and helped him sip some water when two men came into the room. One white guy, one Asian. Both in their twenties, wearing jeans, black jackets and caps, though their boots told Asher they were likely military.

This was a military hospital, after all.

The shorter of the two, the Asian-looking guy, grinned at Harry, seeing his shoulder strapped and his arm tucked up to his chest. "Need me to get you a sippy cup, big guy?"

What the fuck?

Asher didn't care if that was one of the most bogan Australian accents he'd ever heard. No one spoke to Harry like that. He took the teaspoon off the tray and slid off the bed. He'd never stabbed anyone with a spoon before but he was about to.

The taller guy pulled the shorter guy behind him, put his hand up in a show of surrender, but he rolled his eyes and kind of laughed. "Jesus. Sorry."

Hm. Both Australian.

Harry stared at them, and the taller guy put his hand to his chest and said, "Captain." Then he pointed his thumb at the shorter guy. "Medic. Remember us?"

Harry smiled at them, so Asher relaxed, still eyeing the one called Medic.

"We look a bit different in civvies," Captain said.

"I should have recognised the attitude from the little one," Harry said, trying to sit up, wincing at his shoulder.

Asher went to him, fussing, not sure where to touch. "You gotta take it easy," he whispered.

"Told ya your shoulder was fucked," Medic said. "Next time you might listen."

Harry took the spoon from Asher and held it like a weapon. "Come closer."

Captain chuckled as he gave Medic a shove. "Christ, don't upset him."

They both stared at Harry for a long moment, probably remembering what Harry had done to Radovic. Or maybe they finally noticed every single scar on Harry's chest and arms. A decade of war, now silver lines of survival on his skin.

"We just wanted to see how you were holding up," Captain said, softer this time.

Asher felt oddly protective of Harry. He touched his arm, the side of his face, and he smiled at him. "He's doing fine."

"They'd have had better luck trying to stop a tank, huh?" Captain said.

Harry smirked, kind of. "Maybe. Not feeling real invincible right now, I gotta say." Then he sighed. "Thank you. For everything."

"You were almost dead," Medic said. "In that room, when we found you. And in the chopper on the way here." He smiled at Harry with something that may have been respect. "Pretty sure no other man would have survived."

Harry smiled, his jaw obviously sore. He still had the molar but maybe wouldn't have it for long. "Currently held together by surgical glue, stitches and staples. And morphine."

"Not up for another mission?" Captain asked, grinning.

"Fuck no," Harry said. "I'm too old for that shit. You young pups can have it. I'm done."

Asher squeezed Harry's hand, so very happy to hear that. Growing old together had never sounded so good.

"Istomin has been charged," Captain volunteered. "He's finished. And his men, and half a dozen politicians from several countries, and officials in almost every level of government. Cops too." He gave a smile to Asher. "Your run in with the press blew the whole ZBK thing wide open. Once the media got hold of it, reporters, whistleblowers, witnesses, you name it. It's a shitshow. The UN, Nato, the EU. It's big news."

Asher was almost embarrassed. "I didn't do it to blow it open. I mean, I hoped it would. I just wanted some backup to turn up at the old compound we were going to."

"Both your faces on TV," Captain said quietly, "was the reason we got the call, just so you know. We were already watching the situation. We knew Yunho and Lucas were missing but we didn't know where they were. Then there was the murder of Rozga and his whole chapter of men." He made a face. "So we knew where you two were, and we hoped you'd lead us to find Yunho and Lucas."

It was almost as if they'd used Asher and Harry as bait as well. But Asher couldn't bring himself to be mad. They had saved them after all.

Captain smiled. "But when you plastered yourselves on every TV and newspaper across the world, we knew shit was about to go down, and we had to move."

"Our identities are blown. Names, faces," Asher said flatly. Harry would need the Australian government to get him home, but Asher didn't have any government or embassy to help him, and without Yunho's help . . .

"I'm supposed to be dead," Harry said. "So the whole Parrish case is probably fucked."

Captain shook his head. "No. Your friend took care of that." Asher and Harry both stared at him to clarify. "Mr Oh Yunho. With the ADF, he's been an integral part of the whole thing to bring them all down, and to clear both your names. Him and Agent Edwards."

With the Australian Defence Force?

"MI6 and the ADF," Harry whispered. "Together."

"And other agencies," Captain said. "It's a joint effort."

"Like the Milvus Division," Harry added.

The Milvus Division.

Asher couldn't believe it when Harry had told him. It hurt to hear it from him then, like it hurt to hear from this Captain now. Asher needed to speak to Yunho. To see him.

He hadn't wanted to even think about it before now. He'd been so mad, so unsure. He wasn't ready to hear of his closest friend's betrayal. Yunho had been the only family Asher had known, and to think it'd all been a lie. Asher wasn't sure he could cope. Certainly not without Harry by his side, and before his shoulder surgery it wasn't possible.

But now . . .

But now Asher needed to see Yunho.

He needed to know. All the secrets, all the lies. He needed to know it all.

"Have you heard how Lucas is?" Asher asked. They'd had no real updates, and whether that was because it was classified or if they just weren't privy to know.

"He's alive," Medic said. "How on earth he lived through that, I *do not* know. He was . . ." He made a face. "He'll have a very long recovery, and permanent injuries aren't known yet." He put up both hands. "That's all I know."

"We need to go find Yunho," Asher said. "He's here, yes?"

Medic gave a nod. "ICU. You probably wouldn't have been able to see him before now anyway."

Asher nodded. He knew Yunho had some significant injuries. He'd seen him, beaten, drooling blood, gasping for every breath. But hearing the words ICU stung.

He turned to Harry and took his hand. "I need to see him."

Harry gave him a smile. "Of course."

"We should, uh, we should leave you guys to it," Captain said, taking a step back.

"Thank you," Asher said quietly. "For saving us. For bringing Harry to get me."

"No problem."

Medic looked right at Harry and put his hand out as if he were stopping traffic. "No, don't get up. We'll see ourselves out."

Harry snorted, grinning, and beckoned him closer. "Come here, little man."

Medic grinned and took a bravely stupid step closer, but Captain put his arm on his shoulder and turned him toward the door instead. "Nope. Not today," he said, walking him out. He smiled over his shoulder at both Harry and Asher, keeping his arm around Medic as they disappeared through the door.

They were cute. In a not-old-enough-to-shave kind of way.

"So they're letting school kids be tactical officers now," Asher said, nodding slowly. "How old are they, exactly?"

Harry snorted. "Toddlers."

"Medic's funny."

Harry glowered at him. "He's a smartass."

"He's not intimidated by you at all," Asher said. "I like him."

"You were going to stab him with a spoon."

Asher sighed, and taking Harry's hand, he threaded his fingers. "We're too old for this game, Harry."

"I know. All I want is our little house in the woods where there are no people."

"Well, no people trying to kill us, anyway," Asher allowed. "It'd be a good start."

Harry nodded, his blinks getting slower. "I hope we can go home."

"Same, my love." He didn't want to mention the whole passport issue and how he now didn't have one. Didn't have any chance of getting one with Yunho in hospital.

He didn't even have a country with which he could apply to.

He didn't have a clue how he even got into England. He had no clue how he'd leave.

Maybe they'd have to live here now . . .

"Hey," Harry murmured, giving Asher's hand a shake. "We'll be okay. No matter where we are. Remember how once you told me your home wasn't a place, it was me? Well, my home is you. Wherever you are, that's where I'll be."

Asher nodded, teary-eyed. He leaned down and pressed his lips to Harry's. "Wherever you are, that's where I'll be."

He blinked and struggled to open his eyes again. "So tired."

"Sleep. I'll be right here."

Harry extended his good arm. "Lie here with me."

It wasn't likely they'd fit, but Asher wasn't going to say no. He climbed up and gently pressed himself against Harry's side, his huge arm curling around Asher's shoulders.

Asher breathed him in, feeling the warm skin of his naked chest. Asher sighed, everything in this moment, if just for this moment, felt right.

He felt like home.

THE NEXT MORNING, Harry showered and managed some semi-solid food. His jaw still hurt, like most of him hurt, but man, a shower had never felt so good.

His lung was healing, as were all the stab wounds and cuts. His shoulder hurt like a bitch but the drugs helped. Made him more agreeable too, according to Asher.

Harry didn't like the drowsiness that came with it though. Much like he didn't like the hospital policy that he was in a wheelchair when he and Asher went to see Yunho.

Asher was happy to push him though, chuckling as Harry grumbled about it. The ICU was on a different floor and down a corridor, and Asher pushed him slowly. The fetid smell of disease and disinfectant had always made Harry uneasy.

Or maybe it was knowing they were about to see Yunho, about to find out everything.

Harry worried about Asher and how he'd take the news.

They only had a short time, prearranged with the medical staff, of course. And Harry and Asher really didn't know what shape Yunho would be in.

Maybe they wouldn't find anything out today.

Lies and deceit aside, Harry hoped Yunho would be okay. He'd always liked him, and Yunho had done a lot for Harry. And he'd helped Asher immensely over the years; he'd been like a father to him. Asher had trusted him.

And now that trust was gone.

Regardless of what they learned today.

They were escorted into the ICU by a straight-backed, no-nonsense nurse. She told them that Yunho was medicated for extreme anxiety. She gave strict instructions on dos and don'ts and led them past privacy curtains to a bed in the corner of the large room.

Asher let out a deep breath and opened the curtain.

The man in the bed looked old and small, frail. Harry briefly wondered if they'd brought them to the wrong patient, but as soon as he saw Asher, he burst into tears.

It was Yunho.

He just looked like he'd aged a decade in a few days.

It didn't help that half his face was swollen and purple, the other half banged up and bruised. His longish dark hair was unwashed, peppered with more grey than Harry remembered.

Christ, he looked so small.

And he was crying, trembling, and trying to speak but struggling with words. Harry realised then, that Yunho— with his severe anxiety and agoraphobia—had been left alone, no visitors, probably no word on any of them, if anyone had survived.

Harry tried to imagine going through the last few days not knowing if Asher was okay. They would have needed to sedate him with a tranq gun from fifty yards.

It made Harry see Yunho in a different light. Lies and deceit aside, this was a broken man.

Asher went to him, sat on the bed and hugged him, cried with him, and it damn near broke Harry's heart.

Asher pulled back and cupped Yunho's face, taking in the damage. "Is Lucas okay?" Asher asked quietly.

Yunho gave a small nod. "Alive. Barely. I've seen him one time," he mumbled, holding up one finger before sobs wracked him. "What they did to him."

Harry had seen Lucas. Not one inch of him wasn't bleeding.

"He's MI6," Asher said, remaining cool. His guard was up and Yunho knew it.

He nodded again, more tears falling. "I know, I know. I'm so sorry, Asher. I wished I could have told you. So many times."

"You were working with MI6 all these years," Asher said.

"I worked with many governments," Yunho whispered. "Many."

When it all came down to it, Harry wasn't surprised by this. But those waters were really fucking murky, and the fact Asher did Yunho's groundwork, it meant his hands were dirty too.

"I will tell you everything, my darling," Yunho said, reaching for Asher's hand, but Asher pulled his back.

"You knew my real name," Asher whispered. "Ćiro Savić."

Yunho sobbed and nodded. "I wanted to tell you."

"Then why didn't you?" Asher was trying to keep his anger, his pain, in check, Harry could see it. "You knew what it would have meant to me. My whole damn life, I never knew who I was or where I was from. You knew what a single fucking name would have meant to me."

Yunho cried and cried, holding his arm against his side, wincing at his pain. "I'm so sorry, Asher. I was going to tell you, but . . ."

"But what?"

"But there was nothing left. No family, no home. Everyone was dead, killed in the war. I thought learning you had a family only to know they were gone would be too much. You had already been through so much. I wanted to protect you. I'm sorry."

"It wasn't your decision to make," Asher said, his voice just a whisper.

"I know, I'm sorry," Yunho sobbed. "I couldn't bear the thought of hurting you. I'm so sorry, darling. I was going to tell you one day, but I was never brave enough. The longer I left it, the harder it was. And then you met Harry and you were finally happy. Forgive me, Asher, please. I'm so sorry."

Asher was quiet for a long few seconds. He didn't say Yunho was forgiven, and Yunho seemed to understand that he wasn't.

"The Milvus files," Asher said, his voice calm. "You knew what that was years before us."

"I contracted a lot of agents," Yunho said. "Kites, like Harry. I knew where most of them were at any given time, who they were working for, who they were contracted to kill."

This made sense to Harry, as harsh a reality as it was.

But that wasn't Asher's point, clearly. He spoke through clenched teeth. "You had information on Harry."

Yunho's head shot up, his good eye open wide. "Of course I did. Did you think I was going to let anyone get close to you that I didn't have a complete history on? Asher, I needed to know he wouldn't hurt you."

"He's not the one who hurt me," Asher whispered. "You are."

Yunho stared at him, then his ruined face crumpled. He sobbed, and clung to his side, his breaths ragged. "I'm sorry, my Asher. I'm so very sorry."

The nurse came back in, scowling at Asher and putting a sympathetic hand on Yunho's shoulder. "You need to rest," she said. Then her curt glare cut to Asher, then to

Harry. "You both need to leave." She pressed Yunho's meds button and he calmed down in seconds.

Asher stood up and took Yunho's hand. "I'll come back and see you tomorrow," he said quietly. "I can't forgive you. Not yet. I need time, and we need to talk a lot more. But I'm not leaving you. I love you, Yunho. I'm not leaving you." He leaned down and pressed a soft kiss to Yunho's forehead. "I'll see what I can find out about Lucas and let you know."

Yunho blinked slowly, tears running silently down his bruised cheeks.

Asher turned and he never said a word as he pushed Harry back to their room.

Exhaustion crept over Harry and he couldn't shake it. For fuck's sake. He'd been out of bed for half an hour and was about to drop off. He couldn't imagine if he'd walked instead of using the chair.

Maybe the wheelchair wasn't so bad. Maybe the doctors knew what they were talking about. Not that Harry would tell them that . . .

When Harry was settled on his bed, he offered the little spoon spot to Asher.

Asher climbed up, buried his face into Harry's neck, and cried.

"YOU SURE YOU want to do this?" Harry asked. He wanted to save Asher from pain at all costs. Whatever it took.

Asher gave him a sad smile. "I need to do this."

"Okay." Harry understood. He really did. Asher did need to do this. And so did Yunho. But it wasn't without pain, and all Harry could do was reassure him. "I'll be right beside you, baby."

When they arrived, Harry was surprised to see Yunho showered, his hair still damp and brushed back. He looked more put together, more like himself.

His face looked sore and battered. He was bruised and cut all over, Harry noticed. A lot like Harry's injuries. Those assholes learned the same torture skills.

"Harry," Yunho said, swallowing hard. "Sorry for not greeting you properly yesterday. You're in a wheelchair," he said. "And your shoulder . . ."

Harry still wore the sling, and he would for a while yet.

"I'm fine," Harry replied. "The chair isn't my idea. Are . . . are you okay, Yunho?"

Yunho's eyes became glassy, and he patted down his hair with trembling hands. "Well, yes . . . not really. I don't like it here. I want to go home, but I won't leave without Lucas."

It was pretty damn obvious that Yunho's anxiety meds were strong. The sharpness in his eyes and the clarity of his words were now dulled and slow.

At least he wasn't freaking out.

Not outwardly, anyway.

"And you, Asher?" Yunho asked quietly, nervously. "Are you okay?"

Asher sat on the side of the bed and reached out, taking Yunho's hand. "I'm fine. The least injured of all of us."

Yunho nodded, scrubbing a tear from his not-swollen cheek. "I'm just so sorry," he began. "Words cannot convey how sorry I am."

"You were taken," Asher said. "We saw the footage. We saw Narong's body. And Aranya."

Yunho nodded, crying fresh tears. "That poor, sweet girl."

They were all quiet for a moment.

"I knew you would come," Yunho said. "I tried to tell you not to, I didn't want to involve you, but I knew you wouldn't listen."

"Radovic sent men to kill us in Tallowwood," Asher explained. "We were already involved."

Yunho gasped, his hand to his heart. "What? I didn't know, I swear."

"No. It was that young kid, Yixing. He hacked into your system or something. I don't understand all that." Asher sighed. "He was actually pretty smart. For a kid."

"Not too smart though," Yunho said.

"You used some kind of trip key? Or location key? That's what I heard, anyway."

"Yes, when he accessed what he thought was my finances, it tripped the satellite tracker."

"You called Istomin the bait," Asher said. "Before Harry and the rescue team arrived. You told him he was the bait."

Yunho nodded. "To bring them down. The plan was, originally, to send in one of the Milvus teams to bring him down. Before he could plant his men in the senate, and not just in his own government; he had men all over. But them kidnapping us changed the plans. Objectives change, you know this, Asher. When things go sideways, you have to adapt. But the goal never changed. To bring down Istomin. He thought capturing me was the ultimate plan to lure you in. And it worked, but Asher, you have to believe me, you were never supposed to be there. But when he found out that Radovic had you, after the press conference, he came in. He knew he could use you. His friend, Sergey

Volkov, we eliminated him a few years ago. He was not a good man. He and Istomin were setting up for war. I don't know if you remember Volkov—"

"I remember," Asher said. Asher hadn't been too concerned with the whys of it all back then. Maybe he'd been wrong for trusting so blindly. Like Harry had been with the orders he was given by his 'government' all those years.

"But Istomin was the bait all along," Yunho said. "He was our target. Istomin and his drive for war and money."

"A new cold war," Asher whispered.

Yunho nodded. "Political unrest and fascism is never far under the surface, Asher. He got way too close."

Harry wasn't sure what he believed. Everything Yunho was saying made sense, and as crazy as it sounded, Harry knew it was possible.

Asher did too.

He nodded slowly. "Was I the bait?" Asher asked. "In all the years I've known you, did you ever use me as bait?"

"No."

"But you did this time," Asher whispered. "To further your ties with the Australian government, with Lucas and MI6. You did use me. And I can live with that. But you used Harry, like he was a fucking pawn in some fucked-up game," Asher said, his voice a little shaky. "And I'm not sure that's something I can ever forgive."

Oh god. Harry didn't want to be the reason Asher pushed Yunho away.

"Asher," Harry murmured.

Before Asher could say anything, Yunho shook his head. "I did it *for* you," he replied. "For both of you."

"Bullshit," Asher replied sharply. "What did you get in return? What did they agree to for your help, Yunho? Did you have a price? How much was I worth?" Then he spoke through clenched teeth. "How much was Harry worth?"

"I did it for your freedom," Yunho said, crying now. Tears streaming down his face. "And mine. But yours first. Freedom. Citizenship for you, Asher. Your names cleared, for it all to be over so you were free to live as Harry and Asher. No looking over your shoulders. Full government absolution. That was my asking price. For you to be free."

Holy shit.

"I knew my time doing this was coming to an end," Yunho said. "The Milvus Division was up and running, the counsel in place. They know everything we know about the fascist movements. Not just in Europe, Asher." He sighed. "Lucas's work with MI6 was almost over. We were going to hand it all over, everything, every bit of it. Then retire and live out our days on our island."

"You should have told me," Asher said quietly. "You could have told me that, at least."

"We couldn't. Until it was over. But we planned to," Yunho murmured. "When Istomin was behind bars. But he took us first." He let out a shuddering breath and recomposed himself. "I wanted to surprise you when it was all over. So you could use your name. Get married using your real name." His eyes welled with fresh tears. "I knew how much you hated going by the name Joshua Hill and how much you wanted documentation with your real name."

"My real name," Asher whispered. "Ćiro. The sun god. Is it not my real name?"

Yunho deflated. "I'm sorry. Whichever name you want, the Australian government will do it. It was my request. For both of you." He looked at Harry then. "I'm sorry, Harry."

"You said your freedom as well," Harry said. "What did you mean? Were you not free before?"

"When Istomin learned of me, he threatened to inform my government. He said that he'd hand me back as a gesture of good faith to a dictator. Another piece to his political puzzle." He patted his hair down nervously. Then he whispered, "North Korea and Russia don't play to the same rules as the rest of the world. And like Asher, I have no country. I have no government to protect me."

Asher stared at him for a long moment. He inhaled deeply and processed it all. "Why not England?" he asked eventually. "With Lucas?"

"Because Australia held the bargaining chips," he said weakly.

"They plan to use you, don't they," Harry said. It wasn't a question. "To wrap up the Parrish case, and to use the Milvus Division."

Yunho's tired gaze met his, and he nodded. "To an extent. My access, my contacts, my satellite system. Data mining is the future . . ." He let out a shuddering breath. "But I'll be free. No more hiding. No more secrets. No more operatives, no more governments, no more murder. That was my asking price."

Jesus fucking Christ.

All three were quiet for a long time, letting the dust of truth settle over them.

Needing to touch Asher, to remind him he was there, Harry got out of the wheelchair and stood beside Asher, putting his good arm around his shoulder. Asher leaned against him heavily.

Had Yunho kept information from Asher?

Yes.

Was he obligated to tell him?

No.

As his friend, maybe. As his informant? If Asher wasn't on the ground and directly involved, then no. Asher might not like that answer but it was the truth.

Did it all make sense?

Harry was beginning to think it did, yeah.

"Where will you live?" Asher asked eventually. "Your island . . ." He shook his head and grimaced. "What about the police in Thailand? You can't go back there."

"No. I can't. There's a place," he said quietly. "In Far North Queensland. An island . . ."

Asher snorted and shook his head. "Are you serious?"

Yunho nodded and tried to smile, but his chin wobbled. "If Lucas . . ." He cleared his throat. "If Lucas lives. If he doesn't make it, I don't think I'll need it." He shook his head, scrubbing away the tears and wincing when he clearly touched his swollen face too hard. "I can't live without him."

Asher reached over then and took Yunho's hand. "Yunho," he whispered.

Yunho shook his head and let out a teary laugh. "You know, he was planted by MI6. All those years ago. They found me, with help from the Indian government, of all places. He was planted as the project manager of the construction job for my house. That much was true. He was the construction manager. But we fell in love. He confided in me; he told me everything. And he was going to quit, to defect if he had to. I suggested we fake his death, as I had done. But I couldn't leave my island." He shook off more tears. "So we came up with a plan for him to stay. A deal."

"Information," Asher deduced.

Yunho nodded. "Intel. He was still agented. But he

could stay with me if he helped the British ops on the ground. Like I did with you."

"The Milvus files," Harry said. "Managing kites from a bunch of different governments."

Yunho sighed. "It's what we did. It's what we still do." He shrugged and winced again. "Well, it's what we did. Until Istomin and his little Yixing found us."

Harry wondered what would happen to Yixing. He was too good a weapon to put in jail, and there was no way in hell the Australian or British governments would hand him back to the Chinese.

Yunho noticed Harry, and he gave a nod. "The British have him," he whispered. "I can see you're wondering."

Asher looked between them both. "Yixing?"

Harry sighed, it all making more sense now. "And the Australian government gets you."

Yunho gave a nod. "In exchange for immunity, for protection. For me, but also both of you. It didn't all go to plan, but here we are."

Beaten, tortured, left for dead. But alive.

"Come on," Asher said, getting off the bed. He pulled back the blankets to reveal Yunho's legs. His bruised, bandaged legs.

Oh god.

"They had to operate to fix my knee," he said softly in explanation.

"I'm sorry," Asher murmured. "You're like this and I was mad at you, adding to your pain."

Yunho shook his head. "Don't be sorry. You did nothing wrong. I should thank you for coming to rescue me."

Asher put his hand gently to the ruined side of Yunho's face. "Of course we did. I love you, Yunho."

Yunho smiled with a teary laugh. "My sweet boy."

Asher gave him a gentle hug. "We'll be okay," he whispered. Not completely forgiven, but certainly on the way.

"Can you get out of bed?" Asher asked him. "Would you be okay leaving your cubicle?"

"What for?" Yunho asked, his eyes wide with fear. His hands trying to claw into the mattress and sheet.

"We'll go find Lucas. You can use Harry's wheelchair."

Yunho gasped, frozen for a second before he nodded. "Yes, please. Yes."

Asher helped him off the bed, Harry did too, with his one arm, and they eased him into the wheelchair, his IV beside him. Asher fixed the leg prop and Yunho settled back, a film of sweat on his brow at the exertion.

Harry pulled back the curtain and his nurse stood there, arms crossed. "He needs to see Lucas Edwards," Harry said. "We can look into every cubicle, but we'd really appreciate if you could show us the way."

Yunho was trembling. "Please, Sue. Please."

Sue grumbled about how him being well enough to go see Lucas meant he was well enough to be on a ward, which was probably true. She disconnected one of his other machines and led the way to a private room. She knocked quietly, and a male nurse came to the door.

They exchanged a quick conversation, he looked them all up and down, noting Yunho in particular. His injuries, the way he was shaking. He opened the door and held up two fingers. "Two minutes."

Lucas was . . . dear god. He was barely recognisable. The blankets were held up off his legs by a frame. His face was bandaged, one eye completely covered. He was covered in tubes and monitor pads, bandages.

"His ankles needed pinning," the nurse said. "They reset his broken fingers, but they couldn't save his eye. He has moments of lucidity but the sedation helps him heal." He gave a smile. "They didn't expect him to survive, but he's a fighter."

Yunho sobbed, his hand to his mouth, shaking as he tried to stand up on his one good leg. Asher helped him step closer to the bed, holding Yunho up so he could take Lucas's hand. "My love," he cried. "I'm here. I'm not leaving without you. I love you." He sobbed and sobbed, leaning down and lifting Lucas's knuckles to his forehead, to his cheek, to his lips. "I need you. You can't leave me. Take all the time you need to heal but you come back to me, you hear?"

A tear rolled down Asher's cheek and Harry rubbed his back. "Yeah, Lucas," Asher said, sniffling. "You do as he says. Don't make me send Harry in."

Harry snorted quietly, and he waited for Lucas's machines to beep, signalling a reaction or some awareness, but there was nothing. Only Yunho's soft crying.

But then Lucas's lips parted a fraction. "Yunho," he breathed, barely a whisper.

"Yes, yes, my love. It's me," Yunho sobbed, holding his hand to his face. "I'm right here."

Now his machine beeped and he breathed a little harder, but said nothing else. Yet it was somehow enough. It was definitely a positive sign and Harry felt hopeful.

"Okay," the male nurse said, fussing over a machine. "He's had enough. Time to go."

Sue pushed the wheelchair closer to Yunho, and they got him back to his cubicle, and back into bed. He cried as he drifted off to sleep but he was mumbling about seeing Lucas again tomorrow.

"We'll take you again," Asher told him. "I promise."

HARRY AND ASHER moved to a different ward that afternoon. Their own private room, two uniformed guards outside the door.

Harry wasn't sure if it was for their protection or to protect others. Probably both.

The next morning, they were visited by some brass. Two XOs from the Australian army and two uniforms behind them, standing at attention. And a familiar guy leaning against the wall, smirking at them.

Captain. He didn't have Medic with him, and Harry was almost disappointed.

Almost.

What Yunho had told them about the deal was basically what the XO's regurgitated to them. The Australian government were taking them both back, officially, when Harry's lung was given the all-clear to fly.

There was no mention of passports to return with, so Harry assumed it was still under a military operation.

Which name Asher would use for his newfound citizenship was still undecided. He wasn't ready, and Harry understood that. He'd only just found out his true name. He needed more time to process, to adjust.

"There's a box in a storage shed in Thailand I want brought back to Australia," Harry said. He hoped he'd never need the weapons but he didn't know if or when Yunho would ever be able to supply them again, and Harry wasn't taking any chances. He'd never leave Asher unarmed again.

The first XO frowned. "We'd need to verify its contents—"

"I don't give a fuck what you have to do," Harry said

flatly. "I want the box, and its contents, delivered to my house."

The XO schooled his expression and gave a nod. Behind him, Captain smiled.

"And Yunho?" Asher asked.

The second XO replied. "He's staying until Agent Edwards is well enough to be transported."

Asher breathed out a sigh of relief. But still. He didn't trust easily. "We have your word on that?"

The XO cut him a cold stare with a curt smile. He clearly didn't like having his integrity checked. Before he could speak, Captain pushed off the wall and walked over. "You have my word," he said. "He and Agent Edwards will be under our protection."

Harry wasn't sure why, but he was relieved to hear that. He trusted Captain. Whatever his name was. It didn't matter.

Harry trusted him.

He gave him a nod. "Thank you."

Then Medic entered the room like he owned the entire hospital and everyone in it and handed a takeout coffee to Captain. "Aw, sorry," he said cheerfully to Harry. "I asked about those supplement drinks for you, you know the ones for the elderly, but they said no."

The two XOs baulked and the two uniform guards alerted as if Harry was about to go nuclear, but Harry couldn't help it. He snorted.

"I know I shouldn't," Asher said to Harry, "but I do like him."

Medic grinned. "Everyone likes me."

"No they don't," Harry grumbled, snarling at him.

The little fucker grinned some more.

The first XO cleared his throat. "Transport on doctor's clearance. We'll be in touch."

Harry gave a nod. "Understood."

Captain gave Harry a mock salute, and he smiled at Asher. "We will see you in the wonderful land of Oz." He turned for the door, his arm sliding around Medic's waist —those two were far too touchy-feely to be just friends— and escorted him out. "Stop pissing him off. You know he doesn't need a weapon to kill you."

The little punk laughed. "It's why I do it."

The door closed, leaving Harry and Asher alone, the silence like a breath of fresh air. Harry took Asher's hand, threading their fingers. "Ready to go home, baby?"

Back to their little house in the woods. Back to their quiet life. Their quiet, boring, and wonderful life.

Asher nodded, his eyes warm and smiling. "So ready."

EPILOGUE

TALLOWWOOD

IT HAD BEEN a normal day at work. Quiet, mostly, apart from paperwork and fielding questions from the public. Mundane and boring were two things August would never take for granted.

It'd been four weeks since ASIO had swept in and confiscated any and all information pertaining to the three missing men in the national park, and Michael and Joshua Hill.

Or Timothy "Harry" Harrigan, as Michael's real name turned out to be.

August and Jake hadn't tried to follow up or even google anything else. They'd been warned, and even though curiosity gnawed at Jake, August urged him to let it go.

"It's clearly related to the Parrish case," August had said. That high-profile military case involving espionage and treason, and they knew Harry had been special forces.

"We can't do anything that might jeopardise his safety," August had said.

And that was enough for Jake to drop it.

But then, not long after that, there were reports on the evening news of gang wars in Bosnia and Serbia, where twenty-odd gang members had been found dead, head-quarters destroyed. It was a turf-war thing, the news had said.

Jake had quirked a silent eyebrow at August, and August did have to wonder . . . But August had shaken his head. "Nah. It can't be. Just a coincidence."

But then, Deans had come into the station with her phone screen turned to show them a photo of two very familiar faces at a press conference in Serbia.

Michael and Joshua Hill.

It was causing a huge stir, according to the article. One of the men was a ghost, it claimed. The infamous sniper, Asher Garin: unconfirmed kill count in the hundreds, longest distance strike range three kilometres.

Jesus. Fucking. Christ.

And then silence.

No media coverage, no bulletins, no trace online, no anything.

August had wondered what the Australian government had done to shut that down so completely.

And in the three weeks that followed? Silence and normalcy. And boring and mundane.

"Ah, boss?" Deans yelled from her desk, her voice rising in pitch. "Detective?"

August looked around the corner, through the glass panel in the door, to see two men had pulled up out front of the station and were walking in.

Smiling.

Familiar.

"Shit," August hissed, hurrying to get up. He was at the front counter by the time the door opened.

Michael and Joshua Hill walked in, smiling when they saw August. "Hello," August said, feeling stupid the second the word left his lips. Joshua had faded bruising around his left eye, and Michael had his arm in a padded sling, faded bruising and healing cuts all over his face and hands.

What the hell had happened to them?

"You're back," August added.

"We are," Joshua said, grinning. "And we'd love to chat, but I was hoping . . . My Mala; is she okay?"

August almost laughed. "She's fine. Queen of the house, actually." He glanced at Deans, realising she had no clue what they were talking about. He and Jake had never told anyone they were minding Joshua's cat or that Michael and Joshua had dropped her off in the middle of the night after they'd not-so-allegedly disposed of those three men. "Jake's at home. We can go there right now."

Joshua was excited. "Yes, please."

August grabbed his coat and mumbled to Deans to call Jake as he followed Michael and Joshua out.

Jake met them at the door, smiling warily. His eyes asking August *what the fuck* as the three of them stepped inside. "They're here for Mala," August said.

A little bell tinkled as Mala trotted in and Joshua scooped her up, pressing his face into her fur, cooing, a little teary-eyed. "Thank you for keeping her safe," he said.

Michael rubbed Joshua's back, watching him fondly.

"She's been a joy," Jake said. "Scarlet wasn't sure at first but even she warmed to her." Then he looked at

Michael, obviously taking in the cuts and the brace. "Oh, Michael, is your arm okay?"

The big man smiled. "Shoulder, actually. And yeah, it's fine. But, uh, about the name. It's not Michael." He held out his hand for August to shake. "The name's Tim Harrigan, but people call me Harry."

Holy shit.

"And I'm Asher Garin," Joshua said . . . *Asher* said. He shook Jake's hand, then August's. "I want to show you something." He handed Mala over to Harry, pulled out his wallet, produced a NSW driver's licence, and almost bouncing, he handed it to Jake. "Look," he said excitedly. "It has my real name."

Jake took it, reading it over, then handed it to August. It was just a driver's licence. August didn't quite understand his excitement. "Did you not have one before? Because you used to drive . . ."

Asher pulled a face. "Well . . ."

Harry laughed. "You don't get it," he said. "That's his actual name. Asher Garin."

Asher looked up at him, his eyes warm. "My real name. The only name I've ever known."

Harry kissed the side of his head. "It's kind of a big deal," Harry said, giving August a pointed look.

"Oh," August said quickly. "Then that's wonderful." He handed the plastic card back to Asher.

Asher took it, putting it pride of place in his wallet. Then he took out his Medicare card and beamed at them. "I'm an Australian citizen. I have a birth certificate and papers. And this!" He looked at the green-coloured card with huge, happy eyes. He showed it to them proudly. "It has my name on it. And my birthday is April ninth. My real birthday."

Okay, so August very quickly deduced that having his name, his real name, on legal documents was a very big deal. And his birthday. Did he not have one before now? "I'm happy for you, Asher."

Asher's smile was worth it. And the way Harry looked at Asher so proudly made August's heart squeeze.

Yes, he knew who they were, what they were capable of. Yet he still liked them. "I'm glad you're both back, safe and well. And you're staying?"

Asher nodded quickly. "Yes. We just want to go home and live in peace and quiet."

Jake grinned. "August's two favourite words."

"We, uh," Harry cleared his throat. "We might get some media attention, now that our names are out there. The media might come to town, just so you know. There's a legal case ongoing that we can't really talk about. But I promise we won't cause any trouble. We just want . . ." He made a face.

"Peace and quiet?" August guessed for him. "Actually, my two favourite words are boring and mundane, but peace and quiet works."

"I'll take boring and mundane too," Harry said. "For the rest of my life."

Jake collected Mala's things in a bag and handed it to Asher. "There's some food in there too until you get settled."

"Thank you," Asher said quietly. "I cannot thank you enough for looking after her."

"Oh," August said, remembering. Shit, shit. He pulled out his keys and unthreaded one in particular. "You'll need this. I padlocked the gate after ASIO came and cleared out your gun collection."

Both Harry and Asher went stock still and stared at him.

August regretted saying anything but figured honesty was always best. They were about to find out anyway. Best they had some warning. "Sorry," he added. "They didn't touch anything in your house, from what we could tell. Just the guns. And for full disclosure, I may have been the one to put the call in because automatic weapons are illegal and—"

Harry cleared his throat. "You found the door to the tank?"

"Uhhhh." August stared at him, wondering if there was any point in trying to backpedal out of this.

Until Asher snorted and Jake laughed. "Sorry, babe. Your face."

August tried not to blush.

"We know." Harry smirked. "We know what ASIO took. We spent a few days in Canberra when we got back. Getting everything squared away with our names and all the paperwork and bullshit. We know everything. I appreciate your honesty though." He clapped August on the shoulder. "Maybe one day you could come out for lunch. BBQ and a few beers. We can watch the footy and trade stories."

"Uh, sure," August said. Was it odd that he would actually like that?

Jake brightened. "Ooh, I mean it's too late for the football season but we're looking for some players for this year's cricket team. If you're staying in town," he said. "Harry, I bet you'd absolutely kill it with a cricket bat."

August tried not to look horrified. Not as much as Harry tried though.

Jake seemed to realise how his choice of words sounded.

Asher laughed. "He'd love to play!"

Harry narrowed his eyes at Asher, then smiled at Jake. "My shoulder's no good. But I'm sure Asher would love to sign up."

Asher's smile died, and Harry's got wider.

August didn't want to put a cricket bat in either of their hands, especially Harry's. Jesus Christ.

"Well, we better get this little baby home," Asher said, patting Mala who was now tucked into the crook of Harry's padded sling and chest, purring loudly. "Thank you for everything."

"You're welcome," Jake said.

"And I'm glad you're both back," August said, walking them to the door. "When you get settled in, pick a weekend for that BBQ. I'll bring the beer."

Harry gave him a smile. "Sounds good."

August and Jake watched as Harry and Asher drove away, and August sighed as he closed the door. "Cricket, babe? Seriously? You want to give that man a weapon and send him out to a cricket pitch where some poor guy has to bowl at him?"

Jake sighed. "It's not a weapon. It's a . . ." He frowned, because it absolutely was a weapon in Harry's hands. "Look, ex-mercenaries and snipers need love too. Maybe some recreational community sport will be good for them."

August sighed.

For the love of god.

"Could you imagine how good our rugby team would be if we had Harry?" Jake asked. "Next year, his shoulder'll be better. We'd be unstoppable."

August sighed, kissing Jake's lips softly. "No." He was probably going to regret mentioning this . . . "Harry would be better suited with your outreach program in the summer." Jake still ran the program for Indigenous kids, getting them involved in hiking, climbing, rafting. "Harry would be great with those kids."

Jake's whole face lit up. "Holy shit, yes. I'll ask him. I won't tell him it was your idea."

August snorted. "Thanks."

Then Jake smiled. "I'm gonna miss little Mala. Maybe we should get a kitten."

"Also a no."

"I do outrank you, technically," Jake said, sniffing. August shot him a look, making Jake laugh. "Deans called, gave me the heads up that you were on your way with them."

"Thought you might appreciate it."

Jake tilted his head, thinking. "You know, now that I think about it, my kookaburras didn't warn me before they got here."

They had every time before, that was true.

August went to the back door, not sure what he was expecting to see, but there were no kookaburras. "Do you think they're okay?"

Jake chuckled. "Yeah. I also think that maybe Harry and Asher aren't a danger to us anymore. Somehow."

August's eyes met his. "They seemed kinda different, didn't they?"

"Relaxed, like whatever they were fighting is over. Did you see how happy Asher was about his name and birthday?"

August smiled sadly. "Yeah. Makes you wonder, huh? What kind of life he's had."

Jake nodded. "More reason for him to join the cricket team."

August withheld a sigh and walked to the door. "I'm going back to work. Love you."

"I'm getting another kitten. Love you too!" he called back.

August didn't even pause. He didn't mind. If Jake wanted another ten cats, he wouldn't object. He might gripe about it and pretend to be annoyed, but he had to admit, snuggling on the couch on a cold winter night with Jake, blankets, the wood fire raging, and two cats? It sounded kinda nice.

Jake was probably googling animal shelters before August got back to his desk.

"Everything all right?" Deans asked when August walked back into the station.

He fell into his seat with a sigh and a smile. "Yep. Everything's just fine."

OUTTAKE

SIX MONTHS LATER

ACHERON ISLAND, FAR NORTH QUEENSLAND

Rhett Ouston dumped his duffle bag on the floor, and the suit bag onto the large bed in the oversized guest room, and went to the window overlooking the turquoise Pacific Ocean.

Beautiful and luxurious didn't begin to describe this place.

Tropical, private, remote.

Jay Lin came up behind him, his touch warm and familiar. He pressed his lips to Rhett's shoulder blade, then lifted Rhett's arm and squeezed himself into his side, holding Rhett's arm over his shoulder. He fit so perfectly under his arm. All five foot four against Rhett's six feet two, Jay was the perfect size for him.

"Can you believe he owns this whole freaking island?" Jay asked, looking out to the view.

Rhett snorted. "Can't believe anyone owns a whole freaking island."

"Have you seen my favourite cranky tank yet?"

Rhett snorted. "You gotta stop calling him that or you'll say it to his face and he won't find it funny." To be fair, he *was* a tank, and he *was* cranky . . .

Jay sighed. "He likes me."

"If he loses his shit at you, I won't be able to stop him."

Hell, no one would be able to stop him.

They'd watched him crush a man's windpipe with his bare hand. After he'd gutted him like a fish. With one shoulder with severed ligaments. Not to mention the punctured lung and multiple stab wounds.

The man was a fucking machine.

And when they'd seen him in hospital, bare chested, almost every inch of his torso had a scar. God, there was even a line down his sternum that looked a lot like a brass knuckles imprint.

Harry's time as special ops and as a kite had not been an easy one. He reminded Rhett of an old lion. A solitary beast, covered in a lifetime of battle wounds, each one no doubt a story to tell.

Rhett had to wonder if he'd look like that in another fifteen years.

Harry wasn't solitary anymore though. He had Asher.

Like Rhett had Jay.

He pulled Jay from his side so he faced him, his hands cupping his face and kissing him softly. "No rankling the cranky tank," Rhett said. "Not this weekend, okay?"

Jay rolled his eyes. "Fine." Then he smiled wickedly. "The shower has jets, and a built-in seat. It was practically made for fucking."

Rhett smiled, his body thrumming with interest. "Bed looks good too."

"You're such a sap," Jay said, giving him a shove.

"Remember when you'd fuck me raw against the stall wall in the barracks?"

Rhett laughed, but then he spun Jay around and pressed him against the window's edge, rubbing his dick against that pert little ass. "Like this?"

Jay whined, breathily. "Yes. Do it, Rhett." He unbuttoned his shorts and pushed them down, briefs too, exposing the top of his ass.

"Fuck, Jay," Rhett groaned. He was powerless for this man; whatever he wanted, Rhett would give him. He kissed down the back of Jay's neck, enjoying the way he craned his head to give him more room, the sounds he made. Rhett would do anything he asked . . . "I won't fuck you raw though."

He took a step back and went for his bag, reaching for the lube in his toiletries, just as Jay whined impatiently. "It takes away the spontaneity, the rush," he said. "You could have your dick inside me by now if you didn't stop. It's been too long since you fucked me, babe."

Rhett chuckled as he walked back to him. "Then I'd miss this view."

Jay was gorgeous with his pants half pulled down, revealing the globes of his ass. Of course, then he had to stick his ass out, stretch his back and look over his shoulder, totally slutting it up. "Like this?"

He knew damn well Rhett loved it. "Fuck yes."

He closed the distance between them, rubbing his hardening cock over the warm exposed skin of Jay's ass. Jay arched his back for more, pulling his shorts down his thighs.

"Hurry the fuck up," Jay hissed at him. "I'll wait for lube because you insist, but I swear to god if you think I'm waiting for you to stretch me, I will find someone else who will just fuck me like I need it."

Fuck, Rhett loved this game.

He pulled his cock out, squirted lube over his shaft and cockhead, giving himself a few long strokes, smearing the lube with his right hand while his left hand found a fistful of Jay's hair.

He pushed him harder against the wall, squatting down a little so he could press his cock against Jay's hole. He pulled Jay's hair at the same time he pushed into him, in one rough thrust making him cry out and groan.

"No one will ever fuck you like I do," Rhett bit out against the back of Jay's ear.

Jay made a strangled sound, his hands trying to brace on the wall, on the window. His toes barely touching the ground as Rhett impaled him, thrusting up into him, over and over.

Rhett pulled harder on Jay's hair and sucked on his neck, while every inch was buried inside him. "You love how I fuck you."

"Yes," Jay replied, panting, moaning.

"You love my cock inside you," Rhett rasped, already far too close to coming. "My cock, my come."

"Fuck yes, baby," he groaned. "Give it all to me."

Rhett pushed him hard against the wall. The harder he pushed, the harder he fucked, the more Jay loved it.

His tight little ass taking him like a glove. Hot, all-consuming, addictive, and one hundred percent his.

"Gonna come inside you," Rhett bit out, panting, desperate. "Need to come."

"Fuck yes. Give it to me deep," Jay said, his voice tight. "Wanna feel it."

Rhett thrust up hard, once, twice, his cock impossibly

hard and swollen, his balls tight. He slammed up into him one more time, making him cry out, his feet off the floor, and Rhett came with a groan. His cock throbbing, shooting his load in Jay's ass, thick spurts with every pulse.

Fuck.

Fuck, he felt so good.

Head spinning, chest heaving, he kept Jay pressed against the wall until he could catch his breath. And then he pulled his sensitive dick out.

"Don't you dare pull out," Jay said, turning around to shove him. "You're not fucking done, Rhett."

Rhett was used to this. He grabbed Jay easily, and Jay pretended to fight him, demanding to be fucked again. He was too small to fight him off for real, though he did put up a pretty decent struggle.

Until he got what he wanted.

Rhett shoved him onto the bed, roughly grabbed his ankles, and brought his ass to the edge of the bed. He folded him up, his legs near his chest, and he drove his cock into him again.

Jay's eyes rolled closed, a salacious, victorious smile on his pretty lips. Every fucking time.

His feisty little whore loved every fucking minute of it.

Rhett fucked him, his cock sliding in and out of his tight hole, reaching that magic place inside him that drove him crazy. Rhett took Jay's cock in his hand, stroking him to orgasm.

It never took long.

Jay screamed low in his throat, shooting come onto his belly as his orgasm rocketed through him.

And when he was slumped and sated, smiling sleepily, Rhett kissed him. "Feel better?"

Jay laughed. "Fuck yes."

"I'll run us a shower," Rhett said. "We should probably go downstairs. They're probably waiting for us."

"Mm," Jay hummed dreamily.

Rhett pulled out of him, making him whine again. But he went into their private bathroom, turned on the shower, and got undressed. His cock hung heavy, sensitive, but the warm water was amazing, and soon Jay was in there with him.

Rhett lifted his chin and kissed him. "I love you."

Jay closed his eyes and smiled serenely. "I love you too. And your big dick, not gonna lie."

Rhett snorted out a laugh. "Best behaviour when we go downstairs, okay?"

Jay chuckled. "Of course."

Clean, dressed in their suits, and no longer reeking of sex, Rhett and Jay went downstairs. Rhett spotted Harry and Asher and another two men on the patio off the kitchen and headed straight for them. They were all dressed in casual suits, sharp and handsome, each of them.

"Good afternoon," Rhett said to the group. Then focused on Harry. "Looking good, all dressed up."

Harry turned and even cracked half a smile. "Captain," he said, holding out his hand. "Thank you for coming." Then his eyes fell to Jay. "Medic."

"Hey," Jay said. "Thank me for being here too, big guy. You know you want to."

"I really don't," Harry grumbled with half a smile.

Asher gave him a shove, taking Jay's hand. "Thank you for being here," he said with a smile. "For taking the time. I know you don't have much to spare."

Rhett nodded. "We were in the country, so it was good timing."

"Ah, introductions," Harry said, somewhat awkwardly. He gestured to the two men beside him. One taller man, forties, with dark astute eyes, and the other man was younger with a huge bright smile. Clearly a couple, and a gorgeous one at that. "This is August and Jake. Friends of ours from home. This is Captain and Medic."

They shook hands and said quick hellos.

"So," Jay said, smiling at Harry. "You do know our real names, right?"

Harry nodded. "We were told, yes."

"Not gonna be using them any time soon then?"

Harry shook his head. "Nope."

Rhett decided to intervene before these two bickered all night long. He looked around, taking in the bluest water and whitest sand he'd ever seen. "What a place, huh?"

Asher laughed. "Almost as nice as his last place. Harry was just saying he prefers this one."

"Yes," Jay said flatly, rolling his eyes. "My last private island was sooo much nicer too."

Harry huffed. "I've missed you, Captain," he said. "Medic, not so much."

"Be nice," Asher warned, but there was no heat in it.

Rhett had a few interactions with Harry over the last six months. Some professional, mostly friendly, chewing the fat and getting to know the man behind the reputation. The thing was, Rhett respected and admired Harry. He'd survived on his own for a long time, and that deserved a level of respect that not many could grasp.

But Rhett did. And what's more, he liked him. Behind that intimidating glare and hulking body was a man who had lost a lot, who had been pushed to the brink, was abandoned by his government handler, yet he still had more integrity and honour than anyone Rhett had ever met.

And, on a personal level, he was gay and deeply in love with a man who had been with him through thick and thin.

Like Rhett and Jay.

So yeah, Rhett liked Harry. When he'd asked Rhett and Jay to be here today, of course he'd said yes.

And god, it was a beautiful day for it. Warm, sunny, gentle breeze, on an island in Far North Queensland.

Though someone was missing . . .

"I haven't seen Yunho yet." Rhett looked back at the house. "Is he okay?"

"He's doing well," Asher replied. "It took him a little while to get used to being on this island, in this house, but he's okay now. He feels safe here."

"Good," Rhett said. He was glad.

When Rhett had told Harry and Asher back in London that he would look after Yunho and ensure his safety, he took that very seriously. It took another few weeks in hospital before they made the trek home, and for someone like Yunho, with his condition, it took a concerted, medicated effort.

Rhett had never met someone with agoraphobia before. He knew what it was, sure, but he'd never seen it first-hand. Jay had been with them the whole way, of course, which Yunho appreciated.

Rhett really liked Yunho. He was an eccentric little man but extremely smart and tremendously sweet and kind. Alongside his agoraphobia and anxiety, he was injured, had severe PTSD, and had a long medical road ahead of him. Yet he had been nothing but gracious and grateful.

"Oh, hey," Jay said, giving Rhett a nudge and a pointed nod toward the patio doors.

Rhett looked back to the house, and sure enough, Yunho was there. He wore white linen pants, a long blue linen shirt. His face was all healed up, except for the old scar that ran down one side of his face, and he was smiling proudly at someone still coming through the door behind him.

A grin broke out on Rhett's face when he saw who it was. God, it made him so happy to see him. "Here he is. Look at the big fella."

Lucas was walking, very slowly, with the use of a cane, but walking, nonetheless. He had a black patch over one eye and a determined smile. Yunho held his hand out for him.

The last time Rhett had seen Lucas he was bed bound, and barely conscious. He'd been beaten to within an inch of his life, but no matter what they did to him, he never broke. Not one word about the government he worked for, not one word about Yunho or the Milvus Division.

A stronger soldier, Rhett had never met.

"Okay, let's get this party started," Lucas said, smiling at everyone. "Now I'm here."

A woman followed Lucas out and gathered the small crowd, and there on the patio, as the sun was setting over the ocean, palm trees swaying against a pastel sky, Harry and Asher were married.

It was an honour to witness.

The way Harry held Asher's face with such tenderness. The way the big man teared up as Asher said "I do". The way he kissed him softly and swore, in front of us all, that he would love him every day of forever.

Jay slipped his hand into Rhett's and gave him a teary smile as he nodded.

He understood how special it was. Ex-military, special ops, been to hell and back, very fucking gay, and now married.

They were getting their happy-ever-after.

"It'll be us one day," Rhett whispered as the minister announced Harry and Asher husbands, and everyone clapped.

Jay leaned over so only Rhett could hear, giving him his playful but serious eyes. "Better fucking be."

~ The end

ABOUT THE AUTHOR

N.R. Walker is an Australian author, who loves her genre of gay romance. She loves writing and spends far too much time doing it, but wouldn't have it any other way.

She is many things: a mother, a wife, a sister, a writer. She has pretty, pretty boys who live in her head, who don't let her sleep at night unless she gives them life with words.

She likes it when they do dirty, dirty things… but likes it even more when they fall in love. She used to think having people in her head talking to her was weird, until one day she happened across other writers who told her it was normal.

She's been writing ever since…

---

nrwalker.net

ALSO BY N.R. WALKER

Blind Faith

Through These Eyes (Blind Faith #2)

Blindside: Mark's Story (Blind Faith #3)

Ten in the Bin

Gay Sex Club Stories 1

Gay Sex Club Stories 2

Gay Sex Club Stories 3

Point of No Return – Turning Point #1

Breaking Point – Turning Point #2

Starting Point – Turning Point #3

Element of Retrofit – Thomas Elkin Series #1

Clarity of Lines – Thomas Elkin Series #2

Sense of Place – Thomas Elkin Series #3

Taxes and TARDIS

Three's Company

Red Dirt Heart

Red Dirt Heart 2

Red Dirt Heart 3

Red Dirt Heart 4

Red Dirt Christmas

Cronin's Key

Cronin's Key II

Cronin's Key III

Cronin's Key IV - Kennard's Story

Exchange of Hearts

The Spencer Cohen Series, Book One

The Spencer Cohen Series, Book Two

The Spencer Cohen Series, Book Three

The Spencer Cohen Series, Yanni's Story

Blood & Milk

The Weight Of It All

A Very Henry Christmas (The Weight of It All 1.5)

Perfect Catch

Switched

Imago

Imagines

Imagoes

Red Dirt Heart Imago

On Davis Row

Finders Keepers

Evolved

Galaxies and Oceans

Private Charter

Nova Praetorian

A Soldier's Wish

Upside Down

The Hate You Drink

Sir

Tallowwood

Reindeer Games

The Dichotomy of Angels

Throwing Hearts

Pieces of You - Missing Pieces #1

Pieces of Me - Missing Pieces #2

Pieces of Us - Missing Pieces #3

Lacuna

Tic-Tac-Mistletoe

Bossy

Code Red

Dearest Milton James

Dearest Malachi Keogh

Christmas Wish List

Code Blue

Davo

The Kite

Learning Curve

Merry Christmas Cupid

To the Moon and Back

Second Chance at First Love

Outrun the Rain

Into the Tempest

Touch the Lightning

EWB - Enemies With Benefits

Holiday Heart Strings

Bloom

The Men from Echo Creek

Method Acting

TITLES IN AUDIO:

Cronin's Key

Cronin's Key II

Cronin's Key III

Red Dirt Heart

Red Dirt Heart 2

Red Dirt Heart 3

Red Dirt Heart 4

The Weight Of It All

Switched

Point of No Return

Breaking Point

Starting Point

Spencer Cohen Book One

Spencer Cohen Book Two

Spencer Cohen Book Three

Yanni's Story

On Davis Row

Evolved

Elements of Retrofit

Clarity of Lines

Sense of Place

Blind Faith

Through These Eyes

Blindside

Finders Keepers

Galaxies and Oceans

Nova Praetorian

Upside Down

Sir

Tallowwood

Imago

Throwing Hearts

Sixty Five Hours

Taxes and TARDIS

The Dichotomy of Angels

The Hate You Drink

Pieces of You

Pieces of Me

Pieces of Us

Tic-Tac-Mistletoe

Lacuna

Bossy

Code Red

Learning to Feel

Dearest Milton James

Dearest Malachi Keogh

Three's Company

Christmas Wish List

Code Blue

Davo

The Kite

Learning Curve

Merry Christmas Cupid

To the Moon and Back

Second Chance at First Love

Outrun the Rain

Into the Tempest

Touch the Lightning

EWB

Holiday Heart Strings

Bloom

The Men from Echo Creek

Method Acting

SERIES COLLECTIONS:

Red Dirt Heart Series

Turning Point Series

Thomas Elkin Series

Spencer Cohen Series

Imago Series

Blind Faith Series

Missing Pieces Series

The Storm Boys Series

Gay Sex Club Stories

FREE READS:

Sixty Five Hours

Learning to Feel

His Grandfather's Watch (And The Story of Billy and Hale)

The Twelfth of Never (Blind Faith 3.5)

Twelve Days of Christmas (Sixty Five Hours Christmas)

Best of Both Worlds

TRANSLATED TITLES:

ITALIAN

Fiducia Cieca (Blind Faith)

Attraverso Questi Occhi (Through These Eyes)

Preso alla Sprovvista (Blindside)

Il giorno del Mai (Blind Faith 3.5)

Cuore di Terra Rossa Serie (Red Dirt Heart Series)

Natale di terra rossa (Red dirt Christmas)

Intervento di Retrofit (Elements of Retrofit)

A Chiare Linee (Clarity of Lines)

Senso D'appartenenza (Sense of Place)

Spencer Cohen Serie (including Yanni's Story)

Punto di non Ritorno (Point of No Return)

Punto di Rottura (Breaking Point)

Punto di Partenza (Starting Point)

Imago (Imago)

Imagines

Il desiderio di un soldato (A Soldier's Wish)

Scambiato (Switched)

Tallowwood

The Hate You Drink

Ho trovato te (Finders Keepers)

Cuori d'argilla (Throwing Hearts)

Galassie e Oceani (Galaxies and Oceans)

Il peso di tut (The Weight of it All)

Pieces of You - Missing Pieces 1

FRENCH

Confiance Aveugle (Blind Faith)

A travers ces yeux: Confiance Aveugle 2 (Through These Eyes)

Aveugle: Confiance Aveugle 3 (Blindside)

À Jamais (Blind Faith 3.5)

Cronin's Key Series

Au Coeur de Sutton Station (Red Dirt Heart)

Partir ou rester (Red Dirt Heart 2)

Faire Face (Red Dirt Heart 3)

Trouver sa Place (Red Dirt Heart 4)

Le Poids de Sentiments (The Weight of It All)

Un Noël à la sauce Henry (A Very Henry Christmas)

Une vie à Refaire (Switched)

Evolution (Evolved)

Galaxies & Océans

Qui Trouve, Garde (Finders Keepers)

Sens Dessus Dessous (Upside Down)

La Haine au Fond du Verre (The hate You Drink)

Tallowwood

Spencer Cohen Series

Thomas Elkin One

Lacuna

GERMAN

Flammende Erde (Red Dirt Heart)

Lodernde Erde (Red Dirt Heart 2)

Sengende Erde (Red Dirt Heart 3)

Ungezähmte Erde (Red Dirt Heart 4)

Vier Pfoten und ein bisschen Zufall (Finders Keepers)

Ein Kleines bisschen Versuchung (The Weight of It All)

Ein Kleines Bisschen Fur Immer (A Very Henry Christmas)

Weil Leibe uns immer Bliebt (Switched)

Drei Herzen eine Leibe (Three's Company)

Über uns die Sterne, zwischen uns die Liebe (Galaxies and Oceans)

Unnahbares Herz (Blind Faith 1)

Sehendes Herz (Blind Faith 2)

Hoffnungsvolles Herz (Blind Faith 3)

Verträumtes Herz (Blind Faith 3.5)

Thomas Elkin: Verlangen in neuem Design

Thomas Elkin: Leidenschaft in klaren

Thomas Elkin: Vertrauen in bester Lage

Traummann töpfern leicht gemacht (Throwing Hearts)

Sir

So Unendlich Viel Liebe (To the Moon and Back)

THAI

Sixty Five Hours (Thai translation)

Finders Keepers (Thai translation)

SPANISH

Sesenta y Cinco Horas (Sixty Five Hours)

Los Doce Días de Navidad

Código Rojo (Code Red)

Código Azul (Code Blue)

Queridísimo Milton James

Queridísimo Malachi Keogh

El Peso de Todo (The Weight of it All)

Tres Muérdagos en Raya: Serie Navidad en Hartbridge

Lista De Deseos Navideños: Serie Navidad en Hartbridge

Feliz Navidad Cupido: Serie Navidad en Hartbridge

Spencer Cohen Libro Uno

Spencer Cohen Libro Dos

Spencer Cohen Libro Tres

Davo

Hasta la Luna y de Vuelta

Venciendo A La Lluvia

En la Tempestad

El Toque del Rayo

Corazón De Tierra Roja

Corazón De Tierra Roja 2

Corazón De Tierra Roja 3

Corazón De Tierra Roja 4

ECB (Enemigos con Beneficios)

Floral

CHINESE

Blind Faith

Bossy

JAPANESE

Bossy

PORTUGUESE

Sessenta e Cinco Horas